Hope Between Us

By Christy LaShea

Fiction and Literature: Inspirational romance

ISBN: 978-1-947523-75-3

This book is dedicated to all of the single moms out there. I was raised by one. Stay strong and have faith.

To my Granny Hinton and Granny White...I wish I could send this book to Heaven. You two were instrumental in teaching me about my faith and how to persevere when the odds of life are stacked against you.

Acknowledgements

The creation of a novel is said to be a solitary journey. For me, it has taken a community to reach The End.

Thank you, Father God, for being in my heart. Thank You for putting the following people in my life and blessing me with the gift of creating story.

To my dear husband Billy: Your support of this crazy dream has never failed. You are the inspiration behind my strong hero's with soft hearts.

To my sweet children, Downey and William: Raising you two inspired so many things that helped Luke come to life on these pages. Thank you for supporting me and bugging me about when my book was going to be published.

To my Mama: Thanks for all of your hard work to make so many things possible for me growing up. I watched you raise me as a single parent. I don't remember you ever telling me there was anything I couldn't do.

To Nana, my Mom by marriage: You always made it possible for me to attend writer's meetings, conferences and retreats. Without you and Mom, this journey would have been longer, and I may never have followed my dream. I appreciate your encouragement and support.

To my dear friend Margaret: Your encouragement has lasted for almost twenty years. I don't think you ever gave up hope that I would see a story published. You were my first critique partner and plot doctor. You went with me to my very first writer's meeting when I was too afraid to go on my own. Your bravery has fueled mine. Thank you for your continuing support in all areas of my life.

To my cousin Elizabeth: Thank you for allowing me to interview you about blood diseases and cancer treatments. Though I had done a lot of research over the years, your real world experience at Children's Healthcare of Atlanta helped me sew up loose ends and make sure I was current. I am grateful, on behalf of all the families you work with, that God placed you where He did. You are a blessing to many.

With that said, any errors in this novel about Aplastic Anemia and its treatment are all mine.

Many thanks to Patty Smith Hall, long time friend and award winning author, and my first official editor…You had all of the answers, you believed in this book and believed in me. I will be forever grateful.

To Dianna Shuford, my fellow author and critique partner, who has endured this long journey with me. You have always been available to drop what you were doing when I needed to brainstorm.

You are the toughest editor, ever! Thank you for having my back in all things, especially in last minute title help.

Thank you to all of my author friends who read this manuscript in its earliest stages. Your feedback helped this novel grow: Missy Tippens, Lindi Peterson, Cindy Woodsmall, Mindy Obenhaus, Sherrie Lea Morgan, Jennifer Dore, Kim Turner, CiCi Barnes, Debby Giusti, Debbie Herbert, and my fellow writers with Georgia Romance Writers, American Christian Fiction Writers, Seekerville.com, and Romance Writers of America.

Finally, but never least, thank you to Cynthia Hickey and Winged Publications for believing in this story to publish it and share it with the world.

Chapter One

*A*imee McClain turned the ignition a second time as she pumped the gas pedal. "Not today, *dagumit*. Not today!"

Click. Click. Click.

"Momma, is *dagumit* what we call Tank now?" Seven-year-old Luke hopped up between the front seats. "You've said it a bunch today."

"Luke." Aimee turned her head toward her son and wagged a finger.

He shrank against the seat, his lower lip jutted out as if his favorite toy had been pulled away.

"Mommy shouldn't say that word either. I'm sorry for saying it." Aimee acknowledged and turned back to the predicament at hand, mumbling under her breath. *Dagumit* spilled out in a whisper, and, a few other choice words she hoped Luke couldn't hear...

"What's wrong, Momma?"

Steam burped from the hood. Not a good sign.

"Tank's tired, I suppose."

A horn blared from behind them. The rearview mirror reflected what looked like a hundred irate drivers.

What am I going to do? She smacked the steering wheel with the heel of her hand. This made three times in the last month her '78 Grand Wagoneer, Tank, had stalled.

Aimee swiped her palm across her brow. The sun bored stinging rays through the windshield, and her taffeta gown tightened against her sweaty torso by the second, stealing her breath. She stared across the hood as her lack of options flipped like a boomerang through her thoughts: no jumper cables, no tools, and no help.

She glanced at her watch. As Maid of Honor, she should have been at the church forty-five minutes ago.

"Luke," she said through gritted teeth. "Hang tight. Fasten your seat belt." She flipped on the hazard lights, gripped the wheel, and glanced in her side mirror. Cars edged around her, drivers and passengers alike gawked as they passed. Not one Good Samaritan among them.

"Thought you got Tank fixed," Luke settled himself in the back seat.

Stinging rays of sunlight burned her eyes. "Me, too." Aimee swallowed the tight lump blocking her throat, and shifted the gear to neutral. "You've done this once before," she whispered and straightened her spine. Maybe not in heels and a formal dress, but how much different could it be? "It can be accomplished."

Exhaling, she opened the door, set one high-heeled foot on the pavement and lifted the other from the brake. Tank rolled back in protest. She held tight to the doorframe while her other hand gripped the steering wheel. Struggling to find her footing, Aimee braced her hands and feet, and gave the old SUV a hard shove.

A deep voice rumbled behind her. "Excuse me. What are you doing?"

Startled, her ankle wobbled as she turned around. "I'm trying to get out of traf—" Her eyes traveled up a mountain of muscle, a long, lean form of the man who towered above her. Dark sunglasses hid his eyes while his mouth tipped into a smirk.

She tilted her head as she narrowed her gaze. Now, what could he find so amusing at a time like this?

He stepped closer.

Heart pounding, her hold on Tank slackened. The cantankerous heap jerked backward to shove her into the man's boulder-sized chest.

Her face smashed into his sternum, and suddenly, his arms were extended on either side of her shoulders, boxing her in. Time froze as she fought to push herself away, as humiliation washed over her like a cold shower, yet at the same time, his deep voice reassured her.

"I've got a hold on it."

He had Tank. The vehicle wasn't pushing into her anymore, but – oh dear Lord - her face remained against the soft cotton covering his chest, her hands flat against his beating heart as if his presence was an aphrodisiac, and she was paralyzed by him. She inhaled, as if taking her very first breath. She hadn't been this close to a man in three years. Three long years since her cheek had rested against the strong breastbone of a person who had the power to make things right. Three years since she breathed in the male scent, an indescribable combination of strength and tenderness.

When the man spoke, his low voice vibrated against her cheek. "I think it'd be a good idea if you got behind the wheel, ma'am."

She pushed away and slid her hands across her soft taffeta gown. Reality returned as the moment, whatever it was, slid away. Cars passed them on the left, horns echoed across the distance. She eyed his shirt, hoping her makeup hadn't left an imprint on him. Swallowing, she lifted her eyes, wondering how long she had clung to this stranger. Her back rubbed the arm rest of the driver's door. To her left, his hand braced Tank's door and the other hand pressed against the roof.

He released the door long enough to flick his sunglasses to the top of his head. "Have we met?"

"No." There was something familiar about him, but she couldn't place it.

He tilted his head as his gaze lingered.

"I guess I have a familiar face." Her stomach tightened. Had he felt the same connection as she, or was that amusement in his eyes?

His gaze traced a line down the length of her Prom-style dress to the rhinestones on her stilettos that flirted and sparkled in the sun.

"Yep, the one time I dress up, my vehicle won't cooperate."

A smile lit his face. "Happens to me all the time."

She chortled in spite of her predicament. "Can you move Tank all by yourself?"

"Tank?" He smirked. "Um, I think I'm a better bet than you, with all due respect."

Her hand fisted against her hip. "Hey, I was doing fine before you showed up and scared me."

He raised an eyebrow. "You were going backwards."

A sarcastic reply died on her lips as she took in his height and the wide expanse of his chest and shoulders. Two things Aimee hated more than anything; being embarrassed and being proved wrong. Maybe he could move Tank by himself but she wasn't about to be dismissed by someone who was amused at her situation, who thinks he can take over like some superhero. Except he was right, she wasn't making any progress. Heels weren't ideal when moving a vehicle off the road.

"I have help."

She glanced over his shoulder as an older version of her rescuer weaved through the stopped cars toward them. "Who's this?"

"My father. Lucky for you, he's an automotive expert."

"Lucky for me," she repeated. The dude that last serviced Tank at Red's automotive claimed to be an expert, too.

Tall, dark and sarcastic shot her a grin. Straight white teeth shown beneath his mustache and his eyes crinkled. Once he had Tank in park, he headed toward the back. His T-shirt didn't do much to hide his physique. His broad shoulders were ripped with muscle. Feverish perspiration plucked across her temples.

Luke popped out from the open window of the back seat. "Coach Garrett?"

The Hunk turned to face her son.

"Luke!" Dimples framed his wide smile. "Say, are you old enough to start as my pitcher this fall?"

Luke giggled. "No sir, I'm only going into second grade."

"Oh, yeah. I remember now. Well, I guess I'll have to wait on you to grow up a bit. Don't go off and sign with some Major League team before you get to play on my team, okay?"

The Hunk winked at Aimee before turning back to Luke.

"I won't, Coach." Luke's smile beamed as if his favorite superhero stood before him.

"You two know each other?" Aimee looked from her son to her rescuer. How did they have a friendship she knew nothing about?

He extended his hand. "I'm Seth Garrett."

Seth Garrett. "Ah—" She stuttered. Of course he looked familiar! Shutting her eyes tight, she fought to ignore the shiver coursing from her shoulders to her toes.

Her stomach ached all of the sudden, but she swallowed hard and planted her hand in his. "A-A-Aimee McClain. I apologize for snapping at you. I appreciate your help." The warmth of his palm set off bells of bliss.

Oh, God, no! No, she could not feel bliss. She should not even be in this man's atmosphere.

"And I apologize for frightening you." Though he'd let go of her hand, his gaze lingered a moment longer until the older man called his name. "Here's my father. Would you mind getting behind the wheel?" He closed the door once she was seated as his gaze skidded back to her again. "I'll tell you when to put her back in neutral."

Within moments Tank sat on the road's shoulder. Some people may have chunked the aging Jeep long ago, but it had been her mom's and she couldn't let the old clunker go.

Seth's strong hands thumped the hood as he walked to the front of the vehicle.

"Luke, how do you know Coach Garrett?"

He wormed his way to the front seat. "Coach came to the Community Center to talk to us about playing baseball. He's Point Peace High school's coach but he used to play for the Stars. That's a major league baseball team, Mom."

"I've heard of them." In fact, she had followed Seth Garrett's career for a long time. Every high and low he experienced, she had followed by reading any newspaper article and social media post she could get her hands on. Seth also organized a popular race annually in honor of his best friend who died twelve years ago. Proceeds from the race went to an underprivileged youth program which helped kids play sports and get after school help with their schoolwork. She should ask Seth to give her some pointers on the Bone Marrow Drive she was planning for Luke. Except how could she justify asking Seth Garrett for help when she was the one who destroyed his life twelve years ago?

"I'm old enough to play, Mom, he said so."

She caressed his cheek. He may be old enough to play, but his health wouldn't allow it. "I know you're old enough, buddy. Someday you'll get to play again."

Nausea churned in her belly. How had she missed Seth Garrett's appearance at her son's day care and their budding friendship?

Hold it together. It's been twelve years. He won't know who I am.

Seth exchanged words with the older man before he trudged back to her window. His eyes remained steady on her as he neared her door.

She gripped the wheel until her fingers ached. This was not the time for confessions.

"Have you called a tow truck?"

She shook her head. "I-I don't have a phone."

"I can make the call." He yanked his cell from his jeans pocket.

"Yes. Thank you." She twisted her hands on the steering wheel until an awkward fleshy squeak erupted. "I'm sorry to be so much trouble."

His eyes crinkled when he smiled. "You're no trouble."

The older man now stood at the front of Tank. "Hey, Seth." He pointed to the hood.

"Is it okay if my father and I take a look?"

"Sure." She yanked the lever and the hood popped open. Aimee drummed her fingers on the steering wheel as Seth returned to his father's side. The longer Seth stood in front of Tank, the more her stomach churned. No matter what her past and how it intersected with Seth's, she couldn't sit there like a lump while these kind strangers tried to start her car.

"Luke, stay put." She took a deep breath and opened the driver's door. Seth smiled as she approached. An older, attractive lady hustled out of Seth's truck and came to stand beside Seth's father.

Seth introduced her to his parents. Bonnie Garrett had salon styled silver hair and perfect makeup. She nodded politely at Aimee before touching her husband's arm. "Tommy, you need to sit down. Seth can handle this."

"Bonnie, I'm fine." Seth's father gritted his teeth. He was tall like Seth, had the same eyes and tanned skin. He wiped his forehead with his hanky and leaned under the hood. "I may be able to get it started." Mr. Garrett wiggled wires and plugs hooked to the motor and battery.

"You could have a stroke in this heat." Seth's mother fanned herself with a folded magazine. "Remember what your cardiologist said—"

"Excuse me, dear." Mr. Garrett interrupted his wife's stream of excuses and turned to Aimee. "Miss, who serviced this last?"

"Red's automotive."

Mr. Garrett narrowed his eyes. "He did, did he?"

"Do you see something wrong?"

He glanced at her before focusing on the motor. "The plugs look old and worn out. Battery may need to be replaced. How often do you get this serviced?"

"I watch my mileage and take it every five thousand miles."

"That's good." Mr. Garrett prodded and poked

Tank's motor a few more times, then closed the hood and wiped his hands with the handkerchief. "I'm sorry to tell you this, but this old boy needs a lot of work."

Luke sprang out the passenger side window, propping his arms on the roof as he challenged Seth's father. "You know a good mechanic, mister?"

Aimee couldn't suppress her grin. *That's my boy.*

Mr. Garrett strolled over to him. "To answer your question, young man, I do. I know two good mechanics, me and my son."

Luke's eyes widened. "Coach Garrett can fix cars?"

Seth smiled. "He taught me everything I know."

Mr. Garrett winked at Aimee.

Luke grew quiet. He looked back at Seth's father with a frown. "Car repairs take a lot of money, mister. We don't have much of that."

"Honey…" Mortified, Aimee shot her son *the look*. "I can handle this, thank you."

Mr. Garrett turned to her. "Miss McClain, the mechanic you're using charges an arm and two legs to do a tune up. It doesn't look like the oil has been changed in a while."

Aimee shook her head wondering what else that smiley mechanic *hadn't* done.

"Regular maintenance is important." Mr. Garrett wiped his forehead. "But it needs to be running before I can see what else may be wrong."

"You reached that conclusion in just a few

moments of looking at it?"

"Yes ma'am, but I've been working on engines since I was your son's age."

His confidence should have reassured her, yet she'd heard it all before. "So, you know what you're doing?" Seth's father gave a short chuckle as if she'd offended him. "I'm sorry to be so blunt, but I don't know where else to take it. I can't afford to replace it either."

"I understand. If you'd like, Seth and I can give it a once over at no charge and I'll give you an estimate for parts and labor." He extended his hands in offering. "I'm retired. I can work on your car as needed to suit your situation."

Mrs. Garrett stepped beside Seth. "Tom, the doctor told you to stay out of the shop for another full week."

He turned to his wife with a scowl. "Dear, I know what that doctor said, and if I don't get out of the house, I'll go crazy. Now this won't be strenuous, it's a matter of troubleshooting. Besides, Seth will be there to help me with the heavy lifting." He sent her a lopsided smile. "What d'ya say?"

Her gaze volleyed from one man to the other. If she let them fix her car, she'd be forced to see Seth again. She rubbed her fingertips across Tank's chipped paint. Once, his frame stayed waxed and gleaming. She'd let the old wagon down too in the way she neglected caring for it. Tank had brought her family across the country when she was Luke's age. There were good memories tied up in the big dumb vehicle. She wasn't ready to let it go.

Seth smiled at her. He'd smiled at her a lot in this short amount of time. If she risked seeing him again, he could recognize her. She couldn't let that happen. "I appreciate your offer Mr. Garrett, but I'd better take my vehicle back to the mechanic I used before and point out what you've said he didn't do for the last service. I mean, I paid him to change the oil and the plugs."

Frowning, Mr. Garrett nodded. "I understand, Ms. McClain." He hitched his chin at her, as if he'd taken notice of her fancy dress for the first time. "Where're you headed?"

"Hopewell Church. My cousin is getting married, and I'm late."

"Your cousin is Sloan Miller?" Mrs. Garrett asked.

Aimee nodded. "Yes ma'am."

Mrs. Garrett clasped her hands. "Belinda Miller does my hair."

"Belinda's my aunt. I'll be cutting hair at her salon starting next week."

"Belinda hasn't stopped talking about how glad the family is that you're home." Mrs. Garrett's attention moved from Luke back to Aimee.

Sensing the pity in Mrs. Garrett's eyes, Aimee lowered her gaze. While she appreciated people's sympathy, she loathed it. She'd returned home to start over, be self-sufficient. For too long, she experienced loss of loved ones only to find herself scraping the bottom to make ends meet. Aimee didn't keep track of her failures on purpose, but her return home represented attempt number three to make life better for her and Luke. Sick of death and illness, she wouldn't let anything stop her this time.

"We can drop you and Luke off at the church. We'll be driving right by there." Mrs. Garrett angled a look to Seth who nodded his agreement.

"That would mean so much," Aimee replied and turned to Mr. Garrett. "Thank you for offering to fix my car."

He balled up his handkerchief. "If you change your mind, let me know."

Wringing her hands, she walked to the passenger door to gather her items. Towing Tank back to Red's shop irked her. She didn't want to face the touchy mechanic again. He always offered an exorbitant cost to repair her vehicle with a rub to her arm or shoulder. Eck. Her grandfather insisted she take the vehicle there, old ties with Red's dad ran deep between the families. She tried to follow her granddad's wishes since she was living rent free in one of his houses, but Red was a bully she'd always tried to avoid.

Mr. Garrett stood near the faded gold hood. By the look on his face he was amused at something else Luke was saying. Aimee shoved herself in the backseat, while Mrs. Garrett's laugh tickled her heart. For just a moment she longed for a touch the happiness the Garrett's possessed.

Perhaps she should allow Seth's father to work on Tank. Grabbing her bags, she shoved Luke's random items inside. With the task complete, she stepped back and surveyed the inside for anything else of value. She clutched her stomach as dread rose and threatened to buckle her. Yes, she needed a trustworthy mechanic, but the Garrett's wouldn't have offered if they knew the truth.

Chapter Two

Seth brought his black heavy duty truck to a halt in front of the church and hurried to get out. Behind him, Aimee opened the rear passenger door.

"Let me help," Seth extended his hand.

After glimpsing his palm, she focused those clear blue eyes on him. Her hand settled in his grasp and then let go once she was on solid ground.

Luke moved toward the door, ready to exit. Seth grabbed the boy's waist and launched him into the air. Luke hooted in laughter, his blonde hair fanned out like a halo.

"Do it again!"

"Luke, we must hurry," Aimee said her goodbyes to Mr. and Mrs. Garrett before turning to Seth. "Thanks for your help. I appreciate it very much."

"Yeah, glad to help." Seconds snapped by without words.

Her gaze lowered, and then flicked up to his. "Well, goodbye." She turned away and with Luke's hand in hers, rushed to the church.

Seth followed. "Hey, would you and Luke like to—"

"Sorry! We're very late." She called back as she pushed the church doors open and dragged Luke behind.

Seth stood outside the vehicle until she disappeared inside. He took a step following the urge to go after her.

"Seth?" Mom called from inside the cab of the vehicle.

He returned to his place behind the wheel.

"Did you and Aimee already know each other?"

"Never met her until today."

"Oh. You two look about the same age. I know Belinda said she's Michael McClain's widow. Did you go to school with him?"

Seth shook his head. "No, but I heard about it when he was killed."

"He was an Army man," Dad said.

"That's right. Pretty decorated from what I remember. I think he went to school in Bryan or Liberty County."

"I'm sure Aimee's parents lived in Point Peace a long time ago. Belinda told me her sister and brother in law traveled a lot. She was very excited when Aimee made the decision to move back home. Aimee has been through a lot from what Belinda tells me."

He looked back at the church before he pulled away from the curb.

"Maybe you should go by Belinda's shop, Seth. You look like you could use a trim."

Beside him, Dad chuckled. "Bonnie, don't meddle in the boy's life."

"Now, Tommy, I'm not meddling. And who do you think you are getting out in this heat to work on a vehicle? Your doctor gave you strict orders—"

While his parents renewed their discussion, Seth turned the dial on the radio. Still, his mind wandered to the woman trying to push her antique ride out of traffic.

There was something familiar about Aimee, but he couldn't place where he would have met her. He met Luke at the Community Center when he talked to the elementary classes about the importance of physical education. If Aimee was there, he would have remembered her.

And, they hadn't grown up together. He would have remembered her because he dated almost every girl in his class. At the time, that was something to brag about. Now, Seth cringed.

He hung his elbow on the ledge of his open window as the wind whipped by, just as it had whipped Aimee's long, brown hair and the skirts of her poufy dress. She'd been an amusing sight trying to push her vehicle out of traffic. He didn't know many women who would have attempted such a feat.

Seth raked his fingers through his hair. Yep, it may be time for a haircut.

~

High heels in hand, Aimee rushed down the corridor, toward voices and laughter. At the doorway she zeroed in on the bride. Sloan Miller,

17

her cousin, was more beautiful than ever.

Veil in place, it hung below her waist. Her auburn hair twisted up to accentuate her slender neck and shoulders. The bridal crown Aimee had picked out, more as a catty joke than an earnest suggestion, sat on top of her cousin's head.

And it looked absolutely perfect.

She forced a smile and pushed away a horrible pinch of envy. It seemed everything in Sloan's life played out perfectly, while Aimee's life personified the opposite –challenges, losses, and more losses. Her sweet Luke remained her most perfect creation, the one person who helped her forget her wrongs and made her feel like she could do anything.

When one of Aimee's shoes knocked against the doorway, conversation stopped and the ladies surrounding the bride turned her way.

Fueled by a dramatic gasp, Sloan hurried toward her. "Where have you been? I've been worried sick."

Aimee met her in the middle of the bride's dressing room, transformed from a children's classroom. Sloan's gown hung from the bulletin board. Two chairs were set up beside tables littered with cosmetics. Hairdryers and hot irons lay everywhere, plugged into every available outlet. The heat radiating from them filled the air.

She embraced her cousin, crushing her lace-trimmed veil in the process. "Luke had an infusion in Savannah and Tank died on the way back." She didn't want to think about her rescuer at the moment, even though Seth Garrett's hazel eyes were all she could see. "You should be dressed by now."

"I was waiting until the last minute. We couldn't do the group photos without you." Sloan pulled back, sweeping Aimee with a critical eye from head to foot. "You dyed your hair last night?"

Aimee ran her fingers through her tangled chestnut brown curls. "Went back to my natural color."

Her cousin's eyes narrowed. "What's wrong? You never make a drastic change like this except when something in your life is going horribly wrong."

"I do not."

"You do. When your paintings were featured at that art gallery in Charleston, then the columnist trashed your work, you died your hair blue. When your mother went through her chemo, you shaved your head."

"So did you."

"True. Now, what was the reason you died your hair red?" Sloan paused for a moment, remembering as the bride's descriptions garnered the attention of the bridesmaids and the elder family members. The women floated across the room on the tail of curiosity, and landed at Aimee's side.

"Everything is fine. Luke is fine. As a matter of fact, he saw Seth Garrett today. He couldn't be happier." She fisted her hands. Oh, why did she have to mention him?

"Seth Garrett?" Whitney, another bridesmaid and Aimee's cousin on her mother's side, smiled as she approached. "I heard he's single again."

"Did you ask him to help you with Luke's fundraiser, dear?" Aunt Tippy's wide brimmed hat knocked Granny Lena in the head as she barreled her way into the circle surrounding Aimee.

"Seth Garrett?" Sloan glowered.

Aimee turned to her grandmother and aunt to avoid her cousin's stare. "Tank broke down and Seth came to my rescue."

"Ironic." Sarcasm coated Sloan's muttered response.

Granny Lena's polished arthritic hands pushed Tippy aside. She reached out, ready to comfort. "Tell us all about it dear. Did your young man break up with you?"

"I don't have a young man, Granny. The last thing I needed is a man." Aimee shrugged her purse onto the floor as she sank into a chair.

Aunt Velma, whose hearing had suffered for as long as Aimee could remember, strolled over to her sister Lena, "Did you say she's seeing Harold Young?"

"Grandma, Harold Young is at least sixty years old," Whitney chimed in.

"Well, he does like the younger ones," Velma concluded.

"Harold broke up with you?" Another cousin exclaimed. "He's married!"

"She wasn't seeing Harold Young." Sloan piped in. Turning to Aimee, she lowered her voice, as if anything could be kept secret now. "Ignore them and tell me what's wrong?"

Aimee clasped her hands on Sloan's. "You're

jumping to conclusions. I wanted to go back to my natural color. And yes, Seth Garrett got us here, but nothing more." She eyed each person surrounding her. "No, I didn't ask him to help me with the fundraiser. I don't need his help."

Sloan's eyes narrowed as if she didn't believe her.

Aunt Tippy shook her head. "Oh, yes you do need his help. Why, people come all the way from Florida and as far north as Virginia to run in the race for that Ridley boy. The race covers Point Peace and Savannah. If Seth Garrett is that successful in motivating people to run, the man can definitely help raise money for Luke. And get folks to sign up to be a bone marrow donor."

A headache had started behind her eyes. "It wasn't the time or the place to bring up any issues besides what was wrong with Tank." She pushed out of the circle of family, claustrophobic due to their suffocating concern. She appreciated them, really she did, but no one in her family knew about her shared past with Seth.

"Seth's father offered to fix Tank, but I declined."

"Oh, Tom Garrett," Granny Lena purred. "Had I been twenty years younger, I would have given that sassy Bonnie a run for her money."

"He was a handsome devil," Aunt Tippy agreed.

"Still is," Velma said.

Ignoring their rambling elders, Sloan turned to Aimee. "You're happy here, aren't you?"

"Point Peace is great. About the hair, I don't

have the time to keep it blonde. I'm determined to keep Luke well and need to focus my efforts on him. We don't have time to discuss this, *Sloan*."

"You're right. I need to get dressed."

"Aimee needs to date a doctor." Whitney unzipped the bag holding Sloan's dress. "A doctor can help her take care of Luke."

"There are plenty of doctors in Savannah." Granny Lena reassured Aimee with a soft pat on her shoulder.

"Plenty of *single* doctors, I hear." Tippy winked.

"Thank you, but I'm not looking for a man."

Tippy rolled her eyes at Lena. "She knows it all, Lena. Come along, sis, it's time to go into the sanctuary."

"Aimee is doing fine taking care of Luke on her own," Sloan pleaded as the ladies shuffled out of the room. She turned to Aimee. "Everything will work out. By the time Luke begins school, he'll settle into his routine, and so will you."

Aimee nodded in agreement.

Grabbing a hairbrush, she began working the tangles. She swallowed the burning lump that rose in her chest. Negative thoughts weren't allowed today. She held an important role as Sloan's maid of honor and Aimee would do her part. Oh, and she couldn't wait to see Luke walk down the aisle as ring bearer.

Once the bridal party began assembling in the hallway, Aimee found herself beside Sloan.

"So, Seth brought you to the church?" Her cousin nudged her toward the back of the bride's processional.

Nodding, she concentrated on the pink roses of her bouquet and exhaled. Any female with a brain would have been thrilled to announce her rescuer. The Garrett family was like royalty around Point Peace, but her past memories wouldn't allow any joy. "I've followed his career like a paranoid fruit loop."

"It's been ten years, Aimee."

"Twelve, actually… Twelve years." Her lip trembled. She bit down but tears brimmed. "That accident was my fault. No one knows except you and me. It was wrong for me to move back here."

"No pity parties today." Sloan wrapped her arms around her. "You have to let this go. You are not the person you were back then. You've endured more in the last few years than anyone I've ever seen."

"I should have been honest with Seth."

"What if he's already found closure to that part of his life? Do you want to renew his pain?"

"No. Of course not."

"You've decided not to ask him to help you with the fundraiser?"

She nodded. "I'll do it myself. The family said they would help me."

Sloan's eyes looked upon her with doubt. "Yes, and they will. I will help you as much as possible, but I am going to be traveling more this summer with my new job."

"Oh, I forgot about your new schedule." Aimee faced the small corridor ahead where the rest of the bridal party had lined up to enter the sanctuary.

"The reason we suggested you asking the Garrett's for help is that their family owns the perfect venue and Seth's outreach is state wide. I know you want to exhaust all avenues to find a bone marrow donor for Luke, no matter who helps."

Her voice was barely a whisper. "I can't face Seth again."

"I see. It's okay." Sloan squeezed her arm. "Chances are you'll never see him again. Move on with your life and leave the past where it belongs."

Aimee held Sloan's train off the concrete as they exited one part of the church that led outside. Once they reached the entrance of the sanctuary, she fanned the full train out behind Sloan. The groomsmen were already filing toward the altar. Luke stood at the door to walk in beside the flower girl. Perhaps it was the soft light in the room, but his skin looked pasty. Though he'd been in the sun before they arrived at church, his cheeks held no sign of color. She mumbled a hasty prayer. *Just let it be he's tired from the excitement today. Please let that be all.*

He glanced her way, and Aimee smiled, adding a wink for good luck.

He returned the wink and faced the door holding the pillow where the rings were tied. With his bowtie, starched shirt, and shiny gold cufflinks, he was her little man. It was so hard to believe he'd turn eight in three months.

Her throat closed as emotion gripped her and she fought to maintain her composure. She didn't want to face more doctors, more tests alone. She'd had little time to understand Luke's blood disorder before his treatments had began six months before. Then, Luke's response to the chemotherapy, with his immune system so compromised, she'd debated even allowing him around all the people at the wedding, but she'd promised her cousin, her best friend.

She'd been praying consistently, asking why her son had to go through this, asking for healing, for a miracle. But so far, no miracle had come.

Luke needed a bone marrow transplant to beat this illness. The bone marrow registry had his information and they were looking for a match, but finding a match often took time. Time her son didn't have. And so she'd taken it on herself to start searching any avenue she could for a hopeful donor and she wouldn't rest until her son had his cure.

Chapter Three

In all of his thirty-four years, the majority spent in Point Peace, Seth had never set foot in a beauty salon. When he needed a cut he stuck with Dutch, the barber at the corner of First and Main, the same one his father used. Except Dutch was out of town, and for the last two days Seth hadn't been able to put the brunette in the pink bridesmaid dress out of his mind.

Shutting the door of his truck, he headed across the parking lot. The salon's building once belonged to old Frances Miller. The elderly lady had been at least a hundred when Seth was a child and rode his bike along the one lane street. Long before the area became commercialized. When the Piggly Wiggly arrived, the grocery store chain stirred things up and afterwards, Point Peace's development exploded. After Mrs. Miller died, her children transformed the cottage into the hair capital of town. Or so his mother said.

Where rocking chairs once graced the veranda, a box for newspapers sat for purchase. Colorful flowers spilled over window boxes. A handicap access ramp lay to the right side of the entrance across from steps on the left. Willow trees hung low, providing ample shade for the porch. Not far from the brick chimney, a bright pink sign hung near the roof's peak, advertising Belinda's Beauty Spot.

Two women who'd parked in front of the salon now eyed him as they hustled inside.

"This is stupid." He lifted his ball cap and raked his hand over hair he'd neglected. Getting a trim at some place called the Beauty Spot may be dumb, but the opportunity to run into Aimee McClain made perfect sense.

He plopped his cap back on his head as he climbed the front steps two at a time, and pulled open the door.

Tiffany leaned against the counter of Aimee's station. "I want to help you with Luke's party, but I signed up for summer classes and they start tonight."

"Good for you. College is important." Aimee fastened one last pin across the orange roller, holding her customer's silver strands in place.

"Tiff dear," Belinda, their aunt, shifted a box of supplies to her hip as she stopped on her way to the storage closet. "It's not a party. It's going to be bigger. We need to have it at an outdoor venue where we can have a spokesman on sight and entertainment. The idea is to raise money for Luke's medical bills."

"We want to raise awareness for the illness and encourage attendees to test to see if we can find a bone marrow match for him." Aimee didn't want the event for Luke to sound like she was simply asking for money. She could scrimp, save, work hard and earn her own money but she couldn't be a bone marrow match for her son. So far, no one in the country that was already a part of the bone marrow registry was Luke's match. Without a transplant, Luke's health would continue to suffer.

Tiffany greeted her next client as Aimee pinned the last roller in place. "All right, Mrs. Lovett. Let's move you to the dryer and let these curls set."

"Don't let me sit under there too long." Mrs. Lovett's voice cracked. "It gets hot and my skin isn't as thick as it used to be."

Holding her customer's purse, Aimee stood nearby as the eighty-something lady scooted forward in the stylist chair. "I'll be watching the clock, but if you feel too hot, please let me know."

Mrs. Lovett's wrinkles deepened as she smiled at Aimee. Once her feet were planted on the floor, Aimee held her hand alongside the woman's elbow as she wobbled across the tiled floor. The back corner of the salon held six dryers, three on either side of the magazine rack. Belinda kept the latest style issues on display, considering herself Point Peace's go-to when it came to all things beauty. Aimee offered Mrs. Lovett a couple of issues, then froze in place when Belinda called her name.

Her aunt sounded so much like her mother sometimes it startled her. It was silly, though because her mother had been gone for twelve years. Still, being back in Point Peace, spending time at her mother's childhood home, seemed to bring her mother's spirit alive. More than once when she'd been in her Granny Lena's kitchen, she'd thought she heard her mother's voice in the other room. She even dreamed about her mother from time to time.

Belinda shared her sister's blue eyes and peaches and cream complexion. Where her aunt's hair was auburn, like Sloan's, her mother's hair was dark brown, like her own.

Her aunt's smile was similar to Diana's. Even now, the way she pinched her lips together in a quite mischievous manner reminded her of Mom. "You have a customer."

"You already scheduled someone else for me?" Aimee turned the dryer to the appropriate setting, keeping the heat low for her elderly customer.

Belinda strolled toward the middle of the salon as her grin boasted a combination of curiosity and amusement. "No, I didn't. This one is all you."

"Hmm... I haven't scheduled anyone." Following Belinda to her newly appointed station, she grabbed a broom, craning her neck to view the reception area as she started sweeping the floor.

"Oh, he's a walk in." Belinda chuckled as she moved aside. "He asked for *you*."

"He?" The foyer came into view. "Oh..." Seth Garrett took up the center of the room, crushing a ball cap in his hands. A lock of hair swept across his forehead. His red t-shirt stretched across his chest as if it were covering a firm Jell-O mold, except nothing jiggled on his physique. His khaki shorts were baggy over his thighs and showed off firm tanned calves. Even his feet were sun kissed, evident by the exposure granted by his flip flops. He looked like he belonged on a beach, ready to kayak or go fishing. If he held a surfboard, it would have suited him.

Seth raised his hand in a bashful wave.

She waved back. "Be right with you."

Belinda tugged her sleeve. "Says he knows you."

She whirled around and shrugged, "Oh, I met him briefly this weekend."

"You must have made an impression. Bringing in customers on your first day, why I should have hired you months ago."

Sweeping hair into the pan, she tried not to think about her most recent mistakes. "I should have started working months ago." With her checking account balanced, she had ten dollars to her name and payday wasn't for five more days.

"Seth's mother is one of my best customers, but Seth has never set foot in here, doll. When should we pull Mrs. Lovett out of the dryer?"

"Who?"

"Your current client," Belinda thumbed over her shoulder. "Remember her?"

"Five more minutes."

Belinda patted Aimee's shoulder. "Go see about Seth. I'll finish up with Mrs. Lovett."

"No. I'll finish her. Surely, as a walk-in he will understand I already have clients and he'll have to wait."

Aimee walked to the foyer, mashing her fingers against her black apron. She inhaled, but the air seemed too thick all of the sudden. "Hi Seth, how's it going?"

After exchanging pleasantries, he brushed the hair off his brow. It fell back almost covering his eyes. "Um, I need a cut and my normal barber is out of town. Can you fit me in?"

"Sure. I'm finishing up with a client. It'll be a few more minutes, unless you'd like for Belinda to give you a cut. She's available."

"Oh sorry, Aimee, I'm busy with the books." Belinda quipped from behind them at the reception desk.

"I'll wait." Seth took a seat near the coffee bar.

Aimee turned on her heel and hurried toward the dryers. Belinda followed, fast on her heels. Once at the dryer station, Aimee narrowed her eyes at her aunt. "You could have offered someone else to do his hair instead of me."

"Why? He asked for you."

Lifting the dryer from the elderly lady's head, Aimee rolled her eyes. "It's my first day, after all."

Belinda sighed. "Don't be silly. You're doing his hair, Aimee." She swiveled away. "What is your problem?"

"I just hate for any customer to have to wait, that's all."

"Well, we'll vote you stylist of the month for your customer concern."

Twenty minutes later, Belinda snickered as she strolled by Aimee's station, tapping her watch. Aimee smirked in return as she sprayed Mrs. Lovett's curls one last time. Perhaps it wasn't right to procrastinate, but Aimee's plan concerning Seth Garrett was to keep her distance.

It's just a haircut. You can cut hair in your sleep. This is not a big deal.

Aimee led Mrs. Lovett to the reception desk. Along the wall beside the powder room, rows of shampoos, conditioners and other hair products filled the glass shelves. Beside the coffee bar, comfy chairs sat between the displays and bar area. Seth's large frame took up every inch of the yellow Queen Anne. Ankle crossed over his knee, his head remained bent as he focused on his phone. Mrs. Lovett's voice seemed to break his concentration and his attention was suddenly on Aimee.

"I'd like to go ahead and make my appointment for next week, Aimee. Do you have another morning appointment?"

Aimee yanked her gaze from Seth and flipped open the calendar's wide pages. "Yes ma'am. I'll give you our opening spot at ten." She completed the transaction and wrote the date and time on a reminder card which she passed to Mrs. Lovett with her change.

Mrs. Lovett waved Aimee's handful of money away. "Keep it, dear."

"Thank you, Mrs. Lovett. Have a wonderful week." She carefully folded the tip into her money folder, grateful to have this job, and grateful Luke had stayed out of the hospital for two weeks straight. When Luke was healthy, Aimee could work. She had so much to be thankful for, but she tucked her thoughts to the back of her mind so that she wouldn't get all weepy. Her hands shook as she locked the desk.

Pull it together. Straightening her back, she

forced a smile and faced her next customer. "All right Seth," As slow as she moved out from behind the reception desk, she might as well have been walking the plank to her death. "What can I do for you today?"

"I need a good two inches off all over." He stood and wove his fingers through his wavy brown locks. "I'd say I'm overdue."

"Sure, come on back." Her voice sounded normal, but inside her throat constricted and her stomach churned. "Would you like it shampooed?"

Before he could answer, Belinda strutted by. "Aimee is wonderful at shampooing."

Dear God. For the last year and a half, her aunt and cousins had been trying to fix Aimee up with eligible bachelors, even while she was still in Atlanta. Apparently their dating game antics were only going to increase now that she was home.

Seth smiled. "A shampoo sounds great."

She led Seth to the chair under the watchful eye of Belinda, her cousin Whitney – who already had a customer – and another stylist named Adele who had Granny Lena in the chair. Tiffany was on the other side of the room, but her customer was turned toward Aimee, too.

Lena stretched her arthritic hand out to as they approached. "Seth, you get more handsome every day."

He leaned down in front of Lena and cupped both hands around her smaller one. "Mrs. Miller, it is good to see you."

"How is it you're not already married?" Lena

flicked a glance at Aimee.

Aimee emphatically tilted her head at her Granny as she flipped open a towel.

Seth chuckled, "I haven't found the right woman, I suppose." He glanced at Aimee before turning his attention back to Granny. "Marriage isn't something to enter into lightly."

"You're right about that. Paul and I have been married sixty years this December."

"Congratulations." Seth patted her hand and began backing away. "You should contact my mother about having a celebration dinner at Pleasant Lea."

Whitney pulled the comb through her client's wet tresses. "Belinda, have you started making plans for Granny and Grandpa's anniversary? Seth has a great location. Pleasant Lea is my favorite restaurant in town."

Crossing her arms, Belinda smirked. "I may have spoken to Bonnie about a big celebration." She looked directly at Granny Lena. "Mom knows it's supposed to be a surprise."

Lena held on to Seth's hand. "I love surprises. Come see us anytime, Seth."

"Thank you for the invitation, Mrs. Miller. I will stop by." Seth stepped back, but Lena held firm.

"Seth, let me ask you a question." Lena blinked repeatedly, the action in her hey-day was probably a sign she was flirting. "I understand you have been very successful with the race you hold every year."

Straightening into a more business-like stance,

Seth rested his hands on a nearby pony wall that divided each booth. "I like to think the Kevin Ridley race is a wonderful success. You may be aware, but we were able to build the youth community center on Elm out of the race proceeds."

"Oh yes," Lena clasped her hands in front of her heart. "And the community center is so nice. I take line dancing over there every Tuesday. The children always enjoy going there."

His eyes twinkled as he glanced at Aimee and then turned to Granny Lena again. "Thank you. I'm glad to hear someone of your clout in the community enjoys spending time there, and that the kids have a good time. That makes my day."

"Well, Seth, I have a proposition for you. A chance to make a difference in one particular person's life—"

Aimee shut the water off in the basin. "Granny, I—" She could not allow her grandmother to mention Luke or her desire to set up a fundraiser. She did not want Seth's help.

Granny went on as if Aimee had not spoken. "Our family is trying to help Aimee organize a bone marrow drive and fundraiser for her son."

"I didn't know, Mrs. Miller." Seth nodded at Aimee. "I will be happy to help in any way I can."

"Maybe you could point her in the right direction," Granny went on. "Perhaps you could discuss it over coffee—"

"Or lunch," Whitney piped up.

"Or dinner," Belinda breezed by Seth and patted his shoulder. "Dinner will give you more time to iron out details. There's a lot of details as I'm sure you're aware, Seth."

"Sure." He stood there, looking sheepish. Dear God, she needed to rescue him from this craziness. "Yes ma'am." He nodded to Aimee's family, surrounding him like happy vultures.

"Let's get started on your shampoo." Aimee waited beside the wash basin and chair. Seth broke away from Granny Lena, who would have kept talking had she been given the opportunity. Adele turned Granny's chair around so that Granny now faced Aimee. Even Whitney's customer was turned around. Tiffany grinned at her from across the room. Aimee swiveled to Seth and forced a smile.

"Don't pay any attention to them. I'm still trying to decide what I want to do regarding a fundraiser. I don't really need any more help." Aimee turned her head slightly so that the words would carry over her shoulder toward her meddling family.

"Oh, that girl!" Granny Lena bit out the words. "Stubborn like her father."

Aimee flipped the water back on and tested its heat on her palm. Seth closed his inquiring eyes as she slid her fingers along his brow and pulled the water over his scalp. She applied shampoo and massaged it over the thickness of his curls. She tried not to focus on who was in the chair, or how her fingertips tingled as they worked the soap across his perfectly shaped head.

Once in her stylist chair, she pulled her fingers through his hair, finding his strands soft and fine. Lavender from the shampoo mingled with his woodsy scent.

Business, girl, get back to business. "How do you like your style?"

"I used to keep a crew cut, but I guess I'd like something a little longer."

His gaze held hers as he explained his likes and dislikes. "I understand." She broke the connection as she grabbed her scissors and comb.

"When did you move back to Point Peace?"

She ran the comb through, snipping the length off here and there. "May."

"And you and Luke lived in Atlanta?"

"Yes, in the Decatur area."

"Big change. How does Luke like it here?"

"He likes being close to our family again." He wants to start school, Aimee sighed, but that probably won't happen. In the mirror, Seth caught her frown. Equipped with a smile, she went back to cutting his hair. She cleaned up along his neckline with the electric razor, and then moved to his beard and trimmed it slightly as he requested. Working quickly, she held her breath ever slightly as she finished. Her heart pounded because being this close to Seth brought back memories of being close to him twelve years earlier. She had made a terrible mistake and had caused Seth and his friend harm. How could anyone ever forgive someone for those actions?

"Aimee could've come home years ago after Michael died, but she wouldn't listen."

Mouth firm, holding in the slew of words she'd like to say to her nosey grandmother, Aimee turned slightly to face her elder. "Now, Granny, I moved back as soon as I could."

"Harrumph," Granny crossed her thin arms over her ample bosom and shook her head.

Aimee turned back around, hoping Granny would let up on her. The whole family supported her idea to hold a fundraiser and bone marrow drive for Luke. The problem was there were too many ideas and no organization to the madness. Granny's idea of having Seth help was reasonable, but Granny didn't know the secret Aimee held. And she wasn't about to risk the woman's frail health to tell her.

Careful not to make a mistake, she made final snips, careful that each stroke was meaningful and good. Giving Seth a good haircut, something he could walk outside and be proud of, would help her make up for her mistakes. Mistakes she prayed he would never need to find out.

She swallowed hard, trying to break up the thickness of sentiment clogging there, threatening to push forward all of the memories and emotions she'd fought to hide. Stepping aside, she put the razor on the table in front of the mirror. "You're all done."

He eased forward in the chair. "You're faster than my barber." Running his knuckles near his sideburns and beard, he nodded. "You're better."

Aimee rubbed her flushed cheeks and neck with her hands, as she led him to the foyer. Behind the reception desk, she shuffled papers, moving objects around on the desk. She needed some space. The air was too thick, too hot and downright stifling.

He slid cash across the desk.

"Keep it." She handed the bill back to him with a smile. "Consider it thanks for stopping to help me on Saturday."

"You already thanked me."

She shook her head. After a few moments, he took the money back. "I was glad to help." He tucked his wallet away. "How about dinner sometime? What about tonight?"

The salon telephone rang beside her. "I already have plans, but thank you." At the third ring, Aimee whipped the phone off its charging station. "Thanks for coming in today, Seth. Take care."

He nodded as Aimee answered the phone, "Belinda's Beauty Spot, how may I help you?"

As Seth let the door close behind him Aimee exhaled. She made it through the difficulty of seeing him again.

Lord, let it be the last.

Chapter Four

He knew the question even before his mother asked.

"Seth, when *is* your surgery scheduled?"

He'd stopped by his parents to help Dad replace a squeaky door. With the task complete, Seth and his parents gathered in the kitchen. Without anyone else more interesting to discuss, the topic of conversation never failed to rotate to Seth.

Mom carried her new cell phone, swiping her finger across the screen. "How do I find my calendar on here, Tommy?"

Dad took the phone as Mom folded her hands around his arm and then shifted her gaze back to Seth. "I'm afraid your surgery will fall on your grandmother's birthday, which is when we're having the family reunion…"

"It won't, Mom."

"There it is, Tommy, there's the calendar."

Handing the phone back to her, Dad lowered to a chair at the kitchen table and unfolded the newspaper.

"Now, let's confirm these dates."

"Not right now, dear. This can wait." Dad didn't look up from his newspaper.

"I canceled it, Mom. I'm not having the surgery." Seth pressed his palms against the cool granite of the counter.

Mom gripped her phone. "Not again."

"You have to have the surgery." Over the newspaper, Dad narrowed his eyes.

"The therapy has loosened my shoulder up considerably. I'll keep doing the exercises and be back to normal." He smiled in an effort to convince his stubborn parents. The injury to his shoulder dated back to his days of playing professional baseball and was one of the reasons he became a coach.

"We talked about this. The shoulder is going to keep getting worse." Dad reminded him.

Mom huffed. "And then you'll lose time from the team. This year is supposed to be your chance to take Point to the state championship. The whole town thinks so."

"The whole town, dear?" Dad smirked.

Seth silenced Mom's snappy retort by raising his hand. "I've given it a lot of thought. I'm not going back under the knife. I'm not playing ball anymore..."

"Have the surgery." Mom laid her hand on his and squeezed. "You'll can recover while the boys are practicing and can still be out there to observe."

Dad all but finished her sentence. "You'll be ready to go by the first game of the season."

"Why is this so important to you?"

His parents exchanged a look. Dad stood. "Look, son, one day you'll have kids of your own. It's different when it's your kid out there. You remember when we'd stay outside past dark and your mom would be ringing the bell for us to come in? Those were some of the best days."

Seth lowered to the bar stool. "My time's passed for a wife and kids, Dad."

"Don't say that!" Mom's eyes got moist and were blinking.

Oh no. "Don't cry, Mom."

Dad chuckled. "Look at Harold Young; sixty years old and on his third wife. He's got at least a dozen kids by now. And he's still out there pitching the ball, taking them to amusement parks."

Seth raised his brows. "Are you saying I need to follow Harold Young's lead?"

His father shook his head. "All I'm saying is stop being a quitter."

"I'm not quitting."

Mom moved beside him, rubbing his back like she did when he was a kid. "If you'd come to church like I've asked, you'd meet some young women. There are many singles attending there and I'm sure any one of them would love to go out with you."

Seth slid off the stool and walked to the bay window. He appreciated his parent's advice on all things except his personal life. Priceless. He shouldn't egg his mother on, but he asked the question anyway. "So, you want me to come to church to find a date?"

"Not *just* to find a date. Goodness, you make me sound conniving, and I'm not." She paused and studied him. "I don't think I mentioned it, but I like your new haircut, Seth."

"Thanks, Mom."

"You took my advice and let Aimee cut your hair, didn't you?"

Beside him, Dad guffawed as he picked up the paper and sat down at the table.

"Yes, Mom, I did. I also asked Aimee out and she declined."

"At least you tried. It's better than hanging out at those sports bars."

"I don't hang out at bars. Occasionally, Grant and I go by and have some wings and watch the game at the pier. Josh comes with us." Surely, mentioning Josh, the associate pastor at their church, would strengthen Seth's defense.

"Well, I think you're looking in the wrong places. Any respectable woman is not going to be hopping around night clubs looking for a man."

"Mom, yes they do."

She waved the notion away with a flick of her wrist and put a pot of water on the stove.

"Seth, have I ever told you about where I met your mother?"

"No, Dad," Seth grinned, playing along. "I don't think you have."

"I was bussing tables," Mom said.

"At a bar," Dad grinned.

"It was a pizza parlor that happened to sell alcoholic beverages." Mom corrected.

"It was a bar!"

A knock on the kitchen door brought pause to the debate. Josh Martin, Seth's buddy for as long as he could remember, had one hand on the door handle and a sheepish grin on his face. "Is it safe to enter?"

"Your timing is perfect, as usual," Seth chuckled. "Mom and Dad were just having a friendly discussion about how they met."

"Ah…I can come back."

"No, stay!" Seth crossed the room to his friend.

Josh hugged Seth's mother, then shook Dad's hand.

"So, what's up?" Seth retrieved water bottles from the refrigerator. He offered Josh and Dad one before opening one for himself.

"I have selected the artist to paint the murals in the Children's center. Her name is Aimee McClain and her grandparents are Lena and Paul Miller. Bonnie, I'd like you to review Aimee's portfolio and her estimate with your committee. If they approve, then I can move forward on hiring her."

"Aimee!" Mom squealed. "We met her this weekend. She's adorable. And her son Luke is just precious."

Josh set an album on the table. "Take a look at these portraits." He shook his head. "She alluded to the fact that she doesn't paint full time. After seeing these, I'm not sure why she's not displayed in galleries across the country."

They gathered around the table as Josh flipped open the book. He turned several thick pages until he came to a photo of a canvas. The painting was of a meadow and one tree. Seth angled his head to get a better view over his mother's head.

"Wonder where this is located?" Seth pointed to the portrait before Josh could turn the page. The similarities of the meadow looked like one he used to drive by when he was in college.

Josh squinted as he lowered his head closer to the album. "The portrait is titled 'Never Forget' but it doesn't say anything else."

Never Forget.

A portrait of a woman was next, the detail of the crow's feet around the woman's eyes were lifelike.

"She's talented," Seth surmised as he backed away. Talented, but not available. Recalling the cheesecake he'd spied in the refrigerator, he stepped away from the conversation and retrieved a few plates from the cabinet.

"These are wonderful." Mom cooed. "I will be more than happy to work with Aimee."

Seth brought the cheesecake to the table and passed around plates and utensils. Mom took her seat beside Dad and began slicing.

Josh gestured to the portfolio with his fork. "The first page is her estimate. Following that are the sketches she is proposing for the murals. I'll leave it up to you and the committee on which ones you ask her to do."

"When can she start? And did she say how long the murals would take?"

Josh nodded. "She will have it done before Labor Day if she can start by the first of July. We need to give her a decision pretty fast."

"Yes, we need the murals done before the

festival and it's scheduled the weekend of Labor Day." Mom eyed Seth. "How are the plans coming, son? Have you completed the fliers we talked about?"

"They're on my computer." He swallowed the rest of his cake. "I had to finalize the details for the race. We have a new vendor handling the participant's times. They have a new system which is high tech. Pretty impressive. Anyway, it's scheduled for the fourth of July this year. With it changing from June to July, I had to make sure the other vendors were aware."

"When can I expect the fliers on my desk?"

"By the end of the week, Mom."

She raised an eyebrow. "That's cutting it close, but I suppose I'll have to live with it."

Josh wiped his mouth with his napkin and stood. "Thank you, Bonnie. The cheesecake was delicious. And I appreciate you helping me with the artist and the murals. You're a life saver."

"Anything for you, sweetheart," She patted Josh's arm. "You should call Cornelia and check on her. I'm sure she'd love to hear from you."

"Bonnie," Dad warned. "Mind your own business."

The ex-Marine, now associate pastor of Hopewell Church, had always been a regular fixture in the Garrett household. He began coming over because of his friendship with Seth. He continued because he had an interest in Cory, Seth's younger sister.

Seth wasn't sure when his best friend fell for his little sister, but from what he'd observed Josh and Cory's timing had never been right. If Mom had any input, their timing would eventually come together whether they wanted it to or not.

"What?" Mom blinked innocently. "I don't know what you're implying." And with that she wandered out of the kitchen humming a song that sounded a lot like a wedding march.

~

Aimee had never seen a bigger mess. The breakfast table was full of brochures, books, notebook paper and folders full of stuff. Except the table was only part of the mess.

Shoving open the kitchen window, she inhaled, hoping for some sanity and clarity. An unseasonable cool breeze greeted her. While the discussion at the table escalated, she moved to the French doors, popped one open so that the cool breeze rustled through the eating area, blowing several brochures, to the floor. The noisy tête-à-tête going on between her grandmother Lena, both great aunts, Tippy and Velma, her aunt Belinda, and her cousins Tiffany and Sloan, had reached an earsplitting level. She hoped her neighbors didn't mind a little friendly arguing. The Millers were a lot of things and quiet wasn't one of them.

"Aimee needs to have something going on at the drive besides the presence of the National Bone Marrow Registry. It makes perfect sense. You treat this like a party." An actress in her heyday, Granny Lena's hands waved dramatically as she spoke. "Feed people. Entertain them. Make them happy, then they will be glad to stick a Q-tip in their mouth for whatever reason."

"How is Aimee going to pay for all of this?" Belinda asked. "Will she sell tickets?"

"What are the people buying tickets to get in return?" Sloan added. As appointed secretary, she was the only person sitting at the table besides Aunt Velma who couldn't stand for too long due to her bad back.

"We should do a talent show," Aunt Tippy suggested.

Tiffany nearly spewed the Coca-cola she was drinking. "That would be so much fun."

"No, it wouldn't." Granny Lena put her hand on Tiffany's head as she'd done when her granddaughter was a child to make her stop talking. "If you have a talent show, then it takes away from Luke and that's too much for Aimee to handle."

Tippy elbowed Lena. "We could be the judges. Velma was a triple threat back in the day."

"Still am!" Velma lifted her crooked finger to drive the point home.

"Save the talent show idea for something else," Lena scolded. "Bring me a drink, Aimee."

Ice cubes clanging in the glass was like a whisper as the debate escalated. While she appreciated her family's help, their constant bickering threatened her sanity. After sitting the iced tea in front of her grandmother, she headed toward the living room. The front door wasn't far away, maybe she should just leave. Who would miss her?

"Sit down, Aimee. Your fidgeting is making me a nervous wreck." Once she was seated, Lena stood and proceeded to pace the small eating area.

"Do you see why we need someone who knows what they are doing to take the lead on this fundraiser?" Lena eyed Aimee the entire time she paced. "We're all crowing and squawking and not making any progress."

Tiffany pouted. "I like the talent show idea."

"Then you organize that. This is for Luke." Lena stopped at Tiffany's chair which was directly across from Aimee. The diamond on her wedding ring caught a ray of sunlight and glinted as Lena tightened her grip on the chair. "We need to find a donor. We've all donated and no one in this family is his match. If Michael's family was worth a darn, we could call them, but they're going to expect something in return." Lena pointed at Aimee. "Don't ask them again, missy. I mean it."

"I won't, Granny." In truth, she'd already contacted them a second time and some of Michael's relatives had agreed to test for Luke. She worked around Granny's tunnel vision when necessary. People could change. She was proof of that statement and she felt the same for Michael's family.

"We don't need their kind skulking around like hungry barn cats." Now seated, Lena took a sip of her tea, eyeing Aimee over the brim. "What do you want to do for Luke's drive?"

Resting her elbows on the table, Aimee leaned forward. "I've called the registry and they will have a representative on sight whenever I give them a date and time."

"Good, good, but you didn't answer my question."

She looked down at her finger nails, cut short and clean. "I just want to send out fliers, emails, put up billboards asking people to come to the bone marrow drive to help Luke. I can tell his story, and hopefully, we will find a donor. People can donate and go home. I just want something simple, Granny."

"What if we had a dinner party?" Belinda leaned on the back of Sloan's chair. "We could find a nice setting. We'll cook the food but people will buy tickets to come and we'll give the proceeds of ticket sales to Aimee—"

"It's a nice idea, but even if we cook, we have to have a venue." Aimee crossed her arms and sat back in the chair. "I'm speaking with a lady at the Chamber tomorrow. I'm sure she will help us."

"I like the idea Sloan suggested about having a walk/run for Luke. That could draw the biggest crowd." Tiffany sipped on her soda. "I know several friends who participate in those every weekend."

"Yes," Lena purred. "And we all know who to ask about putting on a successful race." She eyed Aimee with frustration. "Stubborn britches just wouldn't ask him yesterday, and I want to know why."

Aimee massaged her temples, trying to work up a good reason not to ask Seth. What about the truth? Granny's health seemed to be just fine, despite what the woman had claimed when Aimee had come home for Christmas. If she told her grandmother the truth, that would surely make Granny understand why she didn't need to be around Seth at all.

The weight of her relative's stares clawed at Aimee's conscience while she pulled together how she would explain her past. As she met the gaze of each aunt and cousin, she realized none of them had held back when they told Aimee something. Honesty coupled with being direct was the best method.

Lena's blue eyes narrowed slightly as Aimee finally faced her. "You know Seth's successful race is for Kevin Ridley. Kevin died in a car accident in Clarke County twelve years ago. The reason I know this is because I was there. I caused Seth's car accident."

The room went silent for all of ten seconds, a record for the Miller women.

Granny folded her hands in front her and leaned forward. "Of all the excuses in the world, you had to dream up a whopper like that? Aimee Louise, I don't know what to make of you."

Beside Granny Lena, Sloan lowered her head to her hand.

She doesn't believe me. Aimee moved to her feet. "It's the truth, Granny. This is something I've had to live with for a long time. Do you all see now why I can't work with Seth? He doesn't know, and I want to keep it that way."

"It is not true. My granddaughters do not cause fatal accidents." Granny sputtered as she pushed herself up from the table. "This meeting is over." The old woman shuffled to the door with her younger sisters following close.

Keys jingling in hand, Tiffany eyed Granny

with confusion and hesitation. Their elders didn't see well and never drove at night. "Hurry up, Tiff." Granny spouted then turned as she touched the door handle. "Aimee, I don't want to hear you speak another word of such a fallacy. I mean it. Now, you will ask Seth Garrett to help you. So help me God, if I have to ask him myself, I will." Granny's arthritic finger pointed toward Aimee. "Do you hear me, young lady? Not another word of this ridiculousness."

"Granny, what I've told you is true. And, Luke is my son. I will handle this without Seth Garrett's help and without your help if that's the way it has to be."

"You are acting just like your father right now, do you know that?" Crossing her arms, Aimee braced for the whip of her Grandmother's tongue. "I tried to warn your mother, but she wouldn't listen. She followed that man and his blind ambition across the country. I didn't even get to see her until her last days. Well, you're going to listen to me because I've got fifty years on you, girl. If you want to help your son, you will put this cockamamie story out of your mind and ask Seth for help. Like I said, if you don't ask him, I will."

Chapter Five

"Aimee, I assure you we replaced those plugs, changed the oil and replaced the battery the last time we had your car here."

Alone in the front office of Red's Auto and Salvage, Red glanced the length of her as he scratched his sternum through his rock band embellished T-shirt. He'd worked on her Granddaddy's cars for as long as she could remember, but she wasn't so sure he was the trustworthy man he'd once been.

Maybe she should have given Seth's father the chance to fix Tank. The list of items Red began puffing off to her wouldn't come cheap.

Aimee glared at him. "If you did the repairs in December, why do we need to do them again?"

"All the traveling to Atlanta and back has worn the motor out. It's probably time to trade." Red's teeth were nearly yellow, stained, she assumed by the cancer-causing glop of tobacco in his jaw. "Did you know I opened a used car lot? I could show you what I've got."

As if she'd buy a car from him."I'm not interested."

"You don't want to take a look?"

She turned her head, hoping to catch a fresh scent, however impossible that may be in an establishment that smelled like burnt tires. She needed some air. Turning away from the counter, she pushed the door opened and walked the short distance to her son.

Next door was the park, abundant with grassy slopes and flat areas for play. An open field was marked for baseball. Right field backed up to Red's property. As the crack of a baseball against an aluminum bat confirmed what commanded her son's attention, Luke leaned in, tightening his fingers around the links of the fence.

When the next batter approached the plate, the group of kids in the dugout hollered behind him. Aimee recalled from her own childhood when kids would gather at the park after school and form an impromptu game. Though the afternoon sun blinded the outfield, the short kid at bat might have an advantage if he could connect with the ball.

Aimee looked down at her son. It should be Luke out there. He wanted to try every sport, but his condition had many restrictions. He didn't have the energy needed to play football or baseball—his sport of choice. Sometimes, he was simply too sick to be around other people. She bit her lip as she turned back toward Red's office.

Red renewed his lecture, pontificating about what Tank needed for survival. Amazing he had figured all of that out in his examination of Tank that took maybe five minutes. "Of course, that'll just get it running. We may find we need more parts, and if we do, well, that could take more time—"

"How much?" she interrupted, more interested in the numbers she didn't have. Family friend or not. "What's the bottom line, Red?"

"Four thousand." He didn't blink an eye. Not one shift to indicate dishonesty.

Her fingernails bit into her palms as she balled her fists. She had to bite her tongue to keep from sounding less than lady-like. "The vehicle's book value isn't worth four thousand."

"I'm just shooting you straight." He winked with a friendly pat on her shoulder, ending with a squeeze. "Maybe we can work out a deal, Sweetheart."

Aimee stepped back, but held the man's gaze. "I'm not your sweetheart." The man was old enough to be her father, for Heaven's sake. "I need to call Granddaddy."

Red tapped a can of chewing tobacco against his hand, then broke the seal. "He'll say to leave it with me, darlin'." He shoved a finger full into his mouth and smiled.

Fists tight, she turned away from Red and his obnoxious offer. Oh, what would Michael do? God, she missed her husband so much at times like this. It wasn't that she couldn't handle Red, but there was no way she could afford that kind of money. Not right now with Luke's medical bills.

She'd managed to speak with the hospital this morning and set up a payment plan. While the

HRISTY LASHEA

conversation kept her accounts out of collections, it didn't help her concerns over when the bills would stop coming in. She'd applied for assistance and received help paying some of her utilities, but those agreements were limited. Her grandparents let live rent free in their rental home, but it wasn't permanent. They relied on the rental income to supplement their retirement. Eventually, help would run out and she'd still be in the red.

This morning, she met with a Point Peace Chamber of Commerce representative to propose a plan to hold the fundraiser and bone marrow drive. Though the woman she was polite and helpful, her calendar wasn't open to assist with such an event until next year. The lady agreed that a run/walk would be ideal for Aimee's situation.

"Perhaps you can speak with the organizer for the Kevin Ridley race about how to get started. Or, if you would like a festival type event, the folks at Hopewell Church could share their knowledge."

Both events had ties to Seth Garrett. He had apparently cornered the Point Peace market on raising money and awareness. It was too late to ask him to allow her cause to couple with Kevin's race. Besides, it didn't seem right to take away from Kevin. If anything, she should devote the rest of her life making amends with Kevin Ridley's family and Seth.

"And I'm sure your aunt wouldn't mind holding the event at her shop."

"Yes," Aimee said. "We've thought about many different venues."

"When you decide, let me know so that we can

56

put your event on the website."

The sooner she could raise money for Luke's medical bills, and more importantly find a bone marrow donor for him, the sooner her son could recover. God willing.

Right now, though, she needed an operable vehicle. As she neared Luke, she glanced back at Red. He approached his employee beside an open bay of the garage and pointed toward Tank, parked alone on the end of the building not far from Red's salvage yard. Laughter rang across the dirt packed yard. Red probably quoted a high price on repairs thinking she would sign Tank over for scrap.

Over my dead body. She turned on her heels and headed toward Red.

"Aimee?"

His voice halted her steps. "Seth, what are you doing here?"

He took off his black ball cap and rubbed his hand through his thick dark hair. "I was at the auto parts store next door getting an air filter." He held up the aforementioned filter. "I saw your Wagoneer, and then you. Is Red going to fix Tank?"

"He wants four grand."

Seth held her gaze. "Do you want my opinion?" Before she could answer, he went on, "I wouldn't let this guy change the tire on a tricycle."

She couldn't hold back her laugh, though there was little humor in her predicament. "I can't afford it, regardless." Rubbing her neck, she exhaled. "My husband always handled these things."

"I'm sorry for your loss." Seth shoved his

hands into his pockets.

She glanced up at him. "Did you know Michael?"

"Not personally, but I remember hearing about the military honors he received."

"He was remarkable." She moved her foot over the sandy gravel.

Seth nodded and shifted his gaze toward Luke. "I understand losing someone you care about." He paused and yanked his cap onto his head. "My best friend was killed right after our college graduation. I still haven't gotten over it." Seth stepped closer, his focus moved from her to Luke who was still watching the game.

She closed her eyes trying to shut out her memories of Seth's loss. Maybe she should say something but what? This wasn't the right time. Not with Luke present. Chilled by her mistakes, Aimee rubbed and stepped toward Luke. She would protect him at all costs, from his illness, from others, from herself.

"Are you cold?" Seth's voice jolted her.

She swallowed her pride and tilted her chin. "Chilled by the exorbitant quote Red gave me."

He chuckled. "It's over ninety degrees today. I couldn't imagine you being cold due to the weather."

She forced a laugh. Let him think what he wanted. Better to think she was cold natured than cold hearted... though the latter was exactly how she felt right now, especially standing beside the man who's life she had ruined.

Her grandmother's words from the night before

ricocheted like a bullet in her mind. She wouldn't put anything past Lena Miller. If the woman said she was going to do something, Lord help whoever got in her way. "Speaking of your friend, I heard your race is coming up in a couple of weeks."

"Yes. You and Luke should come. We always have a lot of fun. There will be games and refreshments at the finish line."

Aimee glanced over at Luke. "Maybe we'll stop by." She couldn't afford to participate in the race, but she wanted to see how he set everything up.

"About your current vehicle situation, do you mind some advice?" Seth's intent gaze held her for so long her heartbeat accelerated. "Since it is just you and Luke, you need to become an automotive expert. Too many out there are looking to take advantage of others."

She dropped her focus on the sandy gravel and kicked a rock. "I'm finding out the hard way."

"Our offer is still open. Don't let this guy take you for a ride." His brows lifted waiting for her reply.

"How much would it cost?"

He shook his head. "Let Dad look over it first. He's reasonable and I'm sure he'll work with you on payment arrangements. He's even exchanged car repairs for skills his customer may have. For instance, my friend, Grant, has done a ton of work around my parent's home. He's a carpenter so he barters his carpentry for Dad's handy work." He scratched his chin.

She angled a glance at him. "I could promise

to cut your dad's hair for the next twenty years."

Seth laughed. "I don't think he has enough hair."

Grinning, she shrugged. "Well, I'm also pretty good with yard work. I can cut grass, use a weed eater, and plant gardens. I paint—"

"I heard you've been commissioned to do some painting for Hopewell Church."

"News still travels fast in Peace," she mumbled. Exhaling her nervousness when it came to talking about her dream job, she focused on her unpolished toes and dollar store flip flops.

"I happened to be related to the chair of the committee. Mom will be calling you if she hasn't already. She and Josh were very impressed with your portfolio."

She shrugged. "I dabble."

"Looked like some pretty detailed dabbling to me."

"You saw my portraits?"

"You've got talent, that's for sure. I'm surprised painting isn't your primary profession."

Their gazes held. "Really? Thanks. Most people are flippant when I mention painting. Michael certainly was. He grew up working on his daddy's farm, planning to follow in the family business. He joined the military to pay for college. Still his mindset was old-fashioned. My desire to paint was never something he considered a steady income."

"It can be for some."

"Well, not for me." She had sold a few paintings, but she was no Monet. When the combination of artist, cosmetologist, and gardener, couldn't make ends meet in the midst of Luke's illness, she'd come home, tail tucked between her legs.

Seth snapped his fingers. "There's your money solution."

"Pardon?"

"Let Dad estimate the cost of repairing Tank. You've already turned in your estimate to the church. Maybe there can be some negotiations here, your painting for Dad's automotive skills."

She tilted her head. "I'm not sure how that could work."

Seth opened his hands. "Leave that to me."

What was she getting herself into? How did her job of painting the murals get her car repaired? However, if Seth was able to orchestrate the two, then she couldn't refuse. She needed the extra income and she needed her car back. She extended her hands in agreement. "Deal."

"We'll have your Wagoneer purring like you drove it off the dealer's lot brand new. All you've got to do is paint a few murals as planned."

It sounded too good to be true. She needed their help and this was a workable solution, but was she playing with fire? It wasn't that she had any reason not to trust Seth and his father. It was interacting with Seth that made the entire situation unwise.

She glanced back at Luke. Without reliable transportation, she would have to continue to rely on friends and family to transport her and Luke to work, to the grocery store. If he got sick in the late hours, she would have to call an ambulance because she didn't have a car…

Her throat closed at the thought of Seth's willingness to help, a kindness she couldn't refuse. She didn't want to rack up more bills, and she didn't want to be dependent on anyone. But, Sloan was right. She didn't have to confess anything. "Sounds like we have a deal." She reached forward, hand open. "I really appreciate this opportunity."

His grip was firm but gentle, like his smile. "My pleasure."

Their hands remained joined another beat, through the uncomfortable pause of silence. Aimee withdrew first. While Seth punched numbers into his cell phone to have Tank towed to his father's garage, she clamped the thin straps of her purse trying to calm her shaking hands. She wasn't concerned about the Garrett's combined automotive skills. It was her unrelenting fate of continuing to be placed in Seth's path that was another worry altogether.

~

Later that evening, Seth took the narrow drive through Point Peace Gardens as the sun dipped toward the horizon. Through the path of twelve oaks, he braked. An older model pickup was already parked in Seth's spot. Exhaling, he folded his arms over the steering wheel and squinted against the western sky. Near the rose gardens, he saw the silhouette of a man who stood alone, head down. Something caused the man to look up, and his shoulders drew tight in defense.

He should leave. It had already been a month

since he'd been here. He could come back tomorrow. No. No, he wasn't leaving. He had to stop running away. It had been twelve years. The situation would never change. He would have to be the one to make the change.

Seth parked and cut the engine as he stared at Mr. Ridley's tailgate. Kevin's dad bought the truck brand new when they were ten. The half a dozen times Seth was at the Ridley's house, he remembered this one time with clarity. Mr. Ridley worked a lot. Seth couldn't remember many times the man was truly happy. This time though, he'd charged into the living room, smiling.

"I got it, Marie, I got it!" He threw the shiny keys into the air and caught them. "Who wants to go for a spin?"

The Ridley's had scrimped and saved a long time for a reliable vehicle. Bringing home the truck was a win for the whole family. Kevin and Seth piled in the bed of the truck with the family's three Labradors while Mrs. Ridley rode up front with her husband. Back then, kids rode in the back of a truck, camper shell or not. He could still hear Kevin's laughter.

Now, Seth tried to do everything he could to make safety his first priority.

Carrying a plastic grocery bag, he strode across the lawn. Inhaling the sweet fragrance of the roses, he rubbed his chest. His heart had never grown accustomed to visiting Kevin here. It never got easier to accept his best friend was gone.

Charles eyes seared him until he reached Kevin's plot. For several moments, they stood silent.

"Don't get any easier, Seth."

His heart pounded as he kept his eyes down. Charles was known for his temper. Normally a quiet man, when provoked he could do damage to whatever, or whoever, got in his way. Charles had gone almost crazy when he found out about Kevin. He'd punched holes in the walls of his home, nearly burned down his small outbuilding.

"No sir." Seth's voice was gruff with emotion. "It's as hard as it was twelve years ago."

Charles knelt down and rubbed a cloth over the granite headstone, taking care to clean around the letters of Kevin's name. "His stone never gets dirty."

"No sir." After Kevin died, once Seth was able to get to the cemetery, he had made a point to come every day, rain or shine, and wipe Kevin's headstone clean. Over the years, his visits lessened from daily to weekly. He was ashamed to admit it had been a month since he'd stopped by to pay his respects.

"I come out here every day and clean it." Charles lifted his head then, staring at Seth with hard eyes. "I guess since I couldn't take care of my boy when he was alive, I'm going to make it up to him now."

He clinched his jaw and his eyes burned. "Kevin loved you."

"He loved you and your daddy more." Charles wiped his nose with the back of his hand. "Don't matter none now. What's done is done."

Yes sir. It was my fault. I'm so sorry. But Seth

didn't give a voice to his thoughts.

Charles walked away without another word. Seth couldn't blame Kevin's father for the hard feelings the man felt against him. He deserved Charles's blame. He'd tried to avoid the Ridley family for the last twelve years, a feat that was nearly impossible living in a town as small as Point Peace and especially when Kevin's baby brother Jeff now played on Seth's baseball team. Luckily, Jeff was skilled like his brother. Had the kid not been able to hit a lick, Seth still would have put Jeff Ridley on his team. Whatever it took to make amends for his actions twelve years ago, Seth would do it.

The grass bent under the weight of his knees. Seth lowered his brow to his fist and tried to talk to God. As always, his memories got in the way and he couldn't think of anything except that afternoon on the outskirts of the University's property on a winding country road.

He'd been driving too fast. As they topped the hill, his cell phone buzzed against his shorts. A bump in the road jolted him and the phone slipped from his grasp. His quick glance toward the floorboard checked out the number on the small screen and he was still looking down when Kevin shouted, "Look out, Seth!"

Darkness covered the gardens by the time Seth sprayed the cleaner on Kevin's headstone. Using his phone as a flashlight, he wiped the granite, taking care to work around the grooves of the letters and numbers comprising Kevin's name, his date of birth and of his death. Once the clouds shifted, the moon came out, keeping Seth company as he laid alongside Kevin's plot, asking God the same question he'd been seeking an answer for the last twelve years.

Why was his life spared?

Chapter Six

Aimee rechecked Tom Garrett's address she'd scribbled on the back of a receipt, expecting his garage to be located in the commercial district of Point Peace. Instead, they had ended up south of town, near the bay.

"Will Seth be here?" Luke asked from the backseat of Sloan's minivan.

"I doubt it." Aimee's grip tightened, crushing the receipt.

"He could be." Sloan shot her a wary grin.

"Ask him to help you with Luke's fundraiser." Granny Lena crowed from the middle row. "And if he asks you for another date, go out with him!"

Aunt Tippy quipped. "You're too young to be alone. Heck, I'm too young to be alone."

Velma giggled. "Just because we're close to eighty doesn't mean we don't still have *it*."

Tippy mimicked her sister's giggle. "You're right, Vel. We could teach Sloan and Aimee a thing or two."

"Teach them what, Aunty?" Luke chimed from the rear seat.

"How to make fluffy icing for your birthday cake, Luke," Aimee called out to her son and shot a glare at her relatives, women she shouldn't have to put a filter on their mouths. "There are little ears in the car, ladies!" She shifted her gaze to the houses passing by. "Look at that little yellow house with the magnolia tree in the front yard. Sloan, wouldn't you love to live in a neighborhood as fine as this?"

"Way to change the subject, Aim." Sloan snickered.

Yards of lush green grass were replaced with sand dunes and palm trees, dotting the sparse area between the quaint, older homes. "They're all so pretty, almost as pretty as Sunset Vista."

Hardly any area in Point Peace could compare with the block along Sunset Vista where Lena's rental home was located. Aimee loved living there and was more than happy to move in when she came home. Her grandparents only had one guest bedroom in their small house, having transformed the other rooms to a craft room and exercise room over the years. Plus, Aimee didn't want to be an imposition. Staying in the Sunset Vista rental allowed her to perk up the painting on the interior in her spare time. Once Aimee moved out, when she was able to afford her own place, her grandparents would begin renting the house to tourists again.

"You'll have a house like this someday." Sloan reassured her. "You'll have your happily ever after."

"My happily ever after is gone. Now I just need to focus on helping Luke get better. And, I'm going to speak to Seth about helping me."

"That's a wise choice." Lena said. "You don't have to date him, but learn what you can from him." Ever since Aimee had confessed her part in the accident, her grandmother had acted cool around her. Once she bubbled with excitement, always asking Aimee to go here and there with her. She'd barely heard from Granny all week.

Gravel crunched under the tires as Sloan turned off the road. The driveway laid a path between lines of magnificent live Oaks. Spanish moss dripped from the arching limbs. A two-story Craftsman-style house with a wraparound porch waited at the end. Though the white siding had weathered, it didn't take away from the charm. Aimee gazed at the front door and the large terrace again. The entire structure encompassed an invitation promising cozy conversation with its twirling ceiling fans and rocking chairs.

She and Michael had talked about moving back to Point Peace. Late nights were spent dreaming about where they wanted to live. Could she fulfill those dreams without him? She still wanted to own something as wonderful as this, even as a widow. Her thoughts fluttered back to Seth.

She said her goodbyes to Sloan, her aunts and Granny Lena as Sloan drove away. Luke stood close, taking her hand in a gesture that confirmed he was nervous, too. Together they walked toward the garage. The garage resembled the main house with its matching siding and a dormer overlooking the front. From its open double door, a country singer's rich voice wafted over with the spring breeze, with lyrics asking, "Why haven't I heard from you?"

"Mom, there's the ocean." Luke pointed in front of them, several hundred yards behind the house, the Atlantic rolled in. She loved the beach, and to be fortunate enough to live on the coast would have been a dream come true.

"Wish we could go swimming." Luke leaned against her with a sigh and tightened his grip on her hand.

"Maybe another time. Today, we're here to pick up Tank and be on our way."

Luke's bottom lip poked out in a full-fledged pout.

Aimee hoisted her satchel on her shoulder and pulled Luke forward.

Luke pressed his face against her side.

She paused. "Do you feel sick?"

He shook his head but wouldn't meet her gaze.

She bent down. "Are you tired?" Cupping his chin in her hands, she studied his face. Under his eyes were dark, half-moons. Though his cheeks and forehead felt normal, no fever, he was several shades lighter than normal. Pale, though it was still a few more days until his next transfusion. She should have paid more attention this morning.

In the beginning, the only sign of Luke's illness was his quick fatigue. Even though he expressed interest in playing outside, or going to baseball practice, by the time they arrived, he would only want to sit on the sidelines. He would feel cold in the middle of the summer when he should be hot.

Six months had passed since that lonely afternoon when Aimee's world was pulled out from under her. Since then, nothing had come before Luke. He was the reason she put her trust in Mr. Garrett, even though she had to face Seth once more, to ensure she had reliable transportation so that nothing would delay her getting her son what he needed.

She held her palms out. "Come here, bud. I'll carry you."

He shook his head and continued forward. Though he was too old to be carried, he did take her hand. She savored the feeling of his smaller hand clasped in hers. Continuing toward the Garrett's home, she shut her eyes, thankful Luke had stayed out of the hospital for two straight weeks, though his physician thought he would need to be admitted until a bone marrow donor was found.

Sometimes her nights were spent restless. Long hours of researching Luke's illness caused her to be tired during the day and full of fatigue. But it was her job as Luke's mother to find the answer, to find the donor, so that her son would live.

She glanced at the house and its large porch as she crossed the grounds, wanting nothing more than to be far from this family. Roller coaster emotions had kept her on edge all week, anticipating this day when she would step foot on Garrett property, a family she had harmed long ago. Even though she harbored a painful secret, she was thankful for them.

Mr. Garrett had called Sunday night after giving the Wagoneer a once over and said he'd be putting the head on today—whatever that was. He listed everything he planned to replace, although hearing what Tank needed was like listening to a foreign language. If only she knew more about alternators, transmissions, and spark plugs, but the depth of her automotive knowledge was limited to checking tire pressure and knowing the location of the dipstick.

Across the yard, her gaze settled on a pair of broad shoulders. As if he sensed her eyes upon him, Seth turned, then raised his hand and waved. Her pulse sped as trepidation bubbled in her stomach. Guilt jolted through her at what she didn't have to share.

Seth strolled toward them. Here was her chance to ask for forgiveness. To confess her sins to one of the lives impacted that night, but if she did, would they still help her? She looked at Luke's pale face. Tank had to be drivable in order for her to take care of her son. And Seth had connections. She'd heard that fact from more than several in the community. He had the means to bring people across state lines to donate money and test to be a bone marrow donor for her little boy.

She bit her lip. "Here we go, Luke." She gripped his hand tighter as she continued toward the garage.

Once Mr. Garrett had Tank running, once she had completed the mural for Hopewell's Children's Department, and once she convinced Seth to help her organize the fundraiser and bone marrow drive,

Aimee would tell him the truth. Then, she could finally leave her past behind.

~

Seth's heart raced as he admired the woman walking toward him. The southerly wind whipped her multicolored dress around her ankles and loosened her hair from its tight bun perched atop her head. Her pinched face communicated distress, so he hurried down the sloped walkway, cutting across the newly cut grass.

"Hi, Luke." He gave the kid a high-five. "Hello, Luke's Mom." Ah, there's her smile. He removed his baseball hat. "You look great."

"Oh?" Her glance bobbed to her toes and back to him. "Your mom and I are going to the church to discuss the murals. Did I overdress?"

He rubbed the back of his neck. "Nah, you're fine. Very fine." Heat raced up his neck and flushed his cheeks. He didn't mean to say what he was thinking.

Aimee's eyes rounded, but her grin had her dimples digging in.

Seth refocused on Luke and rustled the kid's head. "Hey, Champ. Have you been practicing your swing?"

"No sir."

"Next time I'm heading to the park, I'll give you a call and maybe you can come along with me and the team."

Luke's eyes brightened. "With the high school team?"

"Who else?"

"Wow! Can I Mom, please?"

"Sure." But Aimee's smile didn't reach her sky-blue eyes.

"Mom, you can come along." Luke patted her shoulder.

"Hello, there." Dad called from behind them wiping his hands on a red cloth. Seth led Aimee and Luke to the garage.

Luke shook hands with Seth's father and beamed at the smudge of grease on his palm. "Cool!"

Dad handed the child a small towel. Luke wiped his hand clean as he peered around the custom shop. "What are you fixing, Mr. Garrett?"

"Come take a look."

Aimee chuckled softly as Luke ran ahead, following Dad to the lift that held Tank.

"What's this?" Luke pointed to the switch on the wall.

"Why don't you push it and find out." Dad pointed to the button on the right wall. Luke walked to it but hesitated, glancing back at Seth's father. "Go ahead."

The child stared in amazement as the lift slowly rose to reveal the Wagoneer well above their heads. "Mom, did you see that?"

"So cool," she replied, mimicking the boy's excitement. Luke followed Dad to help him choose the right drill for the job, asking questions about what the drill was used for and if he could push the switch on the tool.

Aimee's laughter filled the air as she followed the exchange between Luke and Dad. Her hair slipped from her bun every time she moved, tendrils of dark curls hopping on the breeze wafting through the open doors. Her shoulders were bare exposing the line from her clavicle to her arms.

Aimee looked up and their eyes locked.

Seth turned toward the open garage door, refocusing on the main house across the yard. "I can walk with you—"

A white pickup loaded down with lumber spit gravel as it barreled down the driveway toward the house. His buddy, Grant, was here to start another project for Mom. Seth waved. He made good time crossing the lawn.

Behind him, Aimee spoke. "Is your mother home? She's waiting on me."

"Yes, I'll walk you over."

"It's time to go, Luke."

"Aw, Mom, can't I stay?"

She shook her head. Luke frowned but put the wrench down.

Dad glanced up. "I don't mind watching him while you and Bonnie head to church."

Aimee's hands clasped at her midsection. "That's kind of you, but Luke wasn't feeling well earlier."

"Mom, I feel gooder now!" He hopped up and down in front of her.

Grant pulled off his baseball cap revealing his wavy black hair as he entered the garage. He greeted the Seth and Dad and then stepped toward Aimee. "Well, hello there. I'm Grant Morrow."

Seth crossed his arms over his chest as Grant's dark brown eyes sparkled to match the shimmer of the smile he gave Aimee. She smiled back as Grant offered to shake her hand. "Always nice to meet a pretty lady."

"It's nice to meet you." Pulling free of Grant's grasp she went after Luke as he sailed across the garage and planted himself in front of Dad.

Luke turned back to his mother. "Please? I'll eat my vegetables tonight, and I'll take my bath, and everything."

"Sounds like an offer I couldn't refuse." Grant gave one of his boisterous laughs.

"You're going to do all of that for me?" She then looked from Seth to Dad. "He won't be in the way?"

"Nah," Dad chuckled. "He'll be a good helper, won't you kid?"

Grant eased his palm over the hood of the Wagoneer. "Man, this is some antique."

Aimee turned toward Grant. "Thank you. It was my mother's." She studied him a moment longer. "You sound familiar."

"I'm a sports broadcaster."

Her smile broadened. "Station 660 All Sports?"

"Yes." Grant beamed as if he'd won a lottery. "You listen to talk radio?"

"We're on the road a lot and hearing the same music on the radio gets old. Luke and I love listening to sports updates." Her gaze eased away from her son, landing on Seth for a fraction of a second, and then, of course, went back to Grant.

"Where did you go to college?" Grant asked Aimee.

Good question, Seth clenched his jaw. Why

hadn't he asked her?

"The University of Georgia."

"So, did I," Grant glanced Seth's way. "I mean, Seth and I graduated from there. Seth, you should bring Aimee to one of my tailgate parties."

Aimee's smile faded, and she took a step back. Almost as an afterthought, she smiled at Grant, dismissing his invitation with a toss of her hand. "I'm afraid I don't tailgate anymore. Too busy."

"That's what Seth says." His friend looked his way. "We are too old to get in too much trouble, but we still have fun."

Luke tugged at her hand. "Mom pulleeeezzz! Can't I stay?"

Grant stepped aside. "Do you need a hand, Tom?"

"Sure, Grant. Hang around." Dad raked his fingers through his graying hair.

Aimee rubbed Luke's face in a tender motion.

Seth admired her dedication to her child. "We'll look after him, Aimee." He hoped his reassurance made her feel at ease.

"Yes, I know you will. I don't have a cell phone, so please call your mother if you need me, for anything."

"Come here Luke, I want to show you something." Dad took Luke by the hand.

"Bye, Mom. I'll be good." Luke dashed away toward Tank with Dad. Grant followed, leaving Seth with Aimee.

After another glance at Luke, Aimee followed Seth outside. He touched her arm, stopping her. "Is everything alright?"

Her mouth formed a tight line and she shrugged. "Luke is a handful sometimes. He gets excited about new things but then he tires quickly. He has a blood disorder."

Seth rubbed his neck with his hand, a wave of unsettled nerves coursed through him. "Is there anything we need to do for him?"

"If he starts to whine, that's a sign he needs to rest."

"How long has Luke been sick?"

"Almost two years."

In amicable silence, they strolled across the lawn. When they reached the front porch her attention traveled across the yard, where Luke's laughter grew louder. When she looked at Seth, he sensed her scrutiny, as if second guessing herself.

"Luke is in good hands. Neither Dad nor I will take our eyes off of him."

She nodded. "In the short time I've known you and your family, I know there's no reason to worry." She looked down at her purse and a pink bag she carried. Her fingers were twined in the purse's straps. Unfurling the material, she met Seth's eyes. "I've been told you may be able to help me organize a fundraiser for Luke. Um, actually, it will be more than that. I want to also have a bone—"

Mom opened the front door. "Hello Aimee. I'm so glad you're here."

Aimee greeted Mom and then turned back to Seth. "Maybe we can talk later."

"Sure, thing. I'll see you when you get back."

"This is for you." She passed Mom the pink

bag. "Here are a few things from the salon. We just received those samples."

Cooing, Mom peered inside the bag, "You brought the new deep conditioner, and essential oils. Bath bombs!" She held the items for Aimee and Seth to see. "So sweet of you, thank you."

The women's shared excitement had Seth glancing over his shoulder. "Well, this is getting into unfamiliar waters for me, so I'll get back to the guys."

"We'll be back soon." Mom said as she ushered Aimee inside the house.

"Drive safely," he said.

Mom arched her eyebrow. "I will, son. Don't worry."

He caught Aimee's gaze and she grinned.

Smiling back, he waited until the door was shut, then blew out a breath, turned on his heal, and skipped down the steps.

The heat of the sun bore down on his face as he jogged up the hill. Luke met him at one of the open bays of the garage, holding a baseball in one hand and two gloves tucked under his arm.

"You finished with car repairs?"

Luke giggled. "Yes sir, Mr. Tom's all done and said we could play."

He nodded to the gloves. "Do you want to toss a couple?"

The boy's smile exploded. "Yeah!"

They jogged to a flat area of the property. About a dozen yards away the Atlantic tumbled over the beach and the summer breeze gained strength, blowing intermittent pulses across Seth's back. Luke's ball sailed through the air and slapped his glove on contact.

On the return, Seth held the baseball in his right hand and pulled back. The spasm shot through his muscle like a mean bolt of lightning warning him to limit his activity.

He blew out a breath. The same thing happened during practice with the high school boys. He hadn't put any heat on the ball. This was playing catch with a kid. A gentle sloping throw was all he needed, yet he couldn't deliver.

Maybe he should give in, follow the doctor's direction, and have surgery.

Luke punched his glove as he waited for the next throw. Seth shifted the ball to his left hand and threw the ball back to Luke. His mouth tightened with the pain shooting through his shoulder. He glanced toward a discussion about lumber as Dad and Grant headed to the house.

"Do you want me to take over?" Dad called to him.

Take over so that Seth could rest the arm was what his father meant but didn't say. Seth shook his head, even though his shoulder really hurt. "I'm good, Dad."

Dad paused a moment, then shook his head before turning away.

The boy pulled back, about to throw the ball when he saw Seth rubbing his shoulder. Luke frowned. No way did he want Luke getting upset. Seth started across the yard.

"You've got a strong arm."

"Thanks." Luke handed Seth the baseball.

"You don't want to play anymore?" Seth asked.

"No thanks, Coach." Luke grinned. "But maybe we could hang out on your boat. Mr. Tom said you've got some cool fishing gear."

Seth patted Luke's shoulder. "So you like fishing, too?"

"Yes sir. I also like swimming... and skateboarding... and skating."

He laughed. "Wow, that's some list. Let's take one thing at a time. First, the boat, and then, maybe some ice cream?" Seth held up his fist and Luke bumped it in return.

Chapter Seven

Mrs. Garrett guided Aimee to the garage attached to the house. Inside, an older model truck and a late model sports car gleamed under the fluorescent lights.

"I'm in the mood to drive the convertible, what do you think?" Mrs. Garrett wagged her eyebrows as she fastened her scarf over her hair and tied it under her chin. With her sunglasses in place, she resembled a mid-century movie star. Once they rolled out of the garage, Mrs. Garrett pushed a button to lower the convertible top, and she sped up the driveway.

The wind whipped across the windshield, dissolving Aimee's bun. Her hair fell around her shoulders. She pulled it out of her face and held a side ponytail as they scooted down the highway. "Mrs. Garrett, I hope you like the plans I have for the children's center."

"Please, call me Bonnie. Mrs. Garrett makes me remember that I'm old."

"Okay, Bonnie it is."

Bonnie chatted about the sketches Aimee had provided with her proposal. She had already started one of the first murals. She drew the images first, then added the details and paint.

Accelerating over the bridge, Bonnie smiled. "I love your ideas. Some of the committee members made suggestions about placement, so I'd like to discuss that today."

The conversation moved from murals to the weather. Somehow a discussion about the hurricane ten years earlier lead to Bonnie inquiring about Aimee's personal life.

"So, you grew up in Savannah?" Bonnie made a turn off the highway onto a residential side street.

"My father traveled for work, and Mom and I went with him. She homeschooled me until I graduated. It was about that time Dad changed jobs and we moved just outside of town on the north end. I had friends that went to high school in Savannah, but I never attended. And as you know, my mother's family has always lived in Point Peace. Belinda is mother's sister."

"Yes, Belinda is a sweetheart. She thinks so highly of you and Luke. I didn't know her until just a few years ago when we met through the garden club." A few beats of silence settled between them. "Belinda mentioned Luke has a blood disorder?"

Aimee nodded. Before she could respond, Bonnie reached over and squeezed her hand. "We have been praying for you at church."

A knot formed at the base of her throat, the gesture a balm to her troubled heart. She forced a smile but her weepiness caught her off guard.

"Belinda said what a wonderful husband you had. I'm sorry he passed away." When she didn't reply, Bonnie barreled on. "Oh dear, I don't mean to sound flippant. Anything your aunt has said has been with love and concern."

"Yes ma'am. We appreciate your thoughts and prayers. It has been a tough last few years." Letting go of her hair, it whipped wildly in the wind, blowing across her face, blocking her view of Bonnie as she swallowed her emotion.

The church sat at the end of the road around the curve. As they stepped from the vehicle, she met Bonnie's curious gaze. "Do you mind if I ask how Luke became ill?"

Aimee fidgeted with her purse strap around her fingers and loosened them again. She recalled the Monday in December when she had rushed Luke to the Children's Hospital in Atlanta. Fatigue had successfully pulled Luke's energy down to nothing. "We were going through our normal routine of getting ready for school and work that day. I had already gone in to Luke's room to wake him. Usually, he would spring out of bed and be ready to watch cartoons. But that day, he didn't want to move. I offered him to get in the shower, to eat something, but nothing helped. In fact, he'd been acting strange all weekend. He just wanted to lie around."

"Children can be hesitant about going to school even when they feel fine. My Cornelia hated school."

Aimee chuckled at the older woman's effort at

humor. "Well, Luke loves school. And that morning, he'd cried, refused every bribe I made. I got frustrated and decided I would dress him myself. As I began to peel his shirt off, I saw the purple marks across his skin. I took him to the emergency room. From triage, Luke went through several other tests. Finally, a specialist sat down with me in Luke's hospital room. She explained Luke's blood cells weren't producing as they should."

Bonnie made a concerned sound as Aimee paused. Across the parking lot, a wooded area divided the church property from the beach several hundred yards below. Leaves rustled on the trees as they walked toward the fellowship hall entrance.

"I tried to listen to every word that doctor said, determined that whatever Luke needed to get well, I'd make sure he had it. Whatever medicine he needed, I'd make sure he took it.

"Then the doctor said, 'Your son has a blood disorder called Severe Aplastic Anemia. People with Aplastic Anemia are at higher risk for infection because of the lack of cell production.' I didn't understand what that meant. Luke was sound asleep from all of the tests he'd been through. I remember just staring at the doctor and repeating the diagnosis to memorize it. I'd never heard of the illness. I asked the doctor if Luke was going to die? What a horrible question to have to ask, but I had to know."

Bonnie's eyes welled to the brim. "Oh Aimee. I understand. You have to ask those hard questions."

In front of the double doors of the building,

Aimee patted Bonnie's arm. "I am determined Luke will be cured. The doctor said the disorder can be fatal, but she promised they would do everything they could to make sure Luke gets the best treatment. And I believe he has received their best."

"Luke has been having some good days lately so we've been able to take care of his transfusions at the Cancer Center in Savannah." Aimee's voice cracked, but she smiled at Seth's mother. "I hope to have the mural complete in record time."

The church property had undergone three recent additions. Inside the fellowship hall, which was adjacent to the sanctuary, they took the elevator to the basement level.

Their conversation eased back to church topics which seemed to buoy Bonnie's spirits. "In case you're interested, our singles and young married couples have small group meetings here in the morning on the main level. The youth runs our coffee house every Sunday morning." She pointed to an area that was built just like most coffee shops, complete with seating. Even the room carried a scent of the caffeinated decadence.

At the bottom level, Bonnie led them into the hallway until they reached the area of the hall where the murals would be placed.

"This is Daniel in the Lion's den." Further down the corridor, Aimee took over the tour and shared her ideas. "This large wall will hold Noah's Ark. I thought this wall would hold more images. I am planning to have fun with the different animals. I'll paint unique animals, ones from the jungle. I'll add a couple of pigs, cows and horses in the mix."

"I love it." Bonnie turned around to the wall behind them. "Is this Joseph?"

Aimee smiled. "It's a rough sketch, but you are correct."

As they walked back toward the elevators, Bonnie paused at the entry. "Some of the board members had an idea to have Jesus with children of different nationalities."

"This wall would be perfect." Aimee scribbled a note for the idea in her sketch book. "I'll work on it right away. Was the timeline I proposed acceptable to your committee?"

"Yes, eight weeks is perfect. It's just in time for the fall festival." Bonnie frowned.

Aimee's grip tightened on her notebook. "Is there a problem?"

"I realize you and Tom had worked out payment arrangements between your vehicle repairs and this mural. But honestly, that's not going to work."

Aimee held her breath. It was going to be hard enough coming up with the money for the paint for this project.

"Your vehicle repairs were not as expensive as the other shop quoted." She went over the numbers and clarified what the cost of car repairs totaled as well as the estimate Aimee proposed for the murals. Her murals would cost more. "So you see, the church will advance you the first part of your proposal and the remaining will be due at the completion of the murals."

Reeling over the news she would receive a

payment on this project, and get her car repaired, Aimee could barely speak.

Bonnie clasped her hands and looked around the halls of the children's center. "This will look amazing when you're done. Let's head back. I haven't had lunch and I'm famished."

Excitement bubbled and mixed with fear of the project ahead, one she wanted to do and do well. This was her chance to prove she could paint for someone, for this group, and her work would then be enjoyed by many. "This is too good to be true. Michael wouldn't believe it." It was as if Bonnie sensed her needs and was able to meet almost everyone.

"Tom used to doubt my ability to run a restaurant. For a long time I served as chef until the previous owner stepped down. I knew in my heart running Pleasant Lea was what I wanted."

"I had no idea painting the murals would lead to a paycheck." The opportunity to do something she loved for income was an opportunity she did not want to pass up. "Michael would probably say, it's only one church. You can't bring in a steady income painting pictures. That was one reason I started doing hair. Everyone needs a haircut from time to time, but it's rare for someone to buy a painting."

Bonnie's hopeful eyes squinted with joy. "Perhaps a career change is on your horizon."

"Thank you so much." Her whooping laugh echoed through the halls. She covered her mouth. "Oops, that was loud."

"Quite alright, dear."

Aimee inhaled deeply as the realization of her opportunity sank deeper. "Wow." Bonnie patted her shoulder. "I'm fine. It's just been an emotional last few months."

"I'm sure it has." Bonnie squeezed her arm.

"I don't want to be a charity case. I try to keep Luke's illness quiet because I don't want us to be treated differently once people find out." Add her widow status to being a mother of a child with a blood disorder, people seemed to feel obligated to give special favor to her and Luke. There were many others in their community in situations worse than hers.

While she appreciated a person's generosity, it meant more, for this project, for her to manage it on her own. She met Bonnie's concerned gaze.

She didn't deserve the Garrett's generosity, not when she caused Seth so much pain. What if someone caused Luke pain? How would she feel toward that person? Would she be able to forgive them?

She forced a smile. The Garrett's didn't need to know anything. She would do a good job for them, one they would be proud of and then she could say goodbye.

She glanced around the empty corridor. She could almost picture her paintings on the wall. She inhaled, savoring the moment. "Thank you, Mrs. Garrett."

"So, we've got a deal?"

"Yes ma'am." Aimee extended her open hand.

Bonnie chatted, non-stop, on the drive home.

"I've known your aunt since high school. I

guess I knew your mother. Her name was Diana?"

"Yes, she was Diana Miller in high school."

"And your father was Hank Tucker?"

"Yes. He was actually from Chicago. He and Mom met when Daddy was on a family vacation here in Point Peace. Mama worked at a little seafood restaurant at the pier. She always said it was love at first sight. Dad ordered a lobster and she took him to the tank and showed him which one to pick out."

Bonnie giggled. "Sounds like my daughter, Cory. She lives in California now, but when Seth made friends with Josh Martin, and she saw Josh the first time, she fell in love."

"They aren't together?"

"Not yet," Bonnie smiled. "But I'm working on it. They've both been out in the world and she's been away from home for a while. If I know my daughter, it's time for her to come back and settle down. I guess Cory is like you in that way. You both left for a while. Its better you're here, near your family, so that you can have their support while Luke gets well."

Bonnie made Aimee's story seem so simple. She wished Bonnie's version was her truth.

Once they were back at the Garrett's home, Bonnie parked her car beside the rear porch. Camellias twisted up the railing, their deep red provided a pop of color against the white spindles and siding.

Seth's mother paused at the door and looked left to where Grant had framed an extension to the porch. "Ooh, Grant, that's looking good."

"Thank you, Mrs. Bonnie."

Bonnie led Aimee into the mud room. "Grant is so talented. He's building a gazebo for us right under my favorite willow where it's shady in the afternoon. I can't wait."

Following Bonnie's directions for the powder room, Aimee walked toward the front of the house where the foyer held a grand staircase, covered with a thick woven, cream carpet. Aimee's gaze took in the high ceilings, dark stained wood beams contrasted the white walls, extending the length of the hallway. Wood floors, the same walnut color, provided a continuous path deeper into the center of the home. She closed the door of the powder room and washed her hands in the quaint, scalloped shaped pedestal sink. Smells of garlic and herbs grew stronger as Aimee returned to the kitchen, wrapping her in their comfort. A hazelnut scent tickled Aimee's senses before Bonnie offered her a cup of coffee. The combination of warmth and scents reminded Aimee of the times her grandmother cooked for her and Michael, before his last tour, before Luke's illness, when all was right with the world.

Why did she feel so at home with these people when her guilt was eating her alive? She rubbed her bare arms. She needed to complete the murals quickly and move on.

"I left our dinner in the slow cooker. Let me turn it down and then we can sit on the porch and have some coffee." Bonnie said, though by the looks of the pots over every burner and the mound of dough wrapped in cling wrap on the butcher block counter, Aimee would have thought she was preparing a meal for a small army. "Come on in and keep me company while I finish. I hope Luke likes chicken."

Aimee gripped the bar stool while Bonnie retrieved two coffee mugs. "Oh, we hadn't intended on eating. Please, don't go to any trouble."

"You're no trouble at all." Bonnie situated the two cups beside her dainty Irish patterned cream and sugar containers. "After Tom's stint in the hospital, it's nice to have some happiness in this house." With a pat on Aimee's arm, the older woman smiled. "Why, I may not let you and Luke leave."

Gulping down the hot brew, Aimee averted her gaze. If Bonnie learned the truth, the woman would probably feel much different. She needed to get out of here. "Thank you for the coffee, for the job and for the offer of dinner. I'd better find Luke—"

The kitchen door burst open. Seth plowed through, clutching her son against him. Tom rushed in behind them.

Luke held a white cloth to his nose, a bright tinge of red soaked through. Seth placed Luke on top of the breakfast table.

"Oh, Luke," Aimee rushed forward, grabbing the cloth. Not another nosebleed. Please not now.

"We were on the boat and his nose started bleeding. I can't get it to stop." Seth was frantic.

Aimee lowered the hanky, but Luke's nose still poured.

"Did he get hit?" Bonnie asked.

"No, nothing." Seth looked at Aimee, then to her son. "Did you hit your nose, Champ?" Luke shook his head. "Mom, get a towel." Moments later Bonnie rushed to the table carrying several plush hand towels.

Aimee folded the bloodied hanky away as she handed Luke a fresh towel. "You're all right, buddy." Though his eyes swelled with tears, he nodded in agreement.

Seth patted Luke's back. "The bleeding should've stopped by now." Their gazes clashed over her son's head. "Has this happened before?"

"Yesterday, but we stopped it quickly." Aimee's hand shook as she peeled the soaked towel back. "It wasn't like this. His platelets must be low."

"Platelets? I think he needs to go to the hospital, Aimee." Concern filled Seth's voice.

"It's the plastic anemia."

"What?" Seth looked to Luke who held the towel to his face.

"Aplastic Anemia." Aimee supplied and moved to gather her purse. "Let's go, Luke."

"The closest emergency room is in Savannah." Bonnie stood beside Tom, concern emanating from her voice. "You can be there in twenty minutes."

"Yes, thank you. We're familiar with the staff there." After helping Luke off the table, she looked at Tom. "Is my car finished?"

"Yes, all done."

Seth stepped toward the door, keys in hand. "You're not going alone. I'll drive you."

"It's okay you don't—"

Seth's hardened expression brought pause to her rebuttal. He picked up Luke and swung open the door.

"I need a bag out of Tank. It's an overnight sack for me and Luke."

"I'll get it." Tom followed Seth outside.

Bonnie touched her hand before she walked outside. "Let me know what the doctor's say. I'll be praying."

Nodding, Aimee gripped Bonnie's hand. Would she ever not be indebted to this family?

Chapter Eight

"Are you taking the elevator?"

Seth blinked as he took in the busy corridor. Young and old bustled in front and behind him. Overhead a code was announced on the third floor. But in his mind, he was lying on a stretcher. Nurses and doctors surrounded him and then they were gone. And Seth was alone.

"Where's Kevin?" The answer to Seth's only question came too late.

"Hey, buddy? Are you going up?" The elevator door stood open and a man shrugged out of his raincoat as he waited for Seth's answer.

Seth read the sign beside the elevator and looked back at the double doors facing him. "No, no I'm not going up. Sorry."

He stepped back, clutching Aimee's overnight bag. He'd forgotten to give it to her last night. Theoretically, he had a huge L tattooed on his forehead. Hospitals brought out the worst in him and last night he couldn't walk inside. He pulled to the curb at the emergency room doors. Aimee got

Luke out and held his hand as she leaned in to speak to Seth. "Thank you for bringing us."

The building had loomed behind her. All Seth could think about was getting out of there. As he'd driven back home, guilt kicked him in the tail. Aimee called him around ten looking for her bag. He apologized for the oversight.

"It's okay. Everything was crazy when you first dropped us off. The doctor is transferring us to Atlanta. I'll get the bag from you another time. We'll make do."

But it wasn't okay. He should have stayed with her until they knew Luke's status.

After lying in bed, he got up at three and started the four-hour drive north. Now, standing in front of Luke's hospital room door, his hands, clammy and perspiration beaded on his forehead. He rapped his knuckles against the door, the knock echoed through the hallway.

Her eyes brightened. "Seth, I didn't know you were coming up here."

"I brought your bag." He lifted her duffle.

She ushered him inside the room. Sloan moved from the couch closer to the entrance and greeted him. "Luke is still sleeping," Sloan told him while Aimee moved to her son's bedside.

"Do you want any coffee?" Sloan asked him.

After tucking Luke's blanket higher up around his shoulders, Aimee returned to Seth. "There's a break room on this floor that has a coffee pot. I need to stretch my legs anyway. I'll get us some."

"I'll come with you," he said.

"Why don't I wait for Luke to wake up?" Sloan

suggested. "Bring back plenty of cream."

"Sloan just got here a few minutes ago." Aimee walked beside him with her arms crossed. "She's in Atlanta for a meeting and had stayed overnight."

After he and Aimee prepared the coffee, they each took a seat in the waiting area adjacent to the vending and coffee area. Eyeing him over her mug, she cradled her cup as she blew on the contents. Then she leaned in, touching his shirt where a spot of blood tainted the material. "Did you forget to change?"

He placed his cup on the table, his stomach too unsettled even for this weak brew. "I guess I did."

"I'll try to get my vehicle from you as soon as I can."

Seth took her hand in his. "What's going on with Luke? Is he going to be alright?"

"Luke has a rare blood disorder called Aplastic Anemia that he's been dealing with since last Christmas. We have been in and out of the hospital for the last six months. It's the reason he can't play baseball."

Exhaling, she leaned back against the sofa and shut her eyes. He leaned forward. He shouldn't have left her alone last night.

She stared at the cup of coffee, then Seth. "This time around, we may be in here a while. Luke's counts aren't where they need to be for him to be around people. I've been selfish and tried to do too much lately."

He squeezed her hand. "This isn't your fault." She returned the gesture by squeezing back before pulling away. "What can I do to help you?"

She frowned. "Luke needs a bone marrow transplant, but currently, we don't know who in the world could be a match for him. It's Luke's best chance to beat this." Curling her arms about her waist, she stood and walked to the window. Part of the Atlanta skyline was in view, though many of the buildings were lost in the fog. "Granny would kill me."

Seth slowly crossed the room. "Pardon? I didn't catch that."

She shook her head, though a curious smile held. "Yesterday, at your parent's house, I was going to speak with you about helping me organize a bone marrow drive for Luke. I know you must be busy and I understand if—"

"I'd love to help."

She let out a huge breath and walked toward him. "Everyone says your race for Kevin has been very successful."

He tried to turn a horrible event into something positive for others. Helping Aimee expedite a search for someone who could help Luke was a request he would dive into head first. Ideas had come to him over the years of handling Kevin's race that didn't quite fit. Now, those ideas may be useful for Luke's cause. "I'll handle as much detail for you as you need."

With a quick nod, she turned toward the window. Her fist brushed her nose. When her shoulders began trembling, Seth reached out. "Hey, it's okay. It's going to be okay."

God, he hoped everything would be okay. He'd no idea about Luke's illness or what Aimee was going through, but surely, everything would work out. As his fingers brushed her shoulder, her tremble cascaded through him, but he didn't back off. "Aimee, your focus should be on Luke. Don't worry about anything."

Her eyes glistened as she looked up at him. He brushed her cheek when a tear escaped. Then, she came to him, leaning against him. He rubbed slow circles over her back the way he would have comforted his sister, except holding Aimee was different.

~

Less than twenty-four hours later, Aimee hurried across the cold tile to answer the knocking at Luke's door. A flush of heat rushed to her cheeks. "Seth."

His chest puffed up as if he'd just inhaled and when he spoke, his voice sounded shaky. "Is this a good time to visit? I guess I should have called but—"

"It's okay." She stepped back to let him inside, but he surprised her, wrapping her in a hug. His breath tickled her neck as he hugged her. When he broke away several long seconds later, she stepped back, pushing her hair out of her face. Aimee glanced up at him another second before leading him toward Luke's bed. "I didn't expect you to come back so soon. Luke should be waking up any moment."

"Good. This is for him." He held up a brown fuzzy bear.

"He'll love it." She led him to the guest's couch where the ceiling light cast a soft glow.

Above the couch, a window provided a view of the sunrise. Once she was seated, Seth lowered to the spot beside her.

"I brought you something." He passed the red bag to her. "I wanted to make sure I gave it to you as soon as possible."

At the sight of the box, her pulse increased. "You bought me a cell phone?" She shook her head. "Seth, thank you, but it's too much." She handed it back. "I don't mean to be rude, but I can't accept this." She didn't deserve his kindness. If he knew, he wouldn't be here, wouldn't want to help her with Luke. She stood, but her knees were on shaky legs.

The sound of paper crackling and cardboard unfolding signaled Seth's disagreement with her refusal and she swiveled to face him.

"If you get stranded again, you won't be alone because you'll have a phone and you can call for help. What if Tank broke down on your way to a hospital?"

"Your dad assured me that wouldn't happen again."

"I don't know a better mechanic." Seth's expression was serious. "Still, you shouldn't risk it."

She shook her head. "Look, I know what these phones cost because I've priced them and I'm saving to purchase one on my own. Besides, this one is the latest on the market, and not to sound ungrateful, but I wouldn't have paid the money you paid for it. I'm sorry. I can't accept."

His sober eyes considered her. "How about you

keep it until Luke is well?"

She sighed. How could she win Mom of the Year by refusing a free cell phone given to ensure her only child's safety?

He powered the phone on. "I've been doing a lot of thinking about the bone marrow drive. You mentioned you may be here with Luke for a few weeks. With Kevin's race coming up and practice with the team, I won't be able to drive back and forth to see you guys as much. Calling you will be the next best thing. We don't want to delay finding a donor for Luke, do we?"

She returned to the couch, her shoulders drooped under his blanket of reason.

"You'll have to add your contacts. I've added my number and my parents' numbers in here. I figured you may need to reach Mom about the painting. And if you have a question about the car, you'll have Dad's number…and mine."

Her lips pressed together in a firm frown. "I really don't deserve this."

"How can you say that?" He gave her arm a friendly shove. "Hey. You don't believe that, do you?"

Hands clasped in her lap, she considered going ahead and telling him the truth. As she spoke, her tone barely above a whisper, she averted her attention to the phone. "There are things about me you don't know. Things you should know. I'm ashamed of what I've done. Seth, I—"

"Aimee, everyone has something. I'm sure if you and I shared stories you'd find out your shameful things weren't near as bad as mine." He stood and went to the corner of the room, further from Luke's bed. He glanced at her as if he was going to say more, as if he had something heavy on his mind. She moved to stand beside him so that their conversation wouldn't wake Luke. "We can't change our past, but we can change this moment and tomorrow. I don't know about you, but I'm tired of looking back."

Nodding, she wished things were that simple.

"I need to ask your opinion about the drive. We're going to need a large area for vendors and plenty of parking. The church is already using my parent's restaurant and property near the beach for their festival the weekend before Labor Day. The venue is booked solid until then. I spoke with Josh and Caleb at Hopewell. They agreed to hold the church's festival in conjunction with Luke's bone marrow drive."

"Really?" Her heart beat quickened. "I wasn't sure we'd be able to have it this year. Are you sure Hopewell won't mind if we piggyback on their event?"

"They don't mind at all. Besides, your great grandmother's father was one of the founding members."

She leaned against the armrest. "How do you know?"

"I did some digging. Talked to your grandmother."

She hated to ask what else Granny might have said.

He went on. "The date of the festival is the Saturday of Labor Day weekend. It gives me plenty of time to get vendors on sight and tweak some of the plans the church already had in place."

Rubbing her hands over her thighs, she shook her head. "I've been trying to find a venue for a month and couldn't get anything secured." Shifting her gaze, she took in the small hospital room, the confines of its four gray walls. Luke slept soundly, though hooked up to multiple machines and beeping pumps. She'd worked so hard to create an event for Luke and had a door slammed.in her face every time. She inhaled, but her throat was thick, her eyes grew moist. Shutting her eyes, she forced those blasted tears away and met Seth's gaze with a smile. "You've practically planned the whole thing in under twenty-four hours."

She bounced on her toes toward him. Once again, she was in his arms. Her face turned so that her cheek rested upon his shoulder. His strength cocooned her, and he tightened his hold as if he knew exactly what she needed. Even though there were so many things wrong with her sudden dependence on him, she couldn't let go.

Chapter Nine

The road curved against the tight shoulder until it sloped toward a wooded area. Without a flashlight, walking alongside this road was dangerous but she didn't care. If someone hit her, no one would care. She hadn't been able to help her mother. She'd hurt her father. Now, they were both gone. There was no one else.

In the distance, tires squealed. Yellow lights expanded, surrounded her, as the car came closer.

"Momma…"

Aimee jolted awake. Propping on her elbows, she listened as she scanned the small hospital room. Since Luke was lying on his side, back to her, she knew he was still asleep. Sighing, she eased back against the couch, her bed at nighttime. Her head ached with memory of that lonely country road. Why couldn't she erase that time in her life?

Except for a sliver of morning light peeking through the window shades, the darkness surrounded her. Shivering, she pulled the thin waffle blanket over her shoulders and closed her eyes.

"Mom, are you awake?"

Aimee swung her legs over the side of the couch and hurried to his bedside. She flipped on the light switch, blinding them both.

"I'm right here."

He squinted as she rubbed his forehead, hoping he didn't notice her shaking hands.

"Is Seth coming back today?"

"Maybe."

"He said he would." Luke's smile represented hope.

"Yes, he did."

He had visited Luke two more times since then, and she had shared several more telephone calls with him. The date was set for Luke's bone marrow drive and fundraiser. It would be held in conjunction with the church's festival because venues were limited in Point Peace. A 5K walk/run would kick off the fundraiser and the bone marrow drive would become a part of the church's festival. An event she initially imagined would only last a few hours, now took up an entire day.

It had not taken her long to discover what a special person he was. And when he was around, Luke was truly happy. If she told Seth about her part in his past, not only would she lose Seth, but so would Luke.

"Luke, Seth can't be here every day. He has a job, friends…"

"I'm his friend."

With a short knock on the door, the day nurse,

entered carrying his breakfast tray and her clipboard. "Looking good," she commented as she checked Luke's IV site and noted the fluid levels in the bags hanging by his bed.

"Are you okay, Mrs. McClain?"

"Yes, I'm fine." But she wasn't. The nightmares surrounding Kevin's death had woke her throughout the night. She should have expected it. Besides Luke, it was the only other thing she thought about.

The young nurse flitted around the room emptying the water jug, bringing new sheets in for Luke's bed to be changed after breakfast and his bath. If only she could bottle an hour of the nurse's energy and take it every day. Right now, Aimee doubted she could stand much longer. All she wanted was to sleep, but there was no time for that. She needed to keep Luke's spirits up. She needed to question the specialists to learn the latest developments about Luke's condition, and whatever else moms were supposed to do in hospitals.

But right now, she wanted to rest. She needed to figure out how to let go of her anxiety over her and Seth's shared past. She couldn't afford the distraction his presence caused. She moved back to the couch and plopped down. The couch cushion seemed to scream out, earning the young nurse's attention. "Are you sure you're all right, Ms. McClain?"

"A little tired, that's all."

Emma walked toward her, concern etched across her face. "May I bring you coffee?"

"No, thank you. I'll walk to the cafeteria in a few minutes." Aimee managed a smile.

"Alright. Let me know if you need anything. We need to keep you healthy for Mr. Luke. I'm here for you, too." She slipped out the door. "Oh hello!" Emma said, her tone lifting considerably.

"How are you this morning?" A male greeted the nurse as the door shut, cutting off whatever he said next.

Aimee rose from the chair, raking her hand through her tangled, sleep-mussed hair. "Luke, are you ready for breakfast?"

Her son's gaze was fixed on the door. "Was that Seth?"

"Um, sounded like him." Seth had stayed with them late last night, long after visiting hours were over, playing board games. Aimee hardly expected him to return this soon. The drive from Point Peace to Atlanta took three hours one way. When did the man sleep?

Luke pushed himself up in bed. "Go see, Mom."

"He's coming. Now, you eat your breakfast." She held the fork out for Luke. "Or I'll send Seth home."

"He won't leave just 'cause I haven't eaten breakfast."

Aimee narrowed her eyes.

"Told ya he'd come back." He grasped the utensil. "Just like he said he would."

Her child's retort chided her for all of her broken promises. She stood motionless as Luke ate his eggs. Her stomach clenched in guilt. If she told

Seth the truth he may not come back and then Luke would be upset and disappointed in her.

A knock sounded on the door.

"Come in!" Luke slid his tray to the side.

Dressed in a red polo shirt and jeans, Seth crossed the threshold. His tan seemed deeper. He greeted Luke as if it had been days since they'd last spoken, not hours. When he turned her way, his smile sent electric currents through her that she felt clear to her chipped-polish toes. Grant Morrow followed Seth inside the room.

"How are you, Mr. Luke?" Grant focused on Luke and extended his hand.

Luke took hold of Grant's hand and shook it with all his might as Seth moved to Aimee's side and asked for an update on Luke's progress. "The doctor hasn't been in yet."

Grant turned to Aimee. "I hope you don't mind me coming to visit Luke."

"Not at all."

"You've got a real meal now, huh?" Seth knelt down and peered up at Luke. "When we bust you out of here, I'll take you to practice with me. Maybe we'll go get a cheeseburger and a milkshake."

Luke looked at Aimee for approval. She smiled and nodded her agreement.

She turned her attention to their guest. "Do you play baseball, Grant?"

"A little, but football was my sport."

"Seth said you had an injury in college, too."

"Yeah, I blew my knee out which ended football for me." Grant leaned against the wall and crossed his ankles.

"Did you play football, Seth?" Luke asked.

"A little in high school." He sat on the edge of Luke's bed.

"Don't let him fool you," Grant said. "Seth can play any sport he puts his mind to. College scouts were looking at him for both sports. Seth chose baseball because he liked it best."

"I want to play for the Atlanta Braves," Luke chirped.

"Maybe you will," Seth said. "Working for the majors takes a lot of practice and hard work"

Luke's eyes rounded as he clung to every word Seth spoke. "Wow! What's this?" He put his arms around the large box Seth placed on the bed.

"A present for you, champ."

Luke dug inside the box, pulling out a couple of games, a pack of new baseballs and a new glove. Seth had put some other items inside, a bobble head, sports team stickers and trading cards and in the bottom were the two important items.

"An autographed baseball," Luke's smile stretched from dimple to dimple.

"Wow." She locked gazes with Seth. "That's awesome Seth." *It's too much, Seth,* she wanted to say but didn't want to sound ungrateful.

Seth peered inside the box. "There's more."

Luke pulled out a black bag that held a white envelope.

"Open it," Seth said.

Luke ripped the adhesive tab open. His eyes grew wider. "Tickets! No way!"

"Game tickets for the Sandgnats?" Aimee read

over his shoulder.

"They're the minor league team in Savannah, Mom."

Aimee umm-hmm'd her agreement to Luke. Then she eyed Seth. "It's too much. We can't accept them, but thank you."

Now, Seth's eyes widened. "What do you mean? Of course, you can accept them."

"Tickets to the baseball games, Mom," Luke bounced on his bed, jumping to his knees.

"I know it, honey." She shook her head *no* at Seth. "We will pay you for our tickets."

"I won't accept. They're a gift to Luke."

"There's four tickets. One for me, you, and one for Seth," Luke handed her a tickets as if he were about to leap out of bed. "Grant gets number four!"

Grant chuckled. "Thanks buddy, but you may have a friend you want to take along." He leaned in toward Luke and closer to Aimee. "What seats do you have?" Grant's thumb brushed Aimee's hand as he studied the tickets. He announced the gate and row with a whistle. "Prime seats, man.

"Only the best for Luke," Seth added.

"You're the best," Luke said as he threw his arms around Seth's shoulders and gave him a tight hug.

Seth returned the child's hug as if the embrace was the best gift he'd ever received. Why couldn't she provide for her son like this? Why did it have to come from someone her son had only known for a few weeks? A person who would likely turn away once he knew the truth.

But what if she told him and he stuck around?

With his repeated visits, Seth didn't seem like the kind of person to leave them without another word. Her stomach clenched. She was afraid to hope that Seth could forgive her.

Ecstatic, Luke continued to stare at the tickets. No way would Seth take the tickets back and she didn't want him to, not when she enjoyed the look of pure joy on her son's pale face. She was outnumbered. "Will you two be here a minute? I need to run to the café a moment." She had to get out of the room. Think.

"Sure, do whatever you need." Seth smiled, although his eyes were concerned.

"Thanks." She bit the words out, then hurried out into the hallway and headed to the stairs. She jogged a couple of flights until her heart beat too fast for her to continue. Cold concrete penetrated the thin cotton of her lounging pants as she lowered to the bottom tread. Her shoulders shook as she slumped against the cold brick wall.

"Draw four!" Luke slammed the card on the stack, laughter doubling him over until he slumped against the bed, giggles still leaking out after every other breath.

"Aw man!" Grant exclaimed and begrudgingly chose four cards as instructed.

Seth eyed the door. He'd been watching it ever since Aimee hurried out. Something was wrong. He put his cards down, unable to concentrate.

When the door opened and Aimee slipped in, Seth stood. He studied her pink nose and glassy eyes. He motioned to the hallway. "Can we talk?"

A couple of nurses and doctors passed them as they headed toward the elevators. Seth nudged Aimee toward the stairs. The heavy door clanged shut. He faced her. "Are you okay?"

She rubbed her palms down her thighs, a nervous habit he'd noticed. "No more gifts, Seth. It's too much. I can't compete with game tickets and autographed baseballs."

"Whoa," he spoke softly trying to calm her down. "I would never try to compete with you, Aimee. The ball was one I already owned. I just—"

But she plowed on, "It's better to visit without the added extravagance. He'll start to expect gifts every time. If you can't abide by that rule, then just don't come at all."

He stood back, unsure what to make of her sudden disconnect from him. "The kid's been in a hospital for ten days."

"I know that—"

"He can't do what kids his age can do. He deserves all the gifts and support he can get."

She folded her arms in defense. "I don't want Luke disappointed when the money runs out, and you aren't here anymore."

He stepped back. "Is that what you think of me?"

"I don't know," she sniffed. "I'm just preparing for when you stop coming around."

Though she held tight to her arms, she shook. Rather than fuel her anger with his own misunderstanding and frustration, Seth stood silent.

Where was her family? Why was it that every time Seth visited, none of her cousins, her aunts or her grandparents were there to support her? Here stood a widow, trying to raise her son on her own. Luke's illness could be life threatening. The thought of losing him was probably never far from her mind.

No, Seth couldn't get angry at her lashing out. Not only was she attempting to protect Luke, but she was trying to protect herself. He braced her arms, rubbing his palms up and down. Her head remained down, as if she couldn't look at him. Something was bothering her, but she didn't seem in any rush to tell him. Well, he'd wait, forever, if need be. On impulse, he kissed the top of her head.

She lifted her gaze. Surprise lit her eyes.

"I plan to be around, Aimee." He cupped her face, rubbing his knuckles down her cheek. Her lips parted, but Seth quieted anything more she had to say as he covered her mouth with his.

Chapter Ten

"I can't wait to see Max."

Aimee flicked a glance in the rearview mirror. Luke clutched the teddy bear Seth had bought against his chest. "Well, Max has missed you. Grandpa says he's been patrolling their back yard looking for you."

The three-month-old German shepherd was a gift from Grandpa Paul and Granny Lena when Aimee and Luke moved back to Point Peace. So far, even though the black and gold puppy was a major chewer, he loved Luke. The two had grown accustomed to sleeping together in Luke's bedroom.

"That's 'cause he is looking for me." Luke's seatbelt clanged against the door as Luke pulled himself up between the driver and passenger seat. "Seth's here."

Sure enough, Seth's black truck was parked on the street with a trailer hooked to the back. A lawnmower was parked on the trailer and Seth strolled along the yard, blowing grass off the sidewalk. He proceeded toward the driveway but paused when he saw her car turning into the driveway.

Luke hung out the passenger window so he could send Seth a vigorous wave.

Smiling, he cut the motor on the blower. He opened Luke's door and frowned "Don't tell me you rode home without being in your seatbelt?"

Her son's face fell. Seth hadn't spoken harsh, but Luke had sensed the change in his tone. "No sir, I just unbuckled as Momma turned in the driveway."

"Alright, but you should stay buckled until the car is in park." Seth raised his hand for a high five. "Got it?"

"Yes sir!" Luke returned the high five. He squealed when Seth picked him up and spun him around.

Aimee rounded the front of Tank as Seth carried Luke against his side like a football. "What exactly have you been doing?"

"Cutting grass. Your grandmother mentioned your grandfather had a hard time maintaining the yard due to his bad knee. I told her I'd be glad to cut the grass for her."

Granny and her meddling. Her grandfather hadn't complained of his knee in a decade or longer. "I can cut the grass. We have a mower."

"I have no doubt you would excel at the task." He rubbed her shoulder.

She exhaled. It was hard to say no to Seth. He'd held up his end of the bargain regarding gifts. During the last week Luke was in the hospital, Seth didn't bring Luke any more presents. He did bring his favorite drinks and snacks, but Aimee decided to let her argument rest. The man was stubborn.

And handsome. Though his designer sunglasses covered his eyes, she could tell he watched her and was amused at something. His dimples cut into his cheeks. Despite the fact that she tried to avert her gaze, she couldn't help take in his casual shirt, jeans and sneakers. He was sweaty and probably smelled. She exhaled again, frustrated because she'd like to be closer to find out.

"Come on, Luke," she tried not to sound hateful, but the tone of her words was forced. She stormed toward the front door, irritated at her reaction to Seth being here, cutting her grass so she wouldn't have to, and looking so muscular and fine.

The key wouldn't fit into the lock. She jammed it, bent her fingernail in the process and the keys clattered to the floor. She bobbed down and grabbed them, only to rise up and hit something solid.

And he smelled woodsy... Nice.

"Allow me," Seth reached over her shoulder and had her keys in hand before she could fathom what *allow me* meant.

Seth followed Aimee into the house. Her mood had shifted. When he'd talked to her this morning, she'd been ecstatic that they were awaiting discharge. Since she wouldn't allow him to purchase gifts, he figured he would help her in other ways to which prompted him to stop by her grandparent's house. Lena Miller had a list ready to go of things her husband Paul wasn't able to do. She sent Seth home with some canned vegetables, homemade salsa and jellies, and fresh baked bread as payment for helping them.

It occurred to Seth that the Miller's probably had a management company to help maintain their properties. Why they wouldn't hire the company to help their granddaughter out with household chores didn't make sense to him. However he wasn't complaining. Any excuse to see Aimee was worth whatever task he needed to complete.

Luke ran between them inside and disappeared around a corner.

Arms full with groceries bags, Aimee faced Seth. "Thanks for your help."

He gestured to the luggage he held. "Where should I put these?"

"Oh, yes. I forgot about the bags. One is Luke's and one is mine. Just sit them here and I'll get them when I unpack the groceries. I guess we'll see you around."

He raised an eyebrow. "I'll help you."

She appeared flustered as she shoved cereal boxes onto the pantry shelves. Seth grabbed another box of cereal and held it toward her as she reentered the kitchen.

"Seth, you really don't have to stick around and help with this. I can put up the groceries." She took the box from him.

"You're doing a fine job. Where do you keep your canned goods?"

She grumbled over her shoulder, "In the

pantry."

After following her lead on the other items, Seth leaned against the counter as Aimee grabbed the plastic groceries bags and stowed them in a recycling container.

"Does it bother you that I'm here?"

"No. No, no." She shook her head as she ran water in the kitchen sink. A gasp, a sarcastic one, escaped before she spoke. "No, I'm not bothered by you. Don't be ridiculous."

He edged closer. "You seem irritated with me. When we spoke this morning, you were in a great mood."

"I'm in a fabulous mood."

He blinked at the gruffness of her voice. "You sound about as fabulous as a wet cat on a cold day." He crossed his arms, watching her clipped and quick movements as she dried her hands. "You're not much on accepting help are you?"

Her gaze flicked up. "I accept help just fine, but I know you're busy. I hate to burden you with all of our drama."

"Aimee, your situation is far from drama." He followed her into the sunroom. Two easels sat in the corner with portraits in process on both. "Why aren't your cousins here? Didn't your aunt know you were coming home today? I know your grandparents did."

"Sure, they knew." Her mouth pinched in annoyance. "What does that have to do with anything?"

"Why isn't your refrigerator stocked? Everyone knew you've been at the hospital for the last two weeks. Didn't they realize you'd have to stop on your way home, dragging Luke through a germ-filled store just for milk and cereal? Why is it that the person who's known you the shortest period of time is thinking about these things? They're your family. Family should be there to support you."

"Well, our family is different. Everyone works," Aimee countered.

"Me, too."

"It's June. You're a teacher. Don't you have the summer off?"

"Nope. I'm also a coach, and we practice June and July. Plus, I help my parents with their restaurant. I also work with Dad if he needs me when he's repairing a vehicle."

She stacked her sketch pads, gathered pencils and took the bundle to a white wicker storage cabinet. After she'd tucked everything neatly away, she turned to him. "Maybe, it's me. Maybe, I push everyone away. When someone asks if I need a meal, I usually say no. I don't want to be an inconvenience."

He raised his eyebrows. "Ah, okay. Yeah, maybe you're the problem." He made a show of putting his fist to his chin as if considering her reasoning. "Nope, that's not it. It's hard to believe someone hasn't gone ahead and taken the initiative. I guess I'm used to a tight-knit family and if you were mine, I would make sure you and Luke didn't go without."

Without a word, she studied him.

"I can't go to the bathroom without my mother knowing," he quipped.

Chuckling, she lowered her face to her palm.

"Yes, she thinks that's funny." Seth tittered and took her hands.

"Stop it." Aimee smiled though, and she squeezed his hands amicably. She didn't pull away. "I need to unpack and make dinner."

"Good, I'm starving." He pulled her closer. "What are you cooking?"

She tilted her head. "Are you inviting yourself to dinner?"

"I cut your grass. Isn't a dinner invitation automatic?"

He smiled as she became tongue tied. He liked teasing her, liked the rise he got out of her when she forgot her worries and concentrated on fighting back and standing up to his friendly bullying. His gaze settled on her mouth until footsteps stomped through the kitchen.

Luke gripped the door frame, his smile spread across his face. "Grandpa's here and he's got Max!"

Later that evening, Luke set the table showing off what he had learned last year when he was still healthy enough to be in school. "Mom, Seth, come see."

"Very good, Luke." Aimee said. "You've got the utensils in the right spot. The plates for salad and entrée are correct. Awesome job!" She squeezed him against her.

Seth made a show of studying the table. "Yep, looks nice. I think we can hire you at my mom's restaurant. Are you ready to start working full time?"

His face turned pink as he doubled over with laughter. "I'm not even eight years old yet."

Seth formed his best puzzled face. "What do you mean? A seven-year-old can't set a table like this. No way!" He placed the salad bowl in the center and asked for Luke's approval while Aimee finished the marinara sauce.

The round table was large, with seating for six, but the three of them sat together on one end. Seth had shared in many family dinners, but none filled his soul like this one. After dinner, Luke went to lie down and watch television while Seth insisted on cleaning the dishes.

"Sure, you can wash the dishes." She smirked. "I have no problem with that."

Triumphant, he grinned. "We're making progress. Earlier you admitted you didn't like to accept help."

She blinked coyly. "Well, I've got to admit washing dishes isn't my favorite thing. Especially since Granny never saw fit to add a dishwasher."

Elbow deep in lemon-scented water and bubbles, Seth eyed her. "You tricked me."

Her throaty laugh made him smile. "Yes, yes I did."

He handed her a clean and dripping wet bowl. "Even if this place doesn't have a dishwasher, it is a nice cottage."

"It is. I don't know how much longer I can stay here, though. It was quite stressful while we were in Atlanta, knowing my home, my job was down here." She grew quiet as she toweled the plate and put it in the cabinet. "I had more time to think about the possibility of moving back to Atlanta. I can't keep traveling back and forth from the hospital."

Another bowl slipped through his grasp and splashed water over his shirt. "You're not planning to stay in Point Peace?" Disappointment increased pressure in his chest. "But your family is here." His home is here.

"Yes, but while Luke's health is as precarious as it is, I need to be close to the Children's hospital. I appreciate what my grandparents have done for me, but I need to move back. It's like you asked: where is my family? My family is wherever Luke and I are. He and I depend on each other."

Dishwashing and drying commenced in silence. He shouldn't have brought up the shortcomings he had noticed in Aimee's family. However, her decision seemed to be something she'd already been thinking about before he inserted his opinions.

With the kitchen in order, Aimee led Seth into the living room. She paused midway and raised her finger to her lips. Asleep on the couch was Luke with Max curled up at his feet.

Seth carried Luke to bed. While Aimee straightened his sheets, Max settled on his own bed on the floor. Luke's room held posters of various football and baseball players. Toys filled storage containers on one side of the room, with his desk placed beside the window. Seth moved to turn the lamp off and noticed a large pad of paper and colored pencils. A few sketches hung on the wall but more were on the floor.

"Is Luke an artist like you?" Seth whispered.

Aimee moved beside him and gazed over her son's drawings. She smiled. "He likes to draw, so yes, I guess he's a little like me."

Seth thumbed through the pictures of animals and cars. "Impressive." He held up a portrait of a dog.

"That's my favorite. It looks just like Max."

"Yes, Luke really captured the dog's likeness." He followed Aimee to the foyer, but he wasn't ready to leave. "Thanks for dinner."

"Thanks for helping me organize the fundraiser, for cutting the yard, for being such a kind mentor to Luke. Thanks for the gifts, for everything." She flattened her hand against her stomach. "I don't think I'll ever be able to fully repay you."

"I accept weekly installments."

She guffawed and followed him to the porch.

"You think I'm kidding," his tone remained low. "But, I'm serious. I've decided I'm not doing all of this for free, Aimee."

"Well, as Luke already said, we don't have much money."

"I've got plenty of that."

"Oh, good."

Seth took a seat on the swing as she closed the door behind her. She pulled her hair over her shoulder and began fingering and braiding the strands. A breeze, warm and balmy, curled itself across the porch. Though the swing would fit two, she remained by the door.

"Go on a date with me. Tomorrow."

Chin lowered, she cut her eyes at him. "I don't know, Seth, I—"

"Dinner tomorrow," he insisted. "We can go over the details for the festival and fundraiser."

"I'll meet you to talk about the festival, but it's not a date." Sighing, she moved from the door to the porch railing. She was exasperated and he wasn't even teasing her. "I can't date anyone right now. Kissing you the other day…"

"Was wonderful, right? Okay. No date. We'll talk about the business of bone marrow donations and raising money. I promise that we'll only have dinner if it means life or death." He teased, but his offer was more of a statement, not something she could decline. He didn't think he could handle her rejection of him. She had feelings for him, as he did her, and he wanted time with her, away from the stress for an evening, to figure out if his feelings had depth or if she was a passing infatuation. Except he already knew the answer.

Another breeze whisked around them. Aimee rubbed her arms to stave off the chill.

Dinner. Alone with Seth. It certainly seemed like a date to her, although the only person she'd ever dated was Michael. She shook the thoughts away. This wasn't a date. Her mindset dictated her outcome. She would meet with Seth, discuss Luke's fundraiser, and she would come home. And that would be that. Nothing more.

When she met Seth's gaze, only the lamp of the moon stood between them.

He glanced toward the sky. "Care to sit down?"

"No, I'm fine. I sit there all the time."

"I should be going." He stood and slowly made his way toward her.

Somewhere deep inside she wanted to ask him to stay a little longer, but that was dangerous. Though she knew he should leave, her heart stammered like a schoolgirl, creating chaos and feelings that could only spell disaster. She was a widow with a sick child. She knew where her priorities belonged. Never mind the fact that her grandmother was one step away from signing her up for Match.com, Aimee wasn't about to run to the first man who opened his arms.

His kindness over the last few weeks begged her to ignore truth and to give this man a chance. That scared her. She crossed her arms tighter to hold these strange feelings at bay.

Seth leaned against the porch railing beside her. "It's nice tonight."

"Very nice." She concentrated on the inky sky dotted with pins of stars, the velocity of the wind, the leaves rustling on the crepe myrtle. She kept her eyes and mind focused on anything except the minuscule distance between them.

The wind picked up and Aimee held herself tighter.

"Are you cold?"

She stopped rubbing her arms. "No, I'm fine."

Seth touched her bare shoulder. "You are cold." He turned toward her. "Why didn't you say something before now?" His hand splayed across her arm and somehow, she was pressed against him. Heat flooded from one side of her body to the other. "You always do this, you know?"

"Do what?" she asked, trying to will her body to stop shaking. She shouldn't be this close to him. It was wrong, but she couldn't pull herself away. Standing this close to Seth felt good. She wanted his warmth, wanted to feel this connection with him.

"When you need something, you don't say anything. We've been out here for a while and I'll bet you've been shivering the whole time." He continued to rub his hand up and down her arm.

Since he was several inches taller, she found herself snuggled against his side. Oh, Lord, what was she doing? This couldn't happen. The boundary with Seth was extending beyond friendship and she was teetering along the border. Her only defense was to stand ramrod straight and not put her arms around his waist. Not tuck her head against his chest as she'd done that day at the hospital when she'd been so worried.

"I would have left so you could have gone inside."

And she could joke. Yes, she could joke with the best of them when under pressure in uncomfortable situations. "Oh? So this isn't some old high school move you were trying out so that you could put your arm around me?"

Seth chuckled. "You figured me out."

"Slick, Seth, real slick. It's June and you think I'm cold."

"See, I thought you were pretending to be cold because you didn't want me to go."

"I didn't." Words her heart screamed but her mind wanted to keep tucked in secret, spilled out.

Her mouth betrayed her mind. Thinking the words was dangerous, but safe. Now she was across the border and into a danger zone. What was she doing? This would never work out.

"I didn't want to go either." His hands stilled as his head dipped toward her. As her mouth tilted toward him, she grasped the edge of his shirt, holding on as she committed to sharing a piece of her, unwilling to turn back now.

His lips covered hers, soft and pliant. Her heart pounded, sending sensations of fire to her fingertips. Her hands slid up his neck, grazed through his hair.

Michael's face appeared in her mind, and she stilled. Seth must have sensed her detachment because he slowly raised his head. His hands still rested on her arms though and he looked upon her with uncertainty.

In a reflexive motion, her fingers grazed her lips where Seth had touched her.

He said nothing as he took her hand and kissed her knuckles. His gaze had changed from confusion to sympathy. "I'll see you tomorrow."

She walked to the door but turned as his truck revved to life. Standing in the shadows of the porch, she held on to the railing and watched him drive away. This was brand new to her. She'd traveled with her parents growing up and never learned what it was like to have a boyfriend. In college, she'd had guy friends, but after her parents were both gone, Aimee kept to herself. Michael had been her first everything.

When he died, she truly thought he would be

her last. He'd been so possessive of her, she felt sure he wouldn't have wanted her to consider another man. She loved Michael. She never wanted to disappoint him.

What had she done? She scrubbed her hand over her face and neck and drew herself up into the swing. Now the chill truly set in, as the moist air combed through her hair. The seat beside her remained vacant. "Oh Michael, I'm sorry."

The wind quickened and carried her whispers away.

Chapter Eleven

"Guys, run three laps then meet me at home plate." Seth addressed his baseball team on the field the next morning.

"Can I run, too, Coach?" Luke stood with pride in front of the team, dressed out in his cleats, Point Peace Junior Pirate jersey and baseball pants.

Seth pulled Luke's hat off his head in a playful gesture. "Do you feel up to it?"

Luke grinned, "Yes, I'm ready."

"One lap to start, Luke. I don't want you overdoing it today."

The boy took off at a fast clip and the team ran with him as they rounded first base.

"I see you have a new assistant." Josh stood by the dugout as Seth went to get the bucket of baseballs.

He passed Josh an extra glove. Across the field, Luke pumped his legs hard to keep up with the team as they passed center field. "Luke's great." He hitched his chin at Josh. "What are you doing here? Can you help with practice?"

"Sure." He shoved his keys and phone in his pockets. "I've been at Hopewell all morning trying to get the sound system right in the theater. Saw you guys out here and thought I'd stop by."

Silence fell between them as the team rounded home and started their second lap.

"One more, Coach." Luke bounced on the balls of his feet in a stationary jog. "Please, please."

"Last one, McClain!"

Josh chuckled with Seth. Luke looked back at them and smiled as he gained on the team's captain. Josh's voice pulled Seth's attention from the team.

"I saw Charles Ridley today."

"Oh yeah?" Seth picked up one of the bases and moved it near the opponent dug out.

Using his arm to wipe sweat off his brow, Seth eyed Josh. He didn't need a counseling session. Not now, while he was trying to focus on getting his team conditioned. This wasn't the time to relive his mistakes. One wrong decision cost Kevin his life.

Seth focused on Luke who ran toward him. Pointing to home plate, Luke hurried forward.

Luke stomped home plate with both feet and the team ran by Seth to finish their warmup.

"Good job, Luke," Josh gave him a high five.

"Go get your water and take a seat."

Luke's eyes were hooded by Seth's oversized baseball cap he'd given the kid. "I don't feel tired, Coach."

Seth suppressed his grin. Luke had gone from calling him Seth the whole drive to school to

Coach once he heard it from the players. He wanted to fit in with the big kids so bad. Seth wanted that for the little guy, too.

"Let's take it slow. You were in the hospital two days ago. I'm trying to keep you out of there."

He lowered his head in defeat, but obeyed. Seth squatted down and leveled his eyes. "Rest a minute and then you can come out to catch some balls. I'll show you how to pitch when I finish up with the team. Deal?"

Luke bumped his fist in agreement.

Seth strolled back to Josh. "Yeah, Mr. Ridley's rental company is supplying some of the items for the festival. We started talking about old times."

"I don't get by there enough."

"He said they were okay. Mrs. Ridley had been sick, but is doing better. He asked how you were doing. Said he saw you at the cemetery."

He looked away. He didn't want to talk about seeing Charles at Kevin's grave or the incident. Events from twelve years ago plagued him enough when no one else knew.

Seth moved the bucket holding the baseballs and brought two bats within reach of home plate. Though his shoulder ached, he planned to hit balls into the field to the guys. He switched hands and decided he'd hold the bat with his other hand, on the arm that didn't need surgery.

Josh stood by in silence and finally spoke. "It wasn't your fault. There's no need to avoid the family, Seth. The Ridley's forgave you a long time ago. It's time you forgave yourself."

"Thanks, but I don't need a lecture. I'll get by

and see them soon. If you're not going to help with practice, then go on. I've got to get these guys focused."

Seth turned his back on Josh and faced his team. Jeff Ridley, Kevin's brother, stood front and center. After he gave them instructions, they broke out into groups taking the infield and outfield. He glanced back and saw Josh getting into his truck. Josh didn't deserve the brush off Seth gave him, but he wasn't in the mood to talk out his feelings. Some things took time. How long would it take to forget?

~

"Ms. McClain? Are you still here?"

Caleb, the youth minister, called from a distance down the hall.

"Hi, Caleb." Aimee sat her paint brush on the side of the pan and scooted left. Still on her knees she waved. "I'm here."

Grinning, Caleb walked toward her.

"Please call me Aimee."

Caleb glanced over Noah's Ark. "It's looking great."

A tingling sensation raced from her heart to each finger and toe. If running through the halls singing wouldn't make her look crazy in front of Caleb, she would have done it. Being able to paint, for an actual paycheck, was better than any other job she'd ever had. Her work on these walls was almost as good as having them displayed in a gallery. She hoped these pictures helped what the children would learn in these halls come alive. "I hope everyone likes them." She had finished the

Ark today. Tomorrow she would move on to the second mural. "Is it time to leave for the afternoon?"

"Yes ma'am."

"Let me rinse out my brushes and clean up. I'm at a good stopping point. Can you give me about fifteen minutes?"

"Sure. I'd be glad to help."

Seth's words from other night came to mind about her not wanting to accept help. Unfortunately the truth was it was Seth's help she should avoid. Everyone else she was glad to accept. "Thank you. We'll get done quicker working together."

"How's Luke doing?" Caleb asked as he stacked her paint cans in the storage closet.

"His spirits are good." She handed him one of the cans she carried and forced a smile.

While she was elated at painting today, she'd spoken with Luke's doctor earlier. That conversation had successfully put Aimee's spirits in a foul territory.

And then there was Seth. A month had passed since their meeting on the bridge, and she continued to be dishonest with him about who she truly was so that she could make sure the fundraiser for Luke happened.

Somehow, Seth had managed to secure big names to be at Luke's festival. A couple of Braves players would be there to sign autographs after the race. In just a few short weeks, everything was set for Luke's rally. Food trucks would be on hand. Carnival rides and games would entertain folks at the finish line, and a large percentage of the proceeds were going to Luke's medical bills.

She couldn't tell Seth the truth until after the festival. She was manipulating him and she didn't like it one bit. What about after the festival? The truth was she didn't want to tell him at all. The thought of causing Seth more paint was unbearable. Yet the longer she held the truth from him, the longer the lie continued. No good relationship survived on lies.

"Who's the painter on this job?" Seth's voice rumbled through the hall. Caleb and Aimee turned as Seth rounded the corner holding Luke's hand in his.

Her son wore an oversized baseball cap and his baseball pants were smudged with dirt, but she couldn't take her eyes off of Luke's smile. How could she take this happiness away from him?

Seth met her gaze. Tonight, it would be the two of them. Anticipation and trepidation had been her companions the whole morning.

She welcomed her son with a hug. She lifted her gaze to the man who had made their lives whole these last few weeks. "What do you think?"

He studied her artwork. "You have done an awesome job."

Seth and Luke helped her clean up her workspace and the three of them left the fellowship hall. In the parking lot, Seth finished loading Tank and shut the back door.

Aimee turned to Luke, "Ready to go home?"

"Jimmy's on the baseball field. Can I go say hello?"

Shielding her eyes from the glare, she saw a

batter and pitcher practiced in the cages. "Are you sure you feel like walking? I can drive you over there."

"I want to run over there."

Aimee raised her eyebrows. "Well, take it slow. I'll be right over."

"Thanks Mom." Luke hugged Aimee, then turned to Seth and gave him a hug before he ran down the sidewalk toward the baseball fields.

Beside her, Seth watched Luke until he reached his friend. "He's amazing, Aimee. He ate six pancakes at breakfast, ran one lap with the team. He would have run more, but I didn't let him and then he stayed out there practicing drills with the team. He has more energy than anyone I've ever seen."

Nodding, Aimee leaned against Tank's passenger side for support and stared across the quad. "He has these good days, and he has bad days. His doctor called this morning." She crossed her arms and gripped her sides as she repeated the doctor's news. "The person they thought would be a match for Luke ended up failing a couple of tests." Emotion thickened her throat. Speaking the words made them true, causing her eyes to burn. "I'm sorry to get emotional. I was sure this was the one." She put both hands over her face and gave Tank her full weight.

Strong hands touched her shoulders, slowly turning her until she faced him. He wrapped his arms around her and pressed his lips against her hair.

Aimee wound her arms around his waist and

rested her cheek to his chest.

He leaned back, meeting her gaze. "I spoke with the representative from the bone marrow registry. Their person will be on hand, and whoever volunteers can give a sample of a cheek swab. That's all it takes. I actually donated at the Northside clinic while you and Luke were in Atlanta. Since I've already donated, I can easily explain to everyone how the process works."

Aimee tried to smile but her emotions were so heavy, she could do little more than gaze up at this man who had an answer to her every concern. She lowered her head and tightened her grip around him. He held her and neither spoke.

"What if no one comes to the festival, Seth?"

"Don't even let that cross your mind." He leaned back, sliding his fingers along her cheek. She felt his reassurance and his support by just the expression on his face. "Every person who means anything to you, Luke and me will be there."

He tightened his hold on her. "I have this feeling. We're going to find Luke's donor right here in Point Peace."

Words were difficult all of the sudden. Her throat closed with emotion coiling. "It would be a blessing, a miracle, Seth."

"You're due."

She lowered her gaze. "I don't deserve it, but Luke does."

"Hey," Seth tipped her chin until they were eye to eye. "Don't discount yourself."

She shook him off and stepped out of the comfort of his space. "If you knew, Seth, you would understand when I say I just don't deserve your kindness... I've been selfish where you're concerned."

He frowned and tipped his head to the side. "We'll talk tonight." Seth gently squeezed her arm then eyed his watch. "I need to make a couple of stops before I get back to your house tonight. Pick you up at six?"

She nodded, but she needed to cancel tonight. The last place she should be was alone with Seth. He'd started to walk away and then stopped. He returned to her and scooped her hands in his. "One more thing," he glanced around the parking lot as he cupped her face in his hand. "I want this."

Any protest she could generate became lost as his mouth took hers, and he wrapped his arms around her waist. He grumbled against her neck as she pulled away. His lips brushed her cheek and he squeezed her again. Then, he took an honorable step back. "I actually wanted to ask a favor."

"Anything," she whispered. To be able to help Seth in some way would be like repaying him for all he'd done for her and Luke.

"I'm having shoulder surgery next week. I may have to stay overnight in the hospital. Go under anesthesia and the whole nine yards." He looked to his feet, taking on the likeness of a shy little boy. "I'm going to be unavailable to you for a day or so. If you and Luke need anything, I want you to call Mom or Dad, or even Grant or Josh. I'm serious."

She took his hand and looked into his eyes. "I'm glad you're having the surgery. What changed your mind?"

His gaze held hers for several moments before it shifted to the ball field. "I realized if I didn't have the surgery, I would be missing out on too many good things."

~

Seth closed the door of his classroom as he swiped left to answer his phone. Light construction was going on in the gym down the hall making conversation difficult without raising his voice. "Hey, Scoot! How's it going?"

"Ugh! When are you going to stop with the horrible nickname?"

Cory's dull tone made him chuckle. He imagined his younger sister cradling the phone with her manicured fingers, rolling her eyes at him.

"Never. I need a favor."

"Well, you may be in luck, depending on what you want."

"Are you at work?"

"Yes, today is our last day of filming. I'm getting make up done as we speak. Say hello everyone."

"Hello, everyone. Don't take any of my sister's crap."

Cory laughed. "So, what are you doing? Are you back at work?"

"Yes, it's planning period. The students return next week. But the favor doesn't concern Peace. I'm organizing a Bone Marrow Drive." He told his sister about Aimee and Luke and explained Luke's illness, "I'm asking everyone I know to get in touch with their local Bone Marrow Directory and sign up to be a donor. I shared a link on a couple of my social media pages."

"Sure, I'll be glad to check it out. If we can sign up from anywhere, that won't be a problem."

He pressed his fist on his desk as he proposed the other reason for his call. "Or, you could come home, help us with the Drive. I know you're busy, but it would mean a lot to me, and it would mean a lot to Mom and Dad. It's been a while since you've been home."

Shuffling on her end created a sound like papers ruffling and a squeak from a chair. "I don't know, Seth."

"Come home, Cory. Dad's been out of the hospital a few weeks but Mom is still driving him nuts. If you were here, things may settle. You know you have a way of distracting Mom, and Dad misses you."

A door slammed on her end and her voice came through clear. "My schedule is crazy right now. I doubt I can come home, Seth."

"Just try. Your presence could generate many more to attend. This kid needs as many donors he can get." He explained Aimee's situation and how he was trying to help her.

She sighed. "Wow. You're really serious."

"It is. Luke needs a bone marrow transplant."

"I understand, but I also mean it sounds serious between you and Aimee."

"You're going to love her."

"I don't remember you being this motivated about anything beyond baseball since you wanted to go to summer camp in Florida."

He chuckled. "I was twelve, sis."

"True, but I can tell this means a lot to you."

Though she was over two thousand miles away, his sister could read him. Cory had moved to California after high school to try and make it as an actress. He and his parents had visited her regularly until Dad's heart attack made him unable to travel. Since then, Dad's precarious health issues had him in and out of the hospital. "You haven't been home in four years."

She let out a frustrated sigh. "I've been working. But, with this one wrapping up, I'll be between projects. I may be able to come home for a few months. I'll let you know, okay?"

"I could wire you the money."

"Money isn't the problem and even if it was, I wouldn't ask for your help."

"You sound like someone else I know." No one was more stubborn than Aimee.

"I don't need you coddling and bossing me around."

"Am I that awful?" Seth rubbed his neck.

"Yes."

Her flat response caught him by surprise. "You've been gone a while. I'm a big softy now."

"I'd have to see you to believe it."

"Another reason to come home."

Chapter Twelve

"I'm about to make the biggest mistake of my life."

"Oh, stop being so dramatic." Sloan shoved plastic hangers across the metal rack in Aimee's closet. "Your biggest mistake is some of these wardrobe choices. Had I known your situation was this dire, I would've come over long ago."

Aimee worked her hair into a messy bun and walked to the closet doorway. "Why did I agree to go tonight?"

Face pinched in disdain, Sloan thumbed through sweaters. At the blouses, she pulled one off its hanger and held it for examination. "Because he's going to make Luke's fundraiser a grand success and if you ruin it now, you'll not only ruin your life but Luke's, too."

Sloan tilted her head as she held the blouse against Aimee's chest. "He's also handsome, sweet, funny and sexy."

"Those are the worst reasons in the world."

She unhooked the blouse from the hanger.

"You should wear this."

"No. Look at how thin the material is. It's see-through." The black blouse, trimmed in a dainty red thread across the top and the bottom hem, sloped scandalously low, exposing one shoulder. "Where did I get this?"

"My closet. Here, it will look good paired with these jeans."

In the mirror, the girls stared at the blouse. "This outfit makes me look like I'm on a date. I can just wear what I had on today."

"It had paint on the shirt, and you are not walking out of this house in shorts and tennis shoes." Sloan's eyes were wide and incredulous. Her cheeks were almost the color of her red hair. "You want to be pretty, don't you?"

Aimee widened her eyes and tried to mimic Sloan's expression. "No."

Exasperated, Sloan grabbed Aimee's T-shirt by the tail and whipped it over her head. "Well, that bra won't do. Don't you have a strapless?" Without waiting for Aimee's response, Sloan poked her toward her dresser. "How about panties? No granny panties tonight!"

"No one will be seeing my underwear." Aimee elbowed her cousin out of the way, shoved her underwear and socks around in the drawer until she produced the strapless forgotten in the back. "I hate this thing. It's too small."

Sloan tilted her head. "Even better. I'm kidding." Once Aimee had it on she stood back. "It fits fine."

Aimee reached for the blouse and pulled it over

her head. "This is not a date."

"Yes, it is." Sloan yanked the elastic band from Aimee's hair.

"Hey!"

"No ponytails tonight, girlfriend. You're going out with Seth Garrett. You are not painting or sculpting."

"I don't want Seth to think that I want this night to go anywhere."

Sloan rolled her eyes.

Aimee mimicked her cousin's response in humor, but she had to be honest with herself. They'd already kissed. Not once, but a few times. If she wanted to stop the progression of her relationship with Seth, she had to stop kissing him.

Sighing, she recalled each sweet touch. He made her feel young again and excited. Even tonight, despite all of her arguing, the butterflies in her stomach were because she wanted to go with Seth tonight. That admission scared her most of all.

Stomach roiling, suddenly dizzy, Aimee sat down on the settee and tucked her head between her legs.

Red-polished, pedicure fresh feet shuffled toward her. "Luke loves him."

"Too much," Aimee agreed regrettably. "Luke is going to be devastated when I tell Seth the truth, and Seth doesn't want to see us again."

Sloan rubbed her shoulder. "Seth is a good guy." Sloan squatted down and put her hand on Aimee's knee. "Try to relax. If the thought of a date makes you nervous, then, just go out and have some fun."

CHRISTY LASHEA

"No. Tonight is the night. I'm going to tell Seth the truth. I've waited long enough. He's done everything for Luke's fundraiser and even if he doesn't want to see us again, at least the fundraiser will go on." She closed her eyes. "Oh, I can't believe I just admitted that. Listen to me. I sound awful and selfish." She'd wormed her way deeper into Seth's life to get him to set up Luke's fundraiser because she lacked the time, and the know-how to pull it off on her own. Aimee met her cousin's worried stare.

Sloan covered her hands with her own and squeezed. "No, you are not awful or selfish. Asking for Seth's help was what we all encouraged you to do because we knew how well the race for Kevin goes ever year. This year will be the tenth year and it only gets bigger. Luke needs something that no one in the family can give him. We've all tested. We need to spread the word to help that sweet kid of yours."

Aimee bit her lip to stop its quivering.

"Don't tell him tonight. Go out and have fun. You deserve this."

The door chime echoed through the house. "Seth's here!" Luke yelled from the living room.

Sloan braced her hands on Aimee's shoulders. "For tonight, let the past stay in the past."

~

Luke launched into Seth's arms before he was fully inside the house. "I missed you." The kid snuggled his neck.

"It's only been three hours," Seth chuckled. Picking him up off the ground, Seth gave in to the

144

hug and carried Luke inside. "I missed you, too, Champ."

Ryan, Sloan's husband, stood next to the door and shook Seth's hand. The men exchanged introductions until Luke pulled Seth into the living room. "Come sit down here, Seth." He pointed to a chair in the corner that faced the foyer and hallway. "I told her you were here."

Seth winked. "I appreciate that."

Luke crossed his arms and eyed Ryan before setting his focus back to Seth. "When she comes out, do you know what to do?"

"Um—"

"Tell her she's pretty."

Little did the kid know, Seth didn't have a problem telling Aimee she was pretty.

"She likes the beach. You could take her, you know?"

"I already had that in mind."

"Good. She doesn't like sushi."

"Noted." Seth rested his elbows on his knees and looked up at Luke. "I'll take good care of your mom, Luke. I promise you."

Sloan appeared in the foyer. "Hey, Seth.

He stood and looked toward the hallway as he greeted Sloan.

"Aimee will be right out." Sloan slid her hand around Ryan's arm. "Luke, do you have your bag packed?"

"Got it all packed, Nona."

"What about your toothbrush? And Max's toys?"

"Yup," Luke darted to the hall. "Hurry up,

Momma!"

She answered her son before she appeared in the hall. Seth inhaled, but his heart slammed against his chest as if he was rounding third and trying to beat out a throw to home plate. Her hair was down, but she'd curled it and the waves cascaded around her face. Her blouse, falling off of one shoulder, exposed her slender neck and defined collar bone. She rubbed her hands down her hips, over jeans that were slim and fitted, emphasizing her small waist. Her sandals exposed red tipped toenails.

He walked forward with Luke at his side. "You look beautiful."

Blushing, Aimee dropped her gaze.

Seth felt a tug on his shirt. Luke's smile beamed as he held up his thumb.

Early evening at the marina meant high traffic. Boats came in, some to refuel, while others docked to visit the store or restaurant. Along the pier, several fishermen cast lines in hopes of reeling in dinner.

Aimee paused at the entrance of the dock. "You brought the boat here?"

"Do you mind? I needed to run it. It's been docked for too long." He searched her face. "Are you worried about your hair getting messed up? I didn't think about that. Of course, you said this wasn't a date."

"Right, I did say that." She brushed her hand through the curls she'd spent too long wrapping around the curling iron this afternoon. She could've worn her messy bun after all. "I haven't been on a boat in a while. This will be nice."

"It's a twenty-minute ride to Bogart's and the weather is good."

The twenty-two-foot bay boat swayed as Seth moved about, untying ropes and securing loose gear. Once they took out on open water, Aimee settled in beside Seth at the captain's bench. He guided the boat south, toward Point Peace Bay. Heated by the sun hanging low, she pulled her hair up off her neck and secured it with the ponytail holder she'd stowed in her pocket. Along the bank of the bay, rocky forms held the earth secure and palms and hardwood trees swayed with each brush of wind.

"Is Bogart's okay with you? I thought we could sit near the beach and brainstorm any last-minute details about the fundraiser there."

"I like the beach."

"That's what Luke said."

"Did he? What else did Luke say?"

"That you hate sushi and to tell you that you looked pretty."

Oh! What was Luke thinking?

Seth grinned casually as he turned the wheel. "That kid is pretty awesome."

Warmth spread through her at his compliment and she wanted to wrap her arms around his neck, smack a big kiss on his cheek. Instead, she rubbed her palms down her thighs. "Thanks. I think so, too."

They rode in companionable silence for several minutes until her stomach growled. Seth picked up on the sound as if her stomach had a voice. "I made reservations at the restaurant, but then I recalled your opposition to eating…"

She hopped down from the bench to stand beside him. "I'm not opposed to eating. I hope you didn't take me seriously."

Arching an eyebrow, he tilted his face in surprise. "I did take you seriously. I already ate at the burger and shake. We're just going to Bogart's for the beach access."

"Oh."

"Sorry."

"No worries. I've probably got a cough drop. I'll be fine." When she snuck another glance, her mouth dropped at his brazen grin. "You're messing with me."

"Never," he smirked. "So, Luke's spending the night with your cousin… Nona?"

"Nickname for Sloan."

"Figured."

"That's nice that they cleared your evening for you. It's as if they thought you had a date."

"But this is not a date." She wagged her finger. "I don't mind eating, you know? It's the date I opposed. I'm not dating anyone right now or in the future."

"Dating is highly overrated." Resting a hand on the steering wheel, Seth turned toward her. "This evening is about two people planning a fundraiser for a kid in need."

"Exactly." Aimee startled as the two motors roared behind them.

"Hang on." Overhead, the T-top covered their

bench, and the rest of the boat was exposed to the elements. As the boat picked up speed, gusts of wind whipped her hair across her face, slapping Seth's arm in the process.

She pulled her hair off her face to see where they were going as she wound her hair into a ponytail.

He glanced down at her. "What are you smiling about?"

"I love being out on the water."

"Come here." When she narrowed her eyes, he pointed. "Take the wheel."

"Really?" Saddling up in front of him, she slid her fingers over the steering wheel, warm where Seth's fingers had been. His chest brushed against her as he reached around her to adjust their speed. "You're not trying to leave, are you?"

The feel of the boat was different from driving Tank. The slightest movement of the wheel would turn the boat. She was free like a bird flying over water, with Seth behind her, an anchor. Still, one slip, one turn and she could lose control at any moment. Pushing aside her concerns, she settled against his chest. Seth leaned close with one hand on the steel bar of the console and the other resting around her waist.

"I'm not going anywhere. Keep it straight."

He accelerated and she gulped air, holding tight to the steering wheel, fearful and laughing, scared and excited feelings colliding inside of her. Warring between what was right and what her heart desired.

He slowed down as they reached the public

access areas. Boats of leisure and luxury passed. Pointing to their right, "There's Mom and Dad's house."

"I didn't realize how close they are to my place."

"Six miles by land."

Seth took over the helm while they drove through a narrow channel. More residences dotted this area with docks the further they floated inland. Once they reached the dock, he hurried to the front of the boat while she maneuvered the boat against the bumpers. After Seth secured the watercraft to the dock, he held out his hand. "Just a short walk and we'll be there."

They walked up a wooden path beside tall grasses and wax myrtles where the property came to a peak. Over the rise, a robin blue house beckoned, with a white glow from a porch lamp lighting the way.

The foyer of the restaurant was crowded, but once Seth provided his name, they were seated right away. A handful of tables were set beyond the restaurants back deck, covered with white linen tablecloths and matching napkins. A hurricane lamp sat on each table, its gold flame providing a quaint, and romantic ambiance for each setting.

Seth held her chair as she sat down and then took his place beside to her left. He nodded toward the southern tip, where the coast reached out in a rocky point and beyond that the lighthouse sat alone. "Just on the other side of the rise is Pleasant Lea."

"We could have eaten there."

"We will next time. Whenever I'm there I feel like I need to bus tables or help the servers and cooks. I thought I'd keep tonight free for our fundraiser plans."

The waiter arrived with a bottle of wine and appetizers of cold shrimp and oysters. After their glasses were poured, Aimee raised her hand to their server. "May I have ice water?"

As the waiter agreed and walked away, Seth leaned in. "You don't like wine?"

She shrugged. "I like it, but I don't drink anymore."

"I should have asked and not assumed. I'm sorry."

"It's okay. I'm strong enough to say no. It hasn't always been that way."

He smiled as he reached for her hand, squeezing gently. She held his gaze as she considered telling him about her college days, about her involvement with his past.

Let the past stay in the past.

Sloan's words marched through her mind, a loud trumpet blasting somewhere near her eardrum. Exhaling, she rubbed the heel of her hand over her chest to ease the hammering she felt from inside. No, right now wasn't the right time for confessions.

She glanced up as their waiter returned with her water and Seth spoke up. "Sparkling water for us, please sir."

"Is something wrong with the merlot?"

"Not at all, it was my error, not yours." After the waiter asked about their satisfaction with the appetizers, he left them alone again.

Seth opened his hands and gestured to their surroundings. "How do you like our office? I thought this would be the perfect spot to discuss the fundraiser, seeing how this isn't a date." He quipped with a grin that sent a proverbial arrow straight through her heart.

Her gaze fell upon a bonfire near the shore. "Thanks, Seth."

"For what?"

"For being cool about my decision to abstain from drinking, for this lovely dinner." Smiling, she met his eyes. Fire crackled as they indulged in chilled shrimp and finger foods. Seth held up his wine glass, now filled with a bubbly cider. "Let's toast to the best non-date I've ever had."

She clinked her glass with his and savored the taste of the tart golden liquid. Darkness hovered around them, as their conversation swayed from their families, to their hopes and dreams. They never once talked about the fundraiser.

Rain sprinkled from the dark sky as they left the restaurant. It fell like needles once they reached the boat. Seth grabbed rain jackets stowed in a compartment, but by the time they put them on, they were both soaked.

Concern etched across his brow. "I live close. We'll take the boat there and I'll get the truck. I'm sorry Aimee. I didn't see rain in the forecast."

She lifted her face to the pouring rain and laughed. "Two showers in a day never hurt anyone."

Their eyes met and Seth smiled down at her.

His thumb wiped moisture from her cheek. He eyed her lips, then turned toward the wheel. He gunned the boat once they were clear of the docks. When they reached the pier at Seth's house, the rain had stopped. "It didn't even rain here," he observed as he secured the boat to the port.

"If I didn't have bad luck, I wouldn't have any at all."

Seth grabbed her hand and pulled her up the stairs to the rear porch. He brought her around the side to the front entrance and unlocked the door. "It's a little messy. I'm still working on a few things."

"Is this the project you mentioned?"

Inside, he flipped a switch and white light washed the walls. "Yes. The house isn't much right now, but the beach access is the best on the Point."

Following him through the front entry, she inhaled a familiar scent of paint. On either side were vacant rooms with large windows facing the front lawn. At the entry door, the interior opened, boasting larger windows on the backside of the house overlooking the beach. Brown paper covered the entire floor. Kitchen cabinets were covered in plastic along the counters, on either side of the gas stove were open shelves, also protected by thick plastic. A refrigerator sat awkwardly off to itself.

"I just had drywall finished in this area, so everything is still in the masking phase." Pushing open the French doors, warm salty air mingled with the crisp air-conditioned interior. As if he turned on a stereo system, sounds of waves crashing against the shore grew louder.

Aimee dropped her sandals just inside the door and walked barefoot onto the deck. The gusty wind blew her hair and whipped through her thin blouse, drying her camisole underneath. As she warmed and her skin dried, she leaned against the railing. Closing her eyes, she welcomed the hypnotic hum of waves rushing upon the shore. Drenched in pink, the large sheets of thin clouds hung just above the horizon. Though she committed the view to memory, she longed to sketch the scene as the sky shifted from afternoon to evening.

Beyond the sand dunes, stones were stacked. With a flick of a match, a fire rose from the ashes, the flames reaching high. Seth set up two chairs in front of it and turned toward her.

"Do you need help?"

"No thanks. Do you want to change out of those wet clothes? I can throw yours in the dryer."

She followed him inside and upstairs. He opened double doors which led into the master suite. Aimee inhaled as he disappeared around the corner into the bathroom. Turning she caught a glimpse of her face in the mirror and wanted to sink to the floor. "Why didn't you tell me I have two black eyes?"

He reappeared with a couple of pairs of cotton pants and two knit shirts. "I always liked the Goth look," he quipped as he handed her a set of the clothes, tucking the other pair under his arm. "Go jump in the shower. I'll wait for you downstairs. Oh, and the dryer is up here. You can put your clothes in there." He chewed his bottom lip as he considered her for a second, then bolted out of the room. The doors shut with a loud thud behind him.

His bed was huge with four large pillows covered in charcoal colored cases that matched the duvet. She turned away from the bed and pushed away from the direction her thoughts were going. It was inappropriate to think of herself in his bed. She was simply using his shower because she looked like a nightmare clown and she needed to clean up. The plush carpet crushed under her bare feet as she padded across the room and into the bathroom. His shower was the size of her bathroom at Sunset Vista. When she finally figured out which handle turned which faucet on, she counted four shower heads. Two poured water from the top and two more pushed water out from the side walls. She smelled his soap as she lathered, hurrying through the task so that her thoughts would remain pure.

Once she'd dried off, she changed into his shirt and pulled on his pants that were three sizes too big. Securing the waist band into a tail, she fastened her ponytail holder around it. She combed her fingers through her hair, braided the long strands over her shoulder and walked into the hallway.

Seth stood a few feet away in the laundry room. His tanned bare feet caught her attention. As she padded up the hall, his muscled calf came into view. She hesitated at the door, only moving when she noted the hem of his shorts. Shaking her head, grateful he'd already dressed, she cleared her throat.

He tossed his bunch of clothes into the washer, then glanced back. Looked away and did a double take. "That shirt's never looked so good."

Her heart hammered, and she averted her gaze a moment, but quickly flicked her attention back to him. Her smile broke with her chuckle. "Boy, you're a real charmer." She played off his comment as a joke, but she had a hard time looking away from him. He was a guilty pleasure she couldn't avoid.

He shut his eyes for a second as if he regretted saying it then focused on her. "Do you want to just wash your clothes? It shouldn't take long."

Had her clothes not been drenched, had Luke been waiting at home for her, she would have declined. But she had nowhere to be tonight, and for some reason, the shower and slipping into his clothes had calmed her. She flicked the articles in the washer. He added soap and pushed the buttons. "Thanks for everything."

"I felt bad we got caught in the rain." Water poured inside the machine as he swiveled around, his grin shy and slightly crooked. Totally adorable. "Although honestly, I don't feel so bad now." He lifted his finger and brushed a strand of hair off of her face. "You're beautiful, Aimee."

When she dropped her gaze in disagreement, he gently lifted her chin. "You are."

Stepping back, she lowered her gaze. "We should go downstairs, Seth."

Outside, he stoked the fire while she walked toward the shore, studying the sound of the waves. She turned to each side to take in the north and south ends of the beach.

"What are you thinking?"

She faced him, his house stood tall behind him, protective and beautiful. "Living some place like this would be a dream come true, Seth."

He held her gaze as she moved to his side by the fire pit. The tall grass provided some privacy from other houses that stood on either side of his. He'd brought a picnic basket outside. She knelt on the blanket and picked up a piece of watermelon, offering him a bite first. The breeze pulled strands of his hair over his brow as he sank his teeth into the sweet fruit. He captured her hand before she could draw it away and leaned forward. Resting his elbows on his knees, he studied her as he kissed her fingertips. "It's my dream house, too."

Sensations of excitement trilled through her at his touch. She stood and searched her mind for something to say. "How do you manage this on a teacher's salary?" The intrusive, nosey question presented itself before Aimee could stop herself. She raised her hand. "I'm sorry, that's none of my business."

"I don't mind questions. I have nothing to hide. I've invested wisely. That's my secret. The Hummer is something my parents bought me for graduation from high school and I bought my truck after I moved home a few years ago."

"I thought you told me you had two graduation presents?"

A few moments passed before he spoke. His gaze shifted to the horizon. "Well, Dad restored a 1969 Camaro, but I wrecked it the weekend he gave it to me."

She should have known where this discussion

would lead. Shrinking back in the chair, she concentrated on the flames whipping up from the pit. She should have kept her questions to herself. Except she had to know the pieces of his history the papers had not displayed. "How badly were you hurt?"

"Crushed tibia and fibula. Sprained knee. Broken wrist. Dislocated shoulder."

"Is that why you quit baseball professionally?"

"Nah. I recovered and was able to rehab enough to get to the minors. When I got called up, all went well. I was finding my fit. Then Stars played the Rays, the same team that had signed Kevin." His gaze captured something in the distance, and he shook his head as his frown displayed the difficulty of the memory. "I couldn't concentrate on the game. I kept thinking if Kevin wasn't able to play, and I was the one to blame, then I shouldn't be in the majors either." "You weren't to blame, Seth."

He yanked grass and separated a shell, keeping his focus on the task. "Thanks sweetie, but you weren't there." He lifted his earnest gaze then. "I was very much at fault. I was driving and I looked away for too long. I didn't realize something was in the road."

"Who was in the road?"

"I think it was an animal. Kevin's last words were 'Look out, Seth!'" Shaking his head, he threw down a piece of grass. "It all happened so fast. I saw something and swerved. The brakes didn't seem to work right because the car kept spinning until it left the road. My speed was too fast. I don't remember much until I woke up in the hospital. I asked the doctors where Kevin was but no one would answer. Turned out Kevin's injuries were very serious." He raked his hand through his hair. "He was in surgery while I was lying on the stretcher in the ER. He had internal bleeding and the doctors couldn't stop it."

"I'm sorry."

He nodded and silence fell. "This is the part of my past I can't forget." He stood, took a drink from his water bottle and walked closer to the fire. "It's good you know. That's the darkest part of my past. It's the reason I'm a fanatic about seatbelts being fastened." He turned when she touched his arm and wrapped her in his arms.

"I wish I could take that night away from you."

He brushed his fingers through her hair, each touch loving him more. Gripping him tighter, Aimee shut her eyes. Though her words were true, they were misleading, and he had no idea. She wished she'd stayed out of the road that night. It wasn't Seth's fault his best friend was dead, it was hers.

But she didn't want to tell him the truth. She wanted his arms around her, and she wanted him in her life. He filled the void in her life, the vacant space she didn't deserve to fill.

"I'm glad you're here." Heat from his words caressed her chin.

She dropped her gaze to the sand burying their feet, then she shifted her focus to the dunes a few yards away. "We need to talk."

Yet as she gazed over his lips, his kind eyes,

Sloan's advice returned to the forefront of her mind. But if she didn't go ahead and get this off her chest, when would the time ever be right? "Seth, I-" She lifted her head as he lowered his.

"I know," his lips gently brushed hers while his hands splayed against her neck.

She should have stepped away. She should have put distance between them. Instead, her fingers stretched across the soft material of his shirt and her toes raised her higher. Her mouth parted and she shivered with thrill as their tongues met and played. Her fingers edged around his neck as she held his face and tilted her mouth to strengthen her response.

Her hands were in his hair, his hands caressing her lower back when they parted. Breathless, their gazes held. "I want to be a part of your life. I've never felt like this with anyone else."

"I want you, Seth. I truly do."

He lifted her off the ground as he deepened the kiss. Aimee held tight, not wanting this night to end. But what she wanted and what was right were two very different things.

Chapter Thirteen

Though it was barely light outside, flecks of orange mingled with pink and dotted the Savannah skyline. The hospital's surgical waiting room was a bird's nest of activity. Foot tucked under her knee, Aimee propped her sketch pad for a more amicable position and concentrated on her subject. Though she'd been to this hospital several times recently with Luke, she had not set foot in the surgical area since her mother was there almost fourteen years earlier.

Nausea tumbled her stomach and Aimee couldn't get comfortable. Blaming her upset on painful memories, she'd turned to what she did best. Art.

The receptionist's shiny black hair and olive complexion caught Aimee's eye. She studied the young woman, then began to sketch her. Except her subject was not still and others continued to enter and exit her desk area. Aimee's doodles started off as a rough drawing of the woman at her desk, answering the phone, answering questions every few minutes. Gradually, the reception desk turned into a nest, and the secretary herself was the mother bird, feeding and doting on her babies.

Tilting her head, she questioned the sanity of her work. She'd never drawn anything quite as comical. The woman's face was on the bird but her body was clearly a bird. After the receptionist responded to a coworker with sharp words, Aimee made sure to make her subject's claws sharp.

What would Seth say about her latest masterpiece? He liked her drawings and paintings, the ones she had shared with him. Pressing her lips together, she lengthened the bird's wingspan. If she decided to share this with Seth, she wanted it to be perfect. As crazy as it looked, she wanted it to be its very best for him. He made her feel valued. And, he was very generous in his appreciation of her work.

But what would he think of those drawings she kept hidden? What would he say about the ones of the meadow in Clarke County? What would he think of her having sketched the tree and the back end of his father's restored Camaro? She'd illustrated them so many times after the incident she'd lost track.

Her shrink had said it was good for her to draw what haunted her, but had Aimee ever confided in how many canvases she'd filled of the road where she'd stood that day Seth came barreling around the curve? How many visual renderings were of the field where Seth's vehicle landed once it left the roadway? He never knew what it looked like when they put the Camaro on the tow truck, but she knew.

Her penciled portrayal told the story.

Now, those depictions had been tucked away in a large box, sealed for only her viewing. Perhaps she should just burn them. If she wasn't going to tell Seth the truth, then the drawings should never come to light.

Except, it was wrong to hold onto secrets. Being honest with Seth was right, even if it cost their relationship.

"What are you working on?"

Beside her, Bonnie nodded toward her pencil and sketch pad. Tom lowered the newspaper at his wife's question.

Smirking, Aimee shifted and let them see her whimsical production.

Shifting her gaze from the picture to the subject, Bonnie's eyes widened. "I had no idea you were a cartoonist."

She closed the notebook and shrugged. "This is new for me. It is normal for me to draw when I'm nervous, but I've never drawn anything this silly."

"It means you're happy."

Aimee smiled because she was happy, for the first time in a long while.

Seth's mother crossed her legs as she leaned toward her. "My son couldn't have cared less if Tommy and I were here. He was most concerned with your presence."

She would wreck that happiness as soon as she told Seth the truth.

"Oh, try not to worry, dear." Bonnie patted her knee.

"I'm glad he's having the surgery. With the house he's renovating, all those practices with the team, it seemed to be getting worse."

"I think your influence helped him make the decision to have it done." Bonnie winked, knowingly. "Don't you think so, Tommy?"

Tom leveled his eyes at them over the newspaper. "You're absolutely right, dear."

"How's Luke? I know he had a transfusion yesterday."

"His counts were closer to normal, but not where we wanted them to be."

Tom shifted in his seat then folded the newspaper. "Is there any news about a donor?"

"The search is still underway. I'm told I have to be patient. When we have the festival, the National Bone Marrow Registry will be present. I'm hoping a lot of people will sign up to donate."

"We all donated. I hope someone gets word soon." Bonnie studied Aimee. "You need to get some rest. You're stretching yourself too thin."

"It's okay. I enjoy doing the mural. The children's department will be done this week." If she worked two half days, she could complete it and manage to put her time in at Belinda's salon.

Bonnie covered Aimee's hand with hers. "Is something else wrong? You seem troubled."

Aimee clasped her hands together. "I haven't set foot in this room for fourteen years, not since my mother was in surgery." She lifted her shoulder and gazed toward the floor. "It's just the memories come back when you least expect them. I guess I'm a little sad, missing my mom."

"Your mom had cancer?" Bonnie continued to rub the top of Aimee's hand.

"It started out in her stomach. She fought hard, but it was found too late. She only lasted a year after the discovery."

Bonnie and Tom sympathized with her and for a while they sat in silence until Tom offered to fetch coffee from the cafeteria. Bonnie continued to hold her hand, comforting, just as Aimee remembered her own mother doing during her childhood.

"I wish I'd known your mother. I know I would have liked her very much."

Aimee nodded. "She would have liked you as well." She shook her head trying to steer unfavorable memories away.

"What is it dear?"

Her stomach churned. "I was so angry at my father after she died." What she wouldn't give to go back and change how she'd acted.

Closing her eyes, darkness eased to light and her mother's sweet face appeared before her. "I remember pacing these halls. We were beside ourselves with worry because we knew how dangerous the surgery was." She recalled the embarrassment she felt when her mother came out of surgery, except now it was funny, and she giggled. "Mom never cursed, but when she was coming out of the anesthesia it was as if we were dealing with another person." Aimee smiled, although the incident wasn't one of her mother's best qualities. I slept at Mom's bedside those days. Dad always had to go off to work. He'd taken a new position and was no longer traveling, but I think he worried about losing the job if he was away too much. I stayed with Mom and helped the nurses when they allowed. I thought I wanted to work in the medical field, but after Mom passed, I lost the desire to seek anything except a party where I could get drunk."

Bonnie's hand firmed at her blunt honesty. She hated admitting that part of her life, that dark time when she would drink too much and then slip into a quiet corner where she could lose herself in the numbness. "I just wanted to forget that I'd lost the most important person in my life."

"I understand, dear."

She raised her eyes and found Bonnie crying along with her. "I made huge mistakes back then, Bonnie." Wiping her face, she looked over the many people that waited for their loved ones. "I don't know how I can make up for what I've done."

"Honey, I can't imagine you hurting a fly. Whatever it is, I know you will be forgiven. You only need to ask." Scooting closer, Seth's mother embraced her. "I will be praying for you. It will all work out, dear. You'll see."

A nurse called for Seth's family. After Bonnie and Tom saw Seth in his room, they went home. The outpatient area was at the end of a short corridor and was a large room holding stretchers divided by curtains. It resembled an emergency room due to its multiple beds and lacking privacy. Beside Seth's cubby on the other side of a drawn curtain a woman moaned. Seth lay back in the bed, his lids were almost shut.

Surrounding them were walls in pale gray. Behind the bed a painting of a prairie landscape added hints of pastel greens and blues. A single bag of fluid hung above Seth's bed with the intravenous liquids funneling into his system via the small needle on his left hand.

"I'll bring some ice chips and we'll start him on clear liquids to make sure he can tolerate something on his stomach."

The middle-aged nurse pushed her glasses up the bridge of her nose. "He's coming out of the anesthesia. We need to monitor him a little longer and then the doctor will likely discharge him." The nurse flipped through his chart. "

Aimee rubbed her hands over her thighs and exhaled. If she were honest with herself, she would say that being with Seth, here at his bedside, felt right. She had come a long way since that lonely road twelve years ago. How she ended up beside Seth now seemed unreal. Their acquaintance had grown stronger in the last two months yet she wanted more.

She brushed his hair away from his forehead like she did for Luke, before his treatments had taken his hair.

"Are you awake?" She whispered as she slid her fingers along his cheek.

He stirred and his eyelashes fluttered. "Hey, you're here."

She kissed his temple. "I'm here. Do you need anything?"

"I want a porter house steak, medium well. Lobster tail. Loaded baked potato… and a cold beer."

Aimee giggled. "If you ate that right now, you would be sick. Let's start with ice chips."

He narrowed his eyes and licked his lips and then let out a moan which resembled a grouchy bear "If that's all you're going to give me, then I'll take it." His eyelids lowered. "I need something for the pain."

"I can get your nurse…" But Aimee remained as his eyes closed and his chest found its rhythm to rise and fall as he drifted back to sleep.

Later that evening, after he was discharged from the hospital, after Aimee had gone against her better judgment and given in to Seth's request for a full course meal, he hung his head over the side of the bed as his stomach emptied one more time into the kitchen trash can.

Aimee pinched her nose as she switched trash bags. This was one of the reasons she decided not to go into nursing. Although as a mother, and a friend, nursing sometimes became a necessity beyond a job. Still, she was seeing a side to Seth she didn't realize he was capable of having.

Irritable and hungry made a bad combination. On the way home, she'd called in an order for him at his mother's restaurant. One of the staff delivered it to his home by the time she got him settled into bed. No sooner had he wiped his plate clean, did his stomach rebel.

She eyed the bed. His sheets would have to be changed. "Come on, big guy. Let's move to the guest room. Gee, I'm glad you had some furniture delivered or else you'd be sleeping on the floor." A week earlier, when she first visited Seth's house, the guest bedrooms had been vacant. She was amazed at how much construction had been completed. The floors were no longer covered, and Seth now had a fully functioning kitchen. Three bedrooms on the upper level were fully furnished.

"No, I'm fine here." Grouchy bear grumbled.

"No, you're not. I'm not arguing with you. If you don't get up and move to the other room, I'm going to change the bed with you in it." She rested her fingers on his unaffected shoulder. "You can move back in here if you want."

After a moment of what appeared to be painful deliberation, Seth swiveled his legs to the side and stood. As soon as he had both feet flat and put one foot in front of the other, he stumbled.

"Whoa boy." Slinging his arm around her shoulders, she secured her arm around his waist. "Come on, now."

"You're bossy," he grumbled.

"Well, you're covered from head to toe in steak and lobster, and the smell is making me gag. We have to get you out of those clothes."

"I knew you couldn't resist me."

"Oh, I can, believe me." Ignoring his chuckle, she lugged him across the hall with him trudging like a ton of potatoes beside her. It was all she could do to keep him upright. When she reached the guest bed, she intended to unhook his arm from her neck. But his bottom sank to the mattress like an anchor released from a ship and plunged them both to the bed. Face down she inhaled the industrial scent of fresh from the bag comforter.

Seth reared back to lie down.

"Wait a sec. You have to put on a new shirt and shorts."

"Aw, come on Aimee. I'm not that bad."

She caught his chin with her fingers and forced him to meet her eyes. "Yes you are."

Yanking his shirt up his back, she held her breath. It didn't escape her attention that there was not one ounce of fat on his body. *Dear Lord.* No prayer would be good enough to thank the Creator for a specimen of a man like this. She pulled the shirt over his right shoulder and he was able to pull his arm through with no problem. His drug induced state made him slow and sluggish. The next part was getting the messy side of his shirt off and around his wound dressing without contaminating it. She managed to gently lift the cotton off his shoulder and while she drew the shirt down and off his arm.

His skin, tanned and glorious as it was, also had moisture on it, left from when he couldn't get to the side quick enough and got sick on his lap.

"Are you okay to sit right there?" Barely waiting for a response, she ran to the bathroom, flipped on the hot water and began soaking a washcloth. She filled a bowl with water and grabbed another towel.

Slumped, though sitting on the bedside, he looked like he'd had too many alcoholic beverages. His moaning had quieted, but still lingered. Aimee wrung out the rag and began washing his arms and back, careful to not get the wound wet. A tinge of blood soaked the white gauze dressing. She'd read the instructions on what to do if the bleeding continued. Seeing the blood soaking through the dressing, she knew she needed to change it as well.

She rinsed the rag, finished the left side of his body and repeated so that she could wash his abdomen and chest. Sighing, she glanced over his six pack abs, and she didn't mean a six pack of soda cans. Exhaling, she rinsed the rag the last time and used the fluffy towel to dry him off.

"Your shorts are a mess, too."

"Yeah they feel wet."

"Can you handle it yourself?"

"Of course." He bit the words, as if frustrated she would think anything less, but the pants proved harder to get off than the shirt. He wobbled on his own weight. She stood on his side and held his waist. He stepped on her foot.

"Will you—" his sharp expression cut through her.

"Just trying to help you," her sharp tone caused him to pause.

His eyebrows v'd as he looked down at her.

"Use your good arm to push your shorts down—"

"I know what to do."

"Then do it, you're heavy as lead."

His large body moved to his injured side. "I've got you," Aimee propelled herself toward his right, and her bare hands gripped his waist. She kept her gaze lowered as he fought to pull his shorts over his boxers, she tried to focus on the brand name along the waist band, not anything that was in close proximity below.

Her heart was pounding as she stood. Was her woozy head a result of the amount of physical strength it took to help Seth? Or, the fact that the heat radiating from his half-undressed torso was tantalizing every sense of self control she held by a string? Once his legs were on the bed and he was under the covers, she pressed her fists against her hips.

"Will you be all right for a moment?"

Adjusting his position against the pillows, Seth grimaced. "Don't worry about changing the sheets on my bed."

"I'm not leaving it like that. I'll just throw everything in the wash, and I'll be right back."

When she returned, Seth's snoring filled the room. His arm needed to be propped more, so she shoved another pillow under him. He startled and his left hand clutched hers.

"It's me, Seth."

"I'm glad you're here." His gaze was hooded by heavy eyelids and his words were slower than normal. "I'm sorry for the trouble."

She patted his hand and attempted to move away. "It's okay."

"I love you, Aimee. I love you."

He turned his head and nuzzled the pillow. Soon enough, the snoring ensued.

Aimee lowered her body to the chaise lounge near the window and brought the knit blanket to her chin. She nibbled her bottom lip as Seth's last words rolled through her heart and imprinted in her memory. People tended to say anything under anesthesia.

Did she love him? She tucked her feet under her and studied him in the waning light. Exhaustion seemed to cover her with the soft blanket she clutched, and she gave in to the desire to rest.

~

Darkness cocooned the forest. Standing in the center of the road, she heard tires squealing. She moved her foot, but it wouldn't budge. Breathing hard she gasped. "Please move! Move! Move!"

"Aimee?"

She turned her head as the lights blinded her and she braced for the crash.

"Aimee."

She opened her eyes and found Seth sitting on the edge of the chaise.

"What's wrong?" she scooted back, but there was nowhere to go. She looked around, noting the bed, the dresser and night tables. Through the window, it was still night.

Seth's gaze was intense, and the lamp beside her illuminated his concerned frown. "Are you okay? Do you need something?" Her legs were wrapped tight in the blanket, and he was sitting beside them. Trapped, a tremor coursed through her.

"I'm fine."

With his uninjured hand, his thumb brushed her cheek. "You were crying."

His hand fell away as she swiped the moisture from her face. "I guess I was dreaming."

"It must have been some dream to make you cry."

She swallowed as she flattened her palm against her chest. Her heart pounded beneath. "I was standing in the middle of a dark road. A car was coming. I could hear it, but I couldn't move out of the way." She met his stare. "Then I woke up. I'm alright."

He took her hand. "You're trembling. Come lie down with me." He stood up, but she didn't move. "I'm too weak to be anything less than honorable."

She slipped under the sheets as if the action was something she did every night. And when she snuggled against his body, splaying her hand across his chest, she closed her eyes at how satisfied she felt. She adjusted her neck, moving her cheek against his chest and sighed. His warmth penetrated her shirt and a sensation of heat radiated to her toes.

Since Seth had apparently slept enough that evening, he began talking about his family. One story led to another and soon Aimee was giggling about the Garrett's family vacation to Colorado when his mother learned to ride a horse. Rather, her inability to ride a horse was the moral of the story.

"Did you go on family vacations when you were a kid?"

"No, Dad worked in sales, but it wasn't something that brought a lot of money. Mom and I traveled with him and I remember us going to an amusement park and a beach, but for the most part we just lived hotel to hotel. I think I resented them for moving me around so much. I never had a best friend in school. I never knew what it was like to go to a classroom until I was in college. Mom tried to make each new trip an adventure, but the older I got, the lonelier I became. Then after Mom got sick, Dad bought a house in Savannah. Settling down had been Mom's dream and it seemed Dad was ready, too. He even bought Tank for Mom so that she could travel around town, carrying her art supplies with her. She would set up her easel in the park, or at the beach, and just start painting."

Though her mother had been gone almost thirteen years, the anger over her father's actions washed over her like cold water from a hose. She sat up and pressed her back against the headboard. Beside her, Seth shifted and kept his focus on her alone.

"I haven't thought of my parents, or my father's second wife, Sandy, in a long time." She went on, recognizing Seth's mounting confusion. "The pain seemed to double when Dad met Sandy. I couldn't understand how he could have gotten over Mama so quickly."

"When did he meet Sandy?"

"I think he knew Sandy before Mom died. But one month, no two months, after Mama died, Sandy moved into the house and they started redecorating. The last weekend I was home from college, I found all of Mama's artwork removed from their place on the walls inside the house and they were stacked in the garage about to be sold."

He rubbed his shoulder, but dismissed her when she asked if he needed something for pain.

"No, I'm fine. We're talking about you now. What happened next?" He squeezed her hand, urging her to continue.

"I stormed into the kitchen. Sandy was standing at Mama's stove using her wooden spoon and scrambling eggs in my mother's frying pan. I couldn't accept it. I stood in the center of the kitchen and glared at Daddy. He sat there with his coffee mug in one hand and his newspaper in the other. I demanded to know what he was doing with my mother's paintings.

"They were having a yard sale." She clenched her fists. Saying it out loud brought out her anger. "Dad was so casual about it. He put his coffee and newspaper down and said, 'If there's something you want to sell, put it in the garage. We're going to be ready next weekend. You're welcome to come back home and help us.'

"I made it clear that I could not allow him to sell Mom's things. I got louder and Dad told me to calm down. Sandy said something and I turned to her, pointed toward the garage and said, 'She painted every single portrait out there. Did you know that? Those pieces should be in galleries, on display, not stacked up and forgotten in a garage!'

"I rushed out of the kitchen and decided I was taking Mom's portraits with me. I grabbed as many canvases that I could fit into my Honda Civic. I managed to get about three of the large portraits in the back seat, but the door wouldn't close. And there were many more I needed to take with me. I stood in the middle of the driveway. This house was where Mom's dreams were supposed to finally come true. The house was the smallest bungalow on the block with a big palm tree in the front yard. I thought my dreams would come true there, too. But then Mom got sick. And I looked at the front porch where her rocking chair sat empty. Her flowers were dying because no one tended them anymore. And then, I saw Tank. Dad had a For Sale sign stuck in his rear window. Dad might as well have put an advertisement on a highway billboard. No way would I let him get rid of Tank, too.

"The keys were in the ignition, right where Mama left them. It was a sign from above. She wouldn't have wanted Tank to be sold, just like she wouldn't have wanted the paintings she'd poured her heart and soul into sold either. I emptied the Honda of mom's paintings and loaded them into the Wagoneer. Once the back was filled, I filled up the back seat and the passenger seat.

"The last thing I did was to peel that For Sale sign off Tank's window."

"I would have stuck it in the Honda," Seth said.

"That's exactly what I did. The Honda was paid for. I said goodbye and drove four hours straight to Athens." She shook her head. "One thing I hadn't considered was where I would store all of Mama's things. Then, missing her became overwhelming and soon after I escaped to a party. I drank whatever someone offered. I drank until the pain was gone, but honestly, the pain never went away until I faced it."

She met Seth's gaze. "I realize now that we all deal with grief differently. Maybe Dad needed

Sandy's companionship to work through his sadness."

Seth toyed with the ends of her hair curling near her shoulder. "Now, I understand why Tank is so important to you."

"I'll never let him go."

"Where are your mom's paintings?"

"Some are at the Sunset Vista house. Belinda took some and Granny has many at her house. We even have a few up at the salon. No one could believe it when I told them what Daddy was thinking. He died six months after Mama." Aimee drew her knees to her chest and wrapped her arms around them. She peered over at him. "I didn't realize until now how lonely life without your spouse can be. Luke was diagnosed a little over a year after Michael died. I'm not sure I gave myself time to grieve. But I do know that I don't want to be alone in life."

His hand cradled her jaw. "You won't ever be alone again." His lips brushed her cheeks, her chin, feathering a path along her neck and jaw. Aimee pressed closer as his mouth covered hers, and she tightened her hold on his waist. Did she have the courage to be honest with him about the rest of her past? What if the connection she had with Seth was her second chance? She couldn't lose him.

Chapter Fourteen

After the radio's weather report confirmed
a full day of rain, an upbeat song filled the cab of
the storage van. Seth chuckled as Grant tapped his
fingers to the beat, humming along with the radio
until he joined the artist by bellowing the words.

He and Josh exchanged a glance. "Dude, you
can't sing. Especially not to Petty."

Grant raised his eyebrows. "I can hang with
Tom Petty, no problem." He tapped his hand on the
steering wheel faster, making drumming motions
on the dash, "She-was-an-Amer-i-can- girl…"

Seth looked out the window as Grant's voice
got louder. Despite the blaring radio, Seth couldn't
keep his mind off of Aimee McClain.

Thinking of her included Luke. Seth prayed for
the doctors to find a bone marrow donor so
recovery would become a reality for the future
little leaguer. He refused to consider anything less
than all-star for the kid's future. Unfortunately, the
search for a match had returned only negative
responses. Only one person made it the farthest,

but in the end was not the qualifying full match Luke needed.

Seth refused to stand by and do nothing. His feelings must be inherited because his mother felt the same way. Between the two of them, the plans for the bone marrow drive and fundraiser had grown larger. The church still planned their festival on Hopewell's property, but the festivities would include Luke's event which would happen on the lawn of Pleasant Lea, his mother's restaurant, which bordered the beach and Point Peace Park. With the number of vendors planning to be on hand, Seth had no doubts the fundraiser would raise money for Luke's medical fund. And with the number of people he expected to attend, he felt certain many people would be encouraged to add their name to the bone marrow registry to help more people like Luke.

He clutched the folder of fliers he'd copied at the office store. He planned to distribute some while they were in Statesboro.

"Is Luke excited about the fair?" Josh asked from the backseat.

"He hasn't said much. Aimee wanted him to be surprised so she hasn't told him about all of the activities we'll have."

"Your mother said a circus group will be there?" Grant eased on the brake as they reached an intersection.

"Yeah. It's going to be cool. The circus is coming up from Florida. They were the same group I tried to set up at the end of Kevin's race, but I didn't have any spots available. It worked out better for them to be there at Luke's event."

"It should be a good turnout. I've emailed everyone on my distribution list and shared it on my social media pages." Josh said.

"Aimee's family has been spreading the word."

"Things are getting pretty serious between you two." Grant eyed Seth as he turned onto the highway.

"She's great." Seth rubbed his shoulder that still ached from surgery. He loved having her with him after surgery. He wasn't planning to share his mushy thoughts with these guys, but when she went home the next day, it had been too soon. He missed her presence in his house. It was time to make some changes where she was concerned. Though he made progress in getting her to open up, he still sensed her boundaries, ones more difficult to cross. She still refused his help, so he'd made sure to make himself available for her aunt Belinda and her grandmother. Light bulbs that needed changing at the salon were taken care of during Aimee's shift. And it was pure coincidence that her grandparents needed someone to change the filter on their air conditioner. Seth coordinated that exchange on a day he knew Aimee would be over there helping her grandmother restore an old dresser.

"I'm taking Luke to get pizza this afternoon." He couldn't wait to spend the afternoon with the kid and hopefully spend the evening with Aimee. Being with them, made Seth feel like he belonged.

"You're turning into a family guy." Grant eyed him.

"You say that like it's a bad thing," Josh quipped and held up his hands in frustration. "At least he has someone to go out with. No one wants to date a preacher."

Grant teased Josh while Seth kept quiet. He could picture himself with Luke and Aimee as a family. As they passed the highway where Aimee had stoically tried to move her mother's Wagoneer off the road, he smiled. What other woman would get out, in wedding attire, to push the mammoth Tank off the road? She had no idea how her determination had sealed her in his heart, winning his respect and his admiration.

When he called her this morning, she was already at the church finishing some details on the murals. He liked how she was willing to tackle whatever she faced. Seth had made some decisions where she was concerned. Those decisions were much deeper than organizing a fundraiser for Luke. He couldn't imagine his life without her and Luke in it.

He prayed she felt the same way.

~

The murals were complete. Today, she simply needed to go over each one and make sure no error or detail had been overlooked. An early start on the murals helped her accommodate clients at the salon. While she worked at the salon, Seth would pick up Luke from Sloan's. He had promised to take Luke for an afternoon of pizza and arcade games. And then, Seth would bring Luke home.

Aimee sighed. Her plan, her prayers, of never seeing Seth again had fallen far beyond the wayside. In the shadows of Luke's illness was her messy past where Seth was an innocent bystander.

Nevertheless, she depended on Seth to watch out for her son when she couldn't be there. He was the first person she called to give updates on Luke's doctor visits or his latest childhood antic. When they were together, Aimee imagined herself with him, as a permanent fixture in his life. She allowed herself to wonder what it would be like if Seth became a part of her family with Luke.

They could be so happy.

Until he learned the truth…

She shook her head as she folded the ladder and stowed it in the church's closet. She went back to her workspace and folded two of four drop cloths, then gathered a handful of brushes.

She glanced at her watch. "No." Already ten thirty! Where had the time gone?

She needed to get to work by eleven when her first client was due to arrive. Less than an hour, she cursed the clock. She couldn't be late as this client had proved to be a good tipper, but she was usually early. She hauled a paint can by its handle with her pinkie finger and hurried toward the utility closet.

By the time Aimee washed the last brush, her cell phone alarm chimed. She should be at work by now. Glancing at her paint dotted overalls, she grimaced. No time to change. The drive across town would take twenty minutes, if no traffic. Her stomach clenched. Brushes in hand, she rushed out from the bathroom and grabbed her cell phone.

Dialing Belinda's number, Aimee hurried back to the foyer, phone shoved between her ear and shoulder as the ringing continued. She tucked the two remaining drop cloths under her arm and grabbed four paint cans by their metal handles. Halfway across the room, her cell phone slipped from its precarious position and clanged against the floor. With her hands full, she couldn't retrieve it. She'd call Belinda back. She scurried into the large, dark pantry size-closet. After placing her supplies in the corner the church personnel had cleared for her, she began stacking the cans against the wall.

The storage room door slid against the concrete floor and shut with a thud. Aimee straightened. The wooden door wedge sat beside the shelf at the doorway. She had forgotten to secure it. She rushed across the small space, flipped the light switch. Following a second's flicker OF electricity was a loud pop, then darkness. She yanked the knob, "Oh no! Please open."

Panic shot through her when the door, locked from the outside, wouldn't budge. ~

Seth stepped down from the truck and surveyed the loading bays, already full with customers. He entered the old gray building through a side door and walked to the storefront. He took a place at the back of the service line while others milled around the store. Restaurant supplies of all sizes filled the storefront's shelves from floor to ceiling with items local restaurant owners needed. One clerk manned the cash register. The clerk looked like a kid, no older than twenty by Seth's estimation. The clerk scratched his disheveled shaggy brown hair as he eyed the growing line of customers then punched keys on the register. His eyes glazed over as a customer asked a question.

Seth looked over the fliers for the Bone Marrow Drive as he waited in line. He started conversations with his fellow line-mates, gave them a flier and encouraged them to make copies to distribute at their respective establishments. Others seemed charged by the idea and their excitement fueled Seth's energy.

Finally, a white-headed man waddling with a cane emerged from a room behind the counter and took the next customer in line. Seth reached the counter and the man brought up his mother's restaurant on the computer. The elder peered over his bifocals. "You Tom's boy?"

"Yes, sir."

"I'm Milt. Never missed one of your baseball games over at Peace."

Seth grinned. "No kidding?"

"I sure hated to see you quit the Stars."

"Aw, thanks Milt, I appreciate it."

"What're ya doing now?"

"I'm Peace's baseball coach."

"No kidding? Well, you can tell it's been a while since I've gotten to a game." The old man scribbled a signature across some papers and slid them toward Seth. "You ain't married yet?"

"Not yet, but I have a lady in mind."

The old man grinned, "Atta boy. Give ole Tom some grandchildren. Settle him and Bonnie down."

"I intend to." He glanced at the clock, feeling the morning hours wearing thin.

"Thank you, Seth. Your order is waiting at the

dock." Milt punched a couple of buttons on the keyboard and the receipt spilled out from the top of the register.

After Seth signed the receipt, he pushed a stack of fliers across the counter. "Would you mind if I left these with you?" He explained their purpose.

"Sure. Leave them right here where everyone can see them. I might stop by with my grandchildren."

When Seth reached the loading area, Grant was in the truck. Josh came out from the store and returned to the back seat. While the supplies were being loaded, Seth called Sloan.

"I'm in Statesboro. Hope to be out of here within a half hour. I should be there by twelve-thirty."

"That's fine, Luke's playing. Hey, have you spoken with Aimee? Mom got a hang up call from her and when she tried to call back, no one answered."

"She should be at the salon. She had an eleven o'clock client."

"That's what Mom said, but she's not there."

"Have you called the church?"

"Yes. No one answered."

He turned to Josh. "Who's at the church this morning?"

"No one until the secretary arrives at two. Caleb was in Savannah at a conference this morning. He may not go to his office today."

"Can you let me in? I think something's happened with Aimee."

~

Aimee jerked the knob. "Come on!" She yanked again, pushing and straining until her shoulder and back hurt. The door was shut tight. The thin space along the threshold provided little light from the hallway. Her fingers weren't visible in front of her face. She banged her fist against the cold metal door. "Ouch." Holding her fist with her other hand, she lowered her head and closed her eyes against the black. Getting mad wouldn't get her anywhere. She couldn't wish the predicament away.

She shut her eyes. In the darkness, her mind wandered to twelve years earlier. She didn't want to think about that time in her life, but she couldn't stop the memories.

She could feel the pinch of the gravel under her bare feet. The road curved tight against the shoulder until it loosened around a hill into a wooded area. Without a flashlight, walking alongside this road was dangerous. But if someone hit her, no one would care. She hadn't been able to help her mother. She'd hurt her father. Her grandparents were old and couldn't take care of her. There was no one else.

Tires squealed behind her. Light expanded around her, shooting spotlights across the wooded area below. She looked back and gasped. The charging vehicle was headed straight for her. All would be over soon. She stepped into the car's path and held her breath.

"Aimee!"

"Aimee!"

She opened her eyes and blinked. She must

have imagined hearing her name. Still sitting in the closet in the dark, she plead and prayed for Seth to find her, to save her.

Raking her fingers down her face, she wiped away her guilt filled tears. How could she ask him for anything? Especially after that night? Suffering from her own pain, she'd made a fatal decision, except her plan to end her own life had resulted in someone else losing theirs.

"Aimee!"

That time it sounded close, real. "Seth?" she yelled. Her voice boomeranged. She pressed her palms to the concrete floor and pushed herself up. "Help!"

She screamed help again and again. If she kept yelling, someone would hear her. Her voice grew hoarse and she leaned her forehead against the concrete wall. She should have called for help a long time ago. Long before cancer struck her mother, when she was sad and just wanted steady friends. Once she did enter school, she never trusted anyone. Being on the road had caused that, never knowing what people were good and who to beware of, so she trusted no one. Too soon, her mother was sick, and her family was never the same. She stayed in trouble, hanging out with a crowd that shared her rebellion.

Grimacing, she backed against the wall, darkness still surrounding her. "Why am I thinking of this now?" Oh, how badly she'd handled things with her parents. Now, they were both gone. She never apologized to either one of them for her actions.

"I'm going to stop this. Stop living with these regrets. I can't change my past."

She lifted herself from the wall and started flipping the light switch. The light wouldn't come back on since the bulb blew, but maybe she was due a miracle. She would be standing and ready when someone opened this closet door. She yelled help again and she would keep yelling until someone heard her. Eventually someone would miss her. Luke, if no one else. She wasn't the lonely young adult on the deserted country road anymore. She had faced being a widow and a single mother alone. She was not weak anymore. She was strong, something she should have recognized long ago. Having picked up the shattered pieces of lifetime and again, she would do it once more after she told Seth the truth. It was the only way she would finally be set free.

~

Rain fell in sheets, pouring from the sky so fast and strong Seth could barely see through the windshield by the time Grant entered the town of Point Peace.

Sweat beaded across his brow and his heart raced.

"I'm sure she's okay."

Seth exchanged a glance with Grant. He rubbed the center of his chest where an ache had formed. "I am praying she's okay. She's got a young son. She's just getting settled here again."

"Calm down, Seth." Josh placed his hand on Seth's shoulder. "Aimee's smart. I'm sure we'll be laughing about this later. We'll find her. She's going to be fine."

"She never should have been there by herself."

"She's a grown woman—"

Seth cut Grant off. "I don't care. I should have been there to help her."

"I've seen you two together." Grant quipped. "She wouldn't have gotten anything done because you two can't keep your hands off of each other. Oww!" He covered his outer arm with his hand.

"I'll punch your nose next time," Seth warned, rubbing his knuckles. He glared toward the back seat at Josh. "You keep your mouth shut, too."

"There's her car." Grant said, whipping the truck into the church parking lot. Aimee's Wagoneer sat in front. Seth jerked the door handle before the truck came to a full stop. "I'll meet you at the restaurant as soon as I can."

"Don't worry about the restaurant," Grant said. "Take care of your girl. I'll handle this."

"Thanks, bro. I appreciate it. Sorry about your arm."

Josh was already running up the sidewalk to the fellowship hall.

"She would have been working on the lower side at this point." He yelled to be heard over the downpour. Lightning shot from the clouds, and thunder growled. "She mentioned that mural was the one that needed the most detail added." Seth's chest felt tight. What if she fell off the ladder and hit her head? He would never let her work alone here, or anywhere, again. Oh, but she was stubborn. She would just have to understand her life was too precious to risk injury or worse. In order to protect her, he needed to stop hesitating where his feelings were concerned.

Josh opened the side door to the Children's building, and they hurried inside.

"This was her last painting." Seth jogged ahead of Josh through the hallway.

"Look," Josh pointed to a corner on the floor.

Her purse, duffle bag, and rain jacket lay in a heap with car keys on top. Her cell phone lay a few feet away in the middle of the corridor. Before he slid it into his pocket, he noted multiple missed calls from Sloan and Belinda.

He inhaled, trying to calm down. "She's still here."

"Thank God."

"Aimee!"

They continued toward the end of the hall, calling her name as they ducked into the different rooms, knocking on the restrooms and peaking inside. All other rooms remained dark and undisturbed.

Josh scratched his head as he met Seth in the central foyer. "She wouldn't have gone for a walk, would she?"

"Not in the pouring rain." It didn't make sense. Seth shook his head and retraced steps. On his return back to the foyer, a soft thump stopped him. He listened intently for the sound's origin. His voice broke. "Aimee!"

They followed the muffled sound of her voice and the barely audible thumping until they reached the utility closet. Josh fumbled his keys. "This door has been on the agenda to fix. It just got put on the priority list."

Seth flung open the door and light poured into the dark space. He stepped in and came face to face with her. He didn't give her a chance to move and took her in his arms, circling them around her waist. His mouth covered hers. She held his face as she pressed closer and kissed him back with renewed passion.

She pulled back and focused on his right shoulder. "Did I hurt you?"

"Never." He held her gaze. She buried her face against his chest, her body quaking. He smoothed her hair and spoke softly, so grateful to have her in his arms. "It's going to be okay."

Her chest contracted against his as her breath hitched. She pulled back, tightening her arms around his neck. Her eyes glistened. "I love you, Seth"

He pulled back for a second and studied her with surprise. She started to shrink back, but he held her tight. Before she could wiggle out, because he knew his reaction had startled her and caused her question, he swooped low and captured her lips. His fingers threaded in her hair as he deepened the kiss. When he pulled back, he kept her close, "I love you."

Smiling, she tilted her chin up, then captured his face in her hands. "I like hearing you say that."

"I like kissing you." A loud cough broke through Seth's intentions of continuing. He glanced over his shoulder.

Holding a screwdriver and drill, Josh stood a few feet away. "Sorry to interrupt. Can you two take this party elsewhere so I can fix the lock? I figure it will go a lot smoother if you two aren't in the closet." He grinned, "Just a suggestion."

Chapter Fifteen

Two weeks later, Aimee's heart had declared an all-out war between her emotions.

She made promise to God, to herself, while she was trapped in the church closet. Tell Seth the truth.

But, now she and Seth had taken their relationship to another level. They'd shared their feelings for each other. Sloan's advice to leave the past in the past remained anchored in her mind. Except her past was a ratchet stuck in a tree trunk. Immoveable, stubborn, the past would not leave her mind. And the constant push and pull of being honest with Seth or keeping it to herself was causing her emotions to be a warzone.

Right now, she'd pasted a smile on her face and was determined to feel happy. They'd waited for this day for weeks.

"Where are we going, Seth? I thought the carnival was at the park." Luke squirmed in the backseat of Seth's truck until he could clamp onto the driver's seat. Craning his neck, he fought for a better view of the road ahead.

"The park wasn't big enough. It's been extended to Pleasant Lea." Seth winked at Aimee.

"You didn't mention you changed locations," she said.

"Ah, we just expanded." He raised their clasped hands and kissed her knuckles as he turned off the highway and pulled into the parking lot.

Sloan and Ryan meandered over to Seth's truck as Aimee got out.

"This should be a lot of fun." The cousin's hugged as Seth walked around the truck with Luke's hand in his.

"Do you feel like trying out the carnival rides?" Aimee squatted down to Luke's level and squeezed his arms. His eyes glistened as he took in sights. He'd just been released from the hospital two days ago. She couldn't let him tire out.

She followed his gaze across the grounds. A huge Ferris wheel was set up near the beach. Spinning cars and a mini racetrack were at the center of it all. The stage was set up to the right. A band had already begun to set up as there would be a concert at dusk. Vendors sprawled along the path, selling everything from balloons to cotton candy.

She stood. The crushed shell parking area was full. An American flag whipped from the antenna of each car. Dozens of banners flapped in the wind, advertising different establishments, and sponsors for Luke's event.

Seth slid his arm around her shoulders. "What do you think?"

"I've never seen the area this full." He touched

the bottom of her chin as she gazed around in awe. Her lips shut as he joked. "Better watch that, a sand gnat may fly up for a kiss."

Chuckling, she shooed his hand away only to have him clasp her hand in his and squeeze. "I'm amazed. You really did it."

Sloan stood next to them. "I'm so glad you took over, Seth. You really outdid yourself on this one." She squatted down as Luke moved in front of Aimee. "Guess what buddy? This festival, the carnival rides, all of the people here, are all here for you."

Eyes wide, his gaze did a one-eighty across the grass. "For my birthday, too?"

"This is a party, but not for your birthday. All of the people here want to help find a bone marrow donor to help you feel better." Luke slung his arms around her neck. Aimee squeezed her eyes, except one tear still slipped down her face.

A crowd ambled between the restaurant and the festivities. Tents covered rows and rows of tables. Hundreds of people, or more, had shown up. Just like Seth promised. Upbeat music blared over the laughter and conversation surrounding them.

A banner rippled beside the American flag tethered to the pole above the front entrance. The flag snapped against the hot wind. Aimee raised her hand to block the bright sun and squinted to see the banner as Luke read the words aloud.

LUKE MCCLAIN: BONE MARROW DRIVE AND FUNDRAISER.

"It's my name, Mama!" Luke jumped up and down, energetic and happy. A week ago, he'd been sick and in the hospital. Today, she had her vibrant child back. She prayed today would produce a bone marrow donor for Luke. She wanted her child to be like this every day.

"You bet it's your name, Champ." Seth smiled at Luke. "This day is yours." He met her gaze. "All for you."

They were in the middle of the crowd with people ambling all around them, but she couldn't contain her appreciation. She would be bold while she could. Once he learned the truth, he may not want to be with her any longer. Pushing the thought away, she rose up to her toes and kissed him.

Surprise lit his eyes.

"Thank you. I'll live the rest of my life thanking you for this moment."

He brushed his finger along her chin as he dipped his head. Then, someone called his name.

Seth's parents approached. Bonnie's arms circled her like a warm blanket while Tom lifted Luke effortlessly, reassuring her son all of this was for him.

Could she bottle today's happiness? She didn't want to forget a moment of how special this family made her and Luke feel. And it was all because of Seth. He'd saved her life years ago on that lonely dark road and he'd saved her again. Her throat burned as she fought to keep her emotions calm. She hugged Seth's mother tighter.

"It's okay, darling."

"I don't know how I'll ever repay you all."

Pulling back, Bonnie's eyes held motherly

assurance. "You're in my son's life. Stay there." Bonnie hugged her again. "Oh, Aimee, enjoy the day, dear."

"Thank you for organizing this."

She chuckled. "Honey, I only helped. This was Seth's brainchild." She glanced around. "I want you to meet someone. Where is she? Ah, there she is. Cory!" Cupping her hands around her mouth, she shouted. "Cornelia!"

A young woman about Aimee's age approached. Cornelia Garrett's blond hair hung in a long braid over her shoulder. Her face resembled Bonnie's with her wide blue eyes, high cheekbones and rounded chin. When she smiled, though, her face became similar to Seth. "Aimee, it's wonderful to meet you. I've heard so many good things." Cory opened her arms before she could speak and hugged her.

They exchanged pleasantries, then Aimee had to ask. "You bear a striking resemblance to the actress Cory Garrett."

Before Cory could respond, Bonnie leaned in. "She's the one and only." As her mother sauntered off with Tom, she turned back, "My daughter who doesn't come home near enough."

"Oh, Mom." Cory looped her hand around Aimee's arm as if they were longtime friends and they walked toward the rides. Luke pointed to one thing after another and Seth's laughter rang out over the crowd.

She caught Cory's gaze.

"I've been looking forward to meeting the woman who has made my brother so incredibly happy."

"Seth is amazing." They paused near the ticket booth. "Not only has he made this carnival happen, which is more than I dreamed it could ever be, but he's so in tune to everything we need. I can hardly keep up."

Cory eyed her brother and leaned in, confiding to Aimee. "Don't try to keep up with him. We Garrett's run on some kind of super fuel. When we love someone, we do all we can to make sure that person has everything they need. You just sit back and enjoy the ride."

A masculine voice poured through the loud speakers, hushing the crowd.

"I'm George Dunn, Point Peace Mayor. I want to thank you all for coming today." From the stage, George talked about the town, its growth, and how this rally would no doubt be the first of many. "And now, I would like to recognize our organizer, Seth Garrett."

Ushered toward the front with her family and Seth's family surrounding her, Aimee kept her eyes on the stage. Seth climbed the steps with his head lowered until he reached the Mayor, then he glanced across the crowd, sending everyone a smile.

The crowd cheered, but all Aimee could do was stare. Dressed in khaki shorts and a royal blue polo shirt, his tanned skin seemed magnified by the contrast of colors. He grabbed the microphone and Aimee's body hummed with awareness, even though the distance between them equaled the distance from first base to third. Seth stood front and center, his smile easy and appreciative.

When he spoke, his voice carried through the large speakers hung along the porch of the restaurant and were on stands around the parking area which had been transformed into a tent filled circus.

"Thank you all for coming today. As you know, there is a special young man in our presence, and a part of our community, that is fighting a blood disorder. Luke, would you and your mom come up please?"

Luke raced up the stairs and leapt in to Seth's arms. He returned the boy's bear hug as the crowd waited for Aimee to come on stage. Seth exhaled. Over the crowd, over the squawking seagulls somewhere in the distance, he heard her footsteps. And as the wind shifted, he caught the brush of her perfume.

Seth looked out over the crowd. People he recognized from Hopewell were among many, local business owners, and even people Seth went to school with were in attendance. As he looked over the crowd, their gazes shifted from him, to Luke and Aimee. Standing only a few feet away, he reached for her. She smiled as she took his hand. He had never felt so taken by anyone else.

Between them, Luke waved to everyone. Aimee mimicked Luke and greeted everyone. Seth followed suit until Aimee's gaze hooked his.

"Luke hasn't stopped smiling all day," she said.

"Me either."

And with that, she smiled wider. He wanted this feeling to last. And he knew exactly what he would do next.

The photographer for the newspaper appeared before them, camera poised. "Quick picture, guys. Seth, look this way. Great Luke! Aimee and Seth, I love those smiles!"

Snap! The camera popped.

Luke's arm was slung comfortably around his shoulders. As the photographer took additional photos, Luke reached for his mom. With Luke between them, he made them appear to be a unit.

Seth raised the microphone. "Pl-" his voice caught, and the word croaked out. He cleared his throat again as all eyes turned his way. "Please welcome Aimee and Luke McClain. Luke is turning eight years old in a couple of days but we are celebrating today." He looked at Luke and smiled. "Happy birthday, Champ."

Luke grabbed Seth's neck and buried his face against Seth's head in another tight hug. "I love you, Seth."

"I love you more, buddy."

When Luke loosened his grip, Seth cleared his throat again, feeling his eyes grow moist. "As a present to Luke, I wanted us all to gather here today and help find a donor for him. What Luke needs is a bone marrow transplant. We know the perfect match is out there. That special person could be one of you. By signing up to be a bone marrow donor, you can help this young man's blood cells reform and produce as they should. It is our hope that you will feel lead to consider heading to the booth labeled with a large "A" where you can have your cheek swabbed to be tested to see if you are Luke's match. It's that simple, folks. You'll be contacted if you are selected to donate to Luke."

Applause broke out over the crowd. Seth paused until it subsided. "If you can't be a donor, that's okay. We are glad you cane to offer your support to Luke. For every hot dog you purchase, every snack and refreshment, every game you play here today, the money for your tickets will be placed in a special fund for Luke to pay for the medical bills not covered by insurance."

The crowd cheered again as Seth wrapped up his speech, "Who will be the first to sign up to be a donor today? I'm heading over right now. I encourage you to join me. Thank you."

Grant stood at the back of the crowd. "I'll race you over there, Coach!"

Seth put Luke on his feet and sent Grant a thumb up. As he and Aimee left the stage, a twinge of disappointment nagged him. Several weeks ago he tested at the hospital for Luke. But Seth accepted the chances of him being Luke's match was too high, impossible.

Aimee's cousins waited for them at the bottom of the stage, but she tightened her grip and pulled him away from the group. Luke remained with her family, laughing at the tickles he received from Sloan.

Seth met her concerned eyes. He lowered his head for a quick kiss, which lightened the seriousness that seemed to fall upon her face.

Straightening his collar, she pressed her hands near his shoulders. "Is everything alright?"

He clasped his hand over hers, "I've got you in my arms, what more could I want?"

"I'm being serious." Her eyebrows narrowed, creating a fine line between. "You look like something is bothering you."

Exhaling, he slid his gaze over the crowd. "I just want Luke's donor to be found."

Her arms clasped his neck. "I've never felt more optimistic than I feel today. You've helped me get there." He wrapped his arms around her waist and brought her in for a hug. He needed to hear her reinforce her feelings. "We won't lose hope."

Hand in hand, they rejoined the crowd. Seth pushed the negative thoughts away as Aimee strolled toward Cory.

He just wanted to make a difference in Luke's life.

Laughter broke out between his sister and Aimee easily, as if they were long time friends.

Like family.

Was bringing Aimee and Luke into his family the answer? Fill the void that had remained in his life?

Chapter Sixteen

The following Saturday, Aimee's
doorbell rang a little after eight. Cory stood on the
porch, smiling. "Ready?"

"I thought I was picking you up?"

"Mack's going to take us shopping. I figured
since Luke was already at my parent's house, that
it would make more sense for me to pick you up."

In her driveway, a shimmery white sports car
gleamed in the sun. Cory's bodyguard stood next to
the driver's side, arms crossed. Mack's shoulders
were as broad as a mountain range. Would the tiny
car hold them all?

Tucked in the back seat with Cory, they
whizzed past the Point Peace Square. "Where are
we shopping? The boutiques were that way."

"We're going somewhere fun," Cory winked.

Minutes later, Aimee boarded a small engine
aircraft at the Point Peace airport. "Cory, Seth
wants us at the party by five. Where are we
going?"

"Atlanta. And we'll be home by four."

After landing north of the city, they were shuttled to Buckhead in a stretched, blacked out SUV. Cory posed for a group of photographers while Mack and four other security detail stood nearby. She pulled Aimee beside her for a few shots. As Aimee shied away, Mack led them away from cameras into one exclusive boutique after another.

She lifted a purse from the glass topped table, she searched for the price tag.

"That's nice," Cory said as she thumbed through silk scarves.

Aimee sat the purse back down. "This purse costs what I make in one week."

Giggling, Cory pulled her out of the store and on to the next.

When they stopped for lunch, Cory picked an exclusive restaurant at the top of one of the tallest buildings in the city. Glasses dinged as they waited near the entrance. Pushing her sunglasses to the top of her head, she smoothed her hair back and fought a queasy feeling that accompanied not fitting in with the crowd.

"Cory, I'm underdressed." Her blue sundress, straight from the thrift store rack, was not on par with the designer suits and threads everyone else wore.

"Do you have a reservation, Miss?" The maître'd stood at the narrow podium. His smile was tight and small which fit his narrow head.

Cory, still wearing her sunglasses, raised a manicured finger to her chin. "I'm afraid I don't. I was hoping you'd have room for just two more."

"No," he glanced down the bridge of his nose at the small computer screen. "We're booked for another hour. You two may wait at the bar."

Nodding, Cory took a half step toward Aimee. "What do you think? I'd rather sit beside the window, but I don't want to wait an hour."

Aimee shook her head as she glanced at her watch. "Whatever is faster."

Removing her sunglasses, Cory tossed her long blonde hair over her shoulder and blinked her eyelashes a few times toward the waiter.

"Miss Garrett? Why, I didn't recognize you. I am so sorry for the confusion. I see we do have the seat on the east side of the building, just the one you enjoyed the last time you dined with us."

Cory's mouth formed an O. "I don't want to put anyone out. Are you sure?" Yet there was barely any argument as they were shown to their seats.

Aimee gazed over the menu, before sitting it aside.

"Close your mouth, sweetie, you look like you've this is your first time in a restaurant." She smiled. "Get anything you want. It's on me."

"Cory, thank you, but no. You've already done too much. You've bought me and Luke clothes—"

"Hon, I was buying for everyone today. I wasn't going to leave you two out. You're the newest members of my family. I want to celebrate."

"That's sweet of you, really, but I feel like I'm taking advantage."

"Hush. You're not and I'm not taking anything

back." The waiter arrived and took their orders. "We've only got two more stops after this. Massage and facials. You should change into one of the dresses you bought. The pink one. It emphasized your tan. Then we can go home." Cory sat back in her chair as a frown shadowed her face.

"Is something bothering you?"

She sipped her water a moment, then met Aimee's gaze. "It's just strange, talking about going home. I haven't been home in almost twelve years. Things have changed. And, some things are the same. I guess I'm having a hard time adjusting. I just needed to get away today. There was too much going on at home. Too much excitement, I couldn't relax."

"Shopping helps you relax?"

"Not really. If I really wanted to relax, I'd go to my house in the mountains. I'll make it there one of these days."

"I hope you'll be around for a little while. It's fun having a new friend to hang around with."

"Well, maybe we'll retreat to the cabin next time. I think I'm ready for some rest."

"Rest," Aimee glanced toward the blue gray skyline. "I don't remember what that is. But when you decide to rest, count me in."

Cory's dimples were similar to Seth's when she smiled. "I'd like that."

~

"I wish you would settle down," Dad said as Seth poured charcoal into the bottom of the grill.

Beside them, Luke propped his hands on his hips. He'd been awake since six this morning, excited to help wherever he could with the party. That was fine with Seth since he'd been up even earlier. He couldn't wait to see Aimee. Add to the fact he had Luke in on the plan, and that Luke was all in, fueled Seth's confidence.

He chuckled at his father's impatience. "Dad, I've got this."

"Son, you're about to have a mess. That charcoal goes into the Egg. This charcoal," he held up another bag for emphasis, "goes in here."

"Sorry." Seth dug the lumps out of the grill and put them back into the bag. "Guess my mind is somewhere else."

Dad shooed him away. "Go pick up Aimee and leave this to me."

He backed up as Dad prepared the grills. "Cory's bringing her. Actually, Aimee's bringing Cory. She thinks this is a welcome home party for Cory. They went shopping today."

Dad closed the grill and faced him. "Are you kidding? You put your sister in charge of Aimee and sent them shopping? We may never see them."

Seth, with Luke, followed Dad inside. "Cory said she would bring her home by five. I have faith in her."

"What else do you have going on?" He opened a cabinet and retrieved aluminum pans and spices and began lining the supplies on the bar for easy access.

"Grant's friend is flying across the beach with a message for Mom," Luke said. "But it's a surprise and we can't tell her."

Dad scrubbed his knuckles playfully across

Luke's head, then turned to the refrigerator. "I can keep a lid on it if you can."

Luke's face lit up, then he turned to Seth. "Tell him about the cupcake."

"Mom's made a special cupcake with a crown in fondant. I'll slide the ring on it just before we serve it to Aimee."

"What happened to just getting down on one knee and asking her?" Dad said as he moved the meat they would barbeque from one plate to another.

Seth raked his hand over his neck. "I wanted it to be special."

Arching an eyebrow, Dad sprinkled seasoning across the filets. "If it's meant to be, it doesn't matter where you pop the question. It will be special."

"How'd you propose to Mom?"

He shrugged. "She was working at the Burger and Shake making a sundae for this other dude. When she added the whipped cream and cherry, I said, 'Hey, let's go pick out a ring.' She gave the guy his sundae, but left with me. We got married two weeks later at the courthouse. Bam." Dad clapped his hands together. "Done. Still together thirty-three years later."

"That's romantic, Dad."

"Sounds cool to me," Luke chimed in. "Mom likes ice cream. Sometimes she'll sit on the couch and eat a whole carton herself."

If Aimee heard that come out of his mouth...

Dad chuckled. "Luke, let me tell you something about Seth. He's like Mrs. Bonnie. He's got to go all out. Bells, whistles, and fireworks." His father shook his head. "I know, Seth. Don't worry. All will work out fine. Since your mom's involved, let no man get in her way of romance. She's watched too many chick flicks and soap operas."

An hour later, everyone, except the guest of honor, had arrived.

Seth moved into Dad's study and called his sister. "Where are you?"

"We got tied up at Lenox, but we're on our way back."

"Lenox? Where is that?"

"Buckhead."

"You drove to Buckhead?" Seth choked. "To Atlanta?"

"No silly, we flew, but don't worry. We've landed and will be home in ten minutes."

"She's going to miss the sky writer."

"Can't you postpone it?"

He planted his palm on his forehead and pushed his hair back hard. "It's too late now. Be sure she looks to the sky in about two minutes." Shaking his head, he passed guests in the kitchen and more guests corralled with their cocktails and beverages on the rear patio as he headed to the beach. He nodded to the guy hired to handle fireworks who was setting up near the shoreline.

Seth glanced skyward as the buzz of a small engine peeled through the clouds with a banner trailing behind it that read: BE MINE FOREVER RAIMEE.

He turned as Grant stopped beside him, holding his hands up in surrender. "Sorry Seth. I told them

Aimee. Spelled it and everything."

On his other side, Luke tugged at his shirt. "Maybe you should take your dad's advice and just ask her."

"I think you're right, champ."

~

After the party was over, Luke fell asleep on the drive to Aimee's house. Seth carried him inside to his bed, then moved aside as she pulled his blanket over his legs. Max settled on his bed on the floor, curling into a ball of fur.

Luke's eyes popped open. "I want Seth to tuck me in."

Aimee kissed Luke's forehead, then stepped out of the room as Seth tucked Luke's blankets around his legs. He knelt at his bedside. "Time for bed, champ?"

Luke craned his neck toward his bedroom door. Seth turned in the same direction to find Aimee smiling from the doorway.

"Mom, I have to ask Seth something. Do you mind?"

Her eyes widened. "Oh? No, not at all."

Once she was gone, Luke said, "Are you going to ask her?"

He bobbed his head. "Maybe. Yeah."

"Just go for it, Seth. You've got this." Luke held up his fist. The gesture had become his favorite thing.

He meandered down the hall. Gingerly, he tucked his hand inside his pocket. The velvet pouch was secure.

Her gaze lifted from the magazine as he entered

the living room. "What was that about?" She moved to stand until Seth held a hand up to halt her. Her smile wilted. "What's wrong?"

He stood there a beat, taking in his surroundings. "I like this."

"My messy house?"

Chuckling softly, he stepped closer. "I'm not talking about your house."

She gasped as he bent down to one knee and took her hands.

"I like watching you tuck Luke in to bed. I like walking into this room and having you waiting for me. I like the thought of sharing my day's events with you and hearing yours. I want to keep doing this with you, Aimee."

He pulled the velvet from his pocket and removed the ring from its pouch. The sight of the single stone caused her jaw to drop.

"Seth."

"Will you marry me?"

In his arms, she hugged him with all of the fervor that a champion winning a race accepts the trophy. "Yes, yes," she kissed his neck and his cheek as she pulled back. He slid the ring on her left hand, smiling so wide his face hurt. When he lifted his gaze, her energy and thrill had shriveled. She eased away from him. "Wait. I want to say yes, but there's something I have to tell you."

She'd changed so quick, from absolute happiness to deafening sadness that his heart began pounding.

"When I was in college, I had a problem with alcohol."

"You told me." He moved off his knee to the couch

beside her, still holding her hands.

"It was more than that." Her gaze lowered and she shook her head. "When I found out my father had passed away, I freaked. Instead of coming home, I found a party and...honestly I don't remember much until I woke up on the floor the next evening. I think I lost a day, but it could have been more. I wanted to go home, but wasn't in any shape to drive. I accepted a ride with a friend, who shouldn't have been driving, and we ran off the road. I passed out. When I came to, I was alone in the backseat of his SUV. Instead of realizing I was still in his car, I thought the car's walls were closing in around me. And it probably had to do with what I had taken earlier. Eventually, I got myself out. But I've hated closed spaces ever since."

He rubbed her hands as she continued. "I can understand an event like that would alter how you feel about things. Most everybody has a phobia."

She met his eyes, "Once I started sobering up, it hit me that Dad was gone. Mom had already died just six months earlier. I was all alone. I remembered all I had done. I felt useless, ashamed. My parents had taught me better than that, but it was like I threw all of their love back in their faces and now they were both gone. I just didn't want to live anymore. "

His hands tightened over hers.

When she stood, their connection severed. Pacing the living room, she balled her fists tight. "I have to tell you the rest."

He stood. "I'm here for you."

Sadness filled her gaze and his heart pounded harder.

"I should have been honest with you from the

beginning, but I didn't know how to tell you," she shut her eyes. Then, she faced him again. "I don't want to lose you, but we can't go on like this."

Didn't she know how crazy he was about her? "You won't lose me." Beside her now, he reached for her. "You mean too much to me."

She eased back. Her hand moved over the back of her neck as if she was in pain as her other arm wound across her abdomen. "Come with me."

He followed her through the kitchen to the sunroom. Outside, rain dribbled down the glass roof and window as if the room was under a waterfall. Oblivious to the flashes of lighting outside and the thunder still rolling through the sky, she patiently sorted through her sketches that were leaning against her easel. She startled when he put his hand on her shoulder.

"I didn't mean to scare you." He kissed her hair.

She faced him, gazing up with eyes that were red and swollen.

"What's wrong?"

She took a step back with her hands raised in surrender. "I want you to know that I love you."

His heart thudded hard in his chest as she searched his face.

"I meant it when I said I want to marry you, but I haven't been honest with you." She wiped her cheeks as she walked toward her desk. "I should have said something weeks ago."

Confusion enveloped him, but he stood firm, waiting until he could take her in his arms again, quiet whatever caused her so much despair. "You can tell me anything."

She shook her head as she turned to her desk, shuffling through a file folder.

Swallowing his growing uncertainty, he sought something positive. Her portraits and sketches, each done in uncanny detail, covered the tables. "Your talent is amazing." Dozens of sketches of bridges, waterways, meadows and trees littered the tabletop. He paused over one of a vehicle. The tail end of a vintage Camaro was the center of the board, the vehicle's bumper buried in tall grass. The vehicle resembled the one his dad had given him when he graduated from Georgia. "I had a car like this in—"

"In college. She paced, inhaling fast as she walked across the room and back. He held his breath as she faced him with fear in her eyes. "These portraits were done a long time ago. These are the things I can't forget. Images I won't ever be able to erase from my memory. The Camaro looks like your car because it is your car. What happened to you and Kevin was no accident." Her fingers gripped her sweatshirt near her chest. She trembled and her words came out shaky. "It was my fault."

His gaze circled the room, falling on the sketches on the floor and table. He looked back at the one hanging on the easel. "You weren't there." He stepped to her. Inches away, he studied her blue eyes. His throat tightened. "That wasn't you." He mumbled the words as his mind recalled that night. He'd opened his eyes after the accident and someone with white blonde hair and sad blue eyes had looked upon him, assured him she would get help. Those same eyes looked upon him now, sad and scared. His fist pushed against the desk as his knees shook. "How was that person…you?"

Swallowing she moved closer, hands folded in a prayer-like motion, face wet from her tears. "I was walking on the road that night." Her hands braced each side of her face as she crossed the room to the window. Lightning flashed in front of her but she didn't flinch, only turned and pressed her hands together near her stomach as she moved toward him. "You swerved and you went down the embankment." Raking her fingers through her hair, she turned to him. "You saved my life that day."

Chapter Seventeen

Seth stared at her, unable to move.

Aimee clung to the chair. Shoulders trembling, she lowered her face. "I wanted to die. There is no excuse for my actions."

He lowered to the stool beside her easel. He balled his fists as something foreign gripped his gut. The guilt and hatred he'd tried so diligently to work through had been misplaced. He raised his head and forced himself to look at her. "How long have you known?"

"I've always known who you were."

He turned away. Their first meeting, subsequent cute-meets and activities together flipped through his mind. Now, he was in a room with a stranger. Instead of someone who'd come into his life to bless him, to return some of the happiness he'd lost, she was the person who had changed his life twelve years earlier. He lost everything because of that one night. Nothing had been right since. He thought she was the answer, the person who could feel the void that had been punched into his gut that terrible afternoon. She'd brought peace to him. They'd made promises. He pinched the bridge of his nose. "Kevin died that night."

"I'm so sorry Seth." A sob broke through. "I'm so sorry."

"What did you tell Luke?" His voice remained hard, unshaken, masking his own pain. "Did you lie to him, too?"

She tilted her head as composure seemed to return. "I-I didn't tell him anything about the accident."

Seth lost control. His baritone voice boomed throughout the room. "What did you tell him?" Anger seeped from every pore. He'd lost the desire to cap his unruly emotions.

"Keep your voice down." Her eyes narrowed and she swiped tears from her face. "I never want Luke to know that part of my life, what I did. But you know what? It's none of your business what I tell my son. We have enough on us right now without me dredging up that nightmare. I didn't want you to know," she bit the words out, "but then I fell in love with you and I couldn't keep it from you."

His hard stare met hers. "What do you want from me?"

She didn't reply for several heartbeats. "I want you to forgive me."

Impossible. Seth stalked out to the porch, plowing through the back door, down the short span of wooden steps into the steady rain. He needed air, time to think. For the first time in years he wanted to run. Run until he couldn't think. Run until the ache in his chest melted away. Run until he'd left Aimee's treachery behind.

Behind him, the porch screen door slammed shut. "Seth, please don't leave."

He hated himself for being unable to ignore her.

Above, Live Oak branches with their webby moss provided a slight umbrella against the rain, which continued, heavier with each passing second, plopping around them on the grassy sand.

"Seth—"

She moved in front of him, rain mixed with tears down her blotched and red face. His throat clogged, but he held it in. Close to losing it, his hands balled into fists. He wanted to pound the tree trunk, pound something and he wanted to be alone. Rage was easier than fighting to find calm in this madness. He could put all his pain into anger, and she'd leave him alone.

"I need to explain... what happened... after the accident."

"I've heard enough," he lashed out, ignoring the tiny sensation of grace his heart wanted to extend.

"You deserve the truth."

He backed away, but she kept coming.

"Please hear me out."

Sand sprayed as Seth kicked through it. "Why? What will change?" His keys. He'd left his keys on the table. He stormed past her into the house.

She reached for him. When he faced her, she pulled back.

Words began to spill. "I believed it would be easier to keep burying the accident. I don't want to remember the person I used to be, but that part of me is never far behind. I'm sick of living with my mistakes. I avoided coming home to Point Peace because I wanted to start over. I flunked out of college and left Athens. I thought if I forgot the accident, I'd never have to face it again. But I will never forget." She drew in a breath. "I never expected to fall in love with you—"

He turned away. He didn't want to hear any more.

"I heard you cry out. I went to you." Hands out, she moved ahead of him, blocking his path to the front door.

He closed his eyes and lowered his head.

"You remember."

He stared at the front door. "You said you'd help." He hated how weak he sounded.

"I'm sorry. I tried, but your door wouldn't open, and Kevin's side was smashed against that tree—"

Mouth firm he stared at her. How could he believe her? Everything between them seemed to be a lie.

"Then you left us?"

"I had to get help. We were all alone on that God awful road. I had nothing but the clothes on my back." Her gaze sank to her feet. "I was afraid. I ran until an eighteen-wheeler stopped and he called the accident in to the police."

Seth's jaw tightened.

Aimee shook her head as she covered her face with her hands, as if trying to make it go away. Standing in the dining room, her whispered pleas filled the space. "Seth, I'm so sorry that I got in the way of your car that night." Tears fell. "The police and the ambulance came, and I told them the car went off the road. At first I didn't tell them why you went off the road, but an officer kept questioning me until I told him everything. The officer took me to the hospital to get checked out, too. I kept waiting at the hospital, thinking they were going to take me to jail."

"Your grandparents wouldn't have let you stay in jail. Or Belinda."

She shook her head. "I was a coward." Sniffing she

reached for a tissue on the table. "I thought you both died. Then, I found you in the ER. You were unconscious. When the news began covering your story, I learned you survived, and I was so grateful that you lived." Words tumbled from her lips as renewed tears washed over her face. "I love you. I think I may have loved you since that awful day. And when you stopped and helped Luke and I, well, I couldn't ignore how good you were with him. I've never lied to you. I just couldn't admit to things you didn't know." She wiped a tear, another fell. "You're the best thing that's ever happened to me and Luke. And good things haven't happened in a long, long time." She met his gaze. "Please don't hate me."

"I don't know what to feel." Shoulders slumped he turned away, then paused and looked back at her. "My best friend died that day."

"It should have been me."

He shook his head. "I don't want to hear any more." He turned away. The flicker of rage he'd long buried ignited with anger like flames doused with lighter fluid. He fisted his hands as he left the kitchen.

"Wait, Seth. "Please don't leave."

He gripped the dining room chair as she hurried around him. "How long have you known I was the person driving?"

She rubbed the back of her neck. "I've known ever since the accident happened. You were well known around campus back then. When you stopped for Luke and I on the bridge, I didn't recognize you. With your beard, you look completely different than you did in college."

She had no idea how he felt about the loss of his

friend and now the loss of a promise of a new beginning. "I had to force myself to move on. Every day I feel guilt about that accident."

"I know."

"You could have told me you knew me when I first met you."

She stared at him a moment. "Luke doesn't know about my college life and I don't know if I'll ever tell him. When I saw the adoration in his eyes for you, I didn't know if being honest with you about this was the right thing to do. I had no idea he had met you, but then I remembered he'd come home from school and talked about how you had come in for career day." She crossed her arms over her stomach. "It didn't make sense to say anything while you were trying to get Tank off the road. I didn't think I'd see you again. But then we kept running into each other—"

"You could have told me—"

"I shouldn't have let Tank go with you and your dad. I should have cut ties then." Her fists balled against her abdomen as if she was doubling over as the truth poured out, as if she couldn't handle any more. He couldn't handle any more.

"Then we started spending so much time together. Something clicked with us and I couldn't stop thinking of you, imagining us together. I wanted to be with you. But I knew I needed to tell you and I've been trying to find the right time." She gripped the counter as she looked out the kitchen window. "I thought I could forget the past, but I'll never forget." She extended her arm toward the porch. "I couldn't draw or paint anything else except images of your car, the road, the tree for a long time." She faced him. "Seth, being with you every day has made me realize I couldn't hold the truth any longer."

Pressing his fist against the oak table he considered punching it, punching something. His shoulder throbbed. His head pounded. "It's been twelve years. Twelve awful years…"

"We can get past this, I know we can."

"Kevin may have lived…"

"If not for me," she looked down to the floor. "You're right."

"How can I be with you, knowing this?" He stared at her hair tumbling on either side of her face, tears falling from her sapphire blue eyes. How could he make a life with this woman when she was the reason he swerved that night? "You knew something about my past, and yours, and you chose to keep it to yourself. If I'm going to build a life with someone, I want to know the foundation is built on trust."

When a lone tear streamed down her face, she brushed it away, then wiped the other side of her face with the back of her hand. Her chin lifted, she stepped back and gazed up at him, her clear blue irises staring at him with brutal honesty. His heart pounded as she nodded in agreement to his unforgiving words.

"You're right. You don't know me. It's why I told you that first day at your parent's house you didn't want to know me." More tears fell and she swiped them away.

Her gaze landed on his again and gone was any pity he'd seen in them before. Hardened eyes, her jaw and chin followed suit, her voice shifted, with strength. "I've made more mistakes in my lifetime than you've ever thought of making. I hope you can find someone who can make you happy, whose past isn't riddled with impurity and lies. You deserve the best. And I'm not it. I guess it's a blessing you realized that when you did."

The sound of clicking across the hardwood floor had Seth swiveling around. Max rounded the corner of the hall with Luke by his side, rubbing his eyes. He clutched his blanket.

"Seth, are you mad at Momma?" Luke's sweet voice broke through the smoke and flames of his mind. He walked to the dining table and looked from Seth to Aimee.

"We're talking, Luke." Aimee's voice sounded strong, gentle, though she remained in the dimly lit kitchen. "Just talking. Go back to bed."

Luke's lip puckered as he lifted his gaze to Seth. "Did she say no?"

Across the room, she gasped and turned away.

Seth knelt down. "It's okay, champ." His throat constricted and burned. "Sometimes adults have to work through some things. Sometimes, getting married isn't the right thing to do after all."

"But you said you loved us."

"I do," he lowered his head.

Luke put his hand on his shoulder. "Why are you sad?"

He shook his head, unable to speak at first. "Come here."

Luke's arms clamped around his neck. Seth shut his eyes, holding the small boy against his chest, and tried not to breathe, so that the tears threatening wouldn't come out in front of Luke and confuse him. He couldn't bear to walk away from Luke, but he had no idea how he could stay.

HOPE BETWEEN US

Chapter Eighteen

He was a fool. A fool to rely on his heart and believe he could trust anyone except himself. He'd brought her into his fold, his life, considered a future with her. He'd proposed, only to find out she was not who he thought.

He arrived home, but the thought of rambling around in the large house alone held little appeal. He left his house on foot. He thought about calling Grant or Josh, but it was late. He didn't feel like being gawked at or prayed over right now. He took off to the beach in a jog and ran until his chest ached.

The familiar arm of the Live Oak he climbed as a kid beckoned as he rounded the point and passed the lighthouse. Leaves hung heavy under the steady pounding rain, a canopy for the taupe sand. He walked through the tall grass and slowly climbed the rear deck. Though he didn't want to face anyone right now, it was almost midnight. He needed dry clothes and a ride home.

The door slapped against the cabinet as he

barreled through, and his parent's eyes snapped up in unison. His mother seemed to zero in on his low-hanging jeans and sloshing wet sneakers. Not a stitch of clothing he wore was dry. The kitchen door squawked as it closed, though the sound wasn't as loud since he and his dad repaired it.

Mom and Dad sat across from each other at the kitchen table holding playing cards. Dad guffawed as he sat the deck in the center of the table. "Where'd this muddy dog come from? Did you get lost?"

"No, sir." He looked to his mother before stalking into the mud room. "Do I have a change of clothes here?"

"You should have something in the guest room."

Shirt removed, he turned to his mother who offered a warm bath towel. "Fresh out of the dryer." Mom's happy tone deepened in concern. "Are you all right?"

"Fine." Brushing past her, he rubbed the soft cotton over his head and ducked toward the rear staircase. "I'm going to crash here tonight, if that's okay?"

"You don't look fine." Dad's voice echoed through the hallway. "What's going on, son?"

"Nothing." The stairs were only a few paces away but he doubted a quiet guest room or hot shower would improve his mood.

"Did you ask Aimee?"

He faced her. Mom clasped her hands, smiling.

"Yep." Seth continued to dry his hair and neck as the interrogation began.

"Well, where is she?" Dad leaned against the kitchen counter.

"At home."

"How did you end up out in this weather?" Thunder rumbled outside as rain shrouded the rear windows in repeated caustic bursts. Arms crossed, Dad studied him as if he was wagering Seth's reply. "Did she say no?"

Seth's back stiffened.

"Did you and Aimee have a fight?" Mom asked.

He turned away.

"You hit the nail on the head, Mama." His father slapped his hand on the counter.

"Oh, Aimee sent me a text message." Mom went silent as she read it, then held it out to Seth for him to take it. "She's thanking me for helping with Luke and for befriending her. She makes it sound like we'll never see her or Luke again. Read it."

He shook his head. "I don't want to see it."

"Well, her note doesn't make any sense. What happened?"

Shrugging away the chill creeping across his arms and his legs still covered in soaked underwear and denim, he wrapped the towel around his shoulders. "We're not together anymore. That's all."

His mother gasped. "Why?"

"Mom, I don't want to talk about it." At the stairs, he put one foot on the tread.

"But what happened?"

He gripped the towel tighter. He wasn't ready

to talk about Aimee, because he could barely understand it himself. But Mom wouldn't let up. He met her gaze. "She's been lying to me all this time."

"Lying about what?" Dad walked into the foyer.

Overhead the rain drummed against the roof. Seth gripped the towel between his hands as he stepped off the bottom tread and faced them. "Aimee was in college the same time as me. She caused my car accident. It's a long story, but basically she was walking on the road when I came along." He inhaled, but he couldn't bear to say the words that cut him in two. "She saw my car coming and she walked in front of it."

Mom's hand covered her mouth.

"She walked in front of my car, I swerved and lost control. And you know the rest." He gripped the newel post, gritting his teeth. "Kevin died."

Clutching her throat, Mom moved toward him. "You were critical, too, Seth. Goodness, we were blessed we didn't lose you."

"How is this possible?" Dad rubbed the back of his neck. "When did she find out?"

Seth shook his head. "She's known the whole time." His shoulders sagged as he trudged to the bay window.

Dad scratched his head as he lumbered toward the kitchen. The gesture was the same whenever he couldn't figure out a mechanical problem. "I understand you're angry. This news surprises me, but maybe you should put yourself in her position. It seems to me the girl's been through one thing after another. She's a widow, her son is sick..."

"You're right, Dad."

"Have you considered she may have wanted to tell you all this time, just couldn't find the right moment?"

"That's what she claims, but she should have told me as soon as she figured out our past connection." Head lowered, he pinched the bridge of his nose where a small throb had turned into a heavy mallet slamming behind his eyes.

"Who says you can't build a life together?" Tears bundled in Mom's eyes.

"Don't you understand?" He raked his hand over his head. "I love Luke, but now, everything has changed. I foolishly believed Aimee and I could be together. I thought that being with her would help me get past all of my hang ups, but she's the root cause. If she had not walked in front of my car that day, Kevin would still be here." He trudged toward his parents, pressing his hands on the granite countertop.

"Everyone deserves a second chance." Mom muttered.

Now he'd upset his mother. He turned away. "It's too late now. She wasn't honest with me from the beginning. I can't be with someone I can't trust."

His parents looked at him with doubt. He backed out of the kitchen. "I don't want to talk about this anymore." He needed time to think, get his head sorted out.

Behind the closed doors of the bedroom, he peeled off his socks, wet jeans and started the shower. The hot water stung his skin. He raised his chin to the beads of water shooting from the showerhead.

Even with his eyes shut, Aimee, and then Kevin's face, materialized in his mind. He gasped and water slid in his mouth, suffocating, drowning. How would he ever be able to let go of the past now?

~

Rain fell for days after Seth left them. Though a weight had been lifted from her shoulders, it had cost her. Seeing Luke moping around the house, saddened by Seth's absence, made Aimee want to take her confession back.

That couldn't happen. Truth was best and she had to wade through this mucky time in her life and move on. A check up at the cancer center resulted in Luke being admitted to the hospital. Aimee wasn't sleeping regularly, but she was finally asleep when a persistent knock sounded on Luke's door. Jolted her from cot, she hurried across the room. Hopeful, she lugged open the door.

Grant stood on the other side, wide smile in place. "Good morning!" Then he frowned. "I woke you. I'm sorry, Aimee."

"It's okay, Grant." Noting the frown on his face, she lightened her tone. "Please come in." As he crossed the threshold, Aimee whispered, "Luke is still asleep. I didn't know you wanted to visit today."

"I was in the neighborhood so I thought I'd drop by."

"That's sweet, but I really need you to call or

text me before you come by like this. I was still asleep because Luke had a rough night."

"I'm sorry. I'll go. Here, this is for Luke." He handed her a stuffed teddy bear dressed in football gear. "And, this is for you. I think I ordered the one you like."

Her favorite latte was written across the label of the hot disposable cup. His brown eyes held concern and he brushed away a lock of blonde hair that fell across his forehead. She rose on her toes and kissed his cheek. "I snapped at you. I'm so sorry."

"It's okay, it's not a good time and I understand."

"I'll walk you to the elevators." She put the toy in Luke's bed and followed Grant into the hall. "He's going to love the bear. I really appreciate you coming by."

"Is something else wrong?" His gaze seemed to take in her whole appearance, locking in on her eyes.

"I must look horrible." She pulled her hair over one shoulder.

"I don't think you're capable of looking bad, but I can tell you've been crying. Are things worse with Luke?"

"Luke's health issues are as we expected. I'm upset because Seth and I had an argument. It's been a week and I haven't heard from him. Not that I really expected to," but she'd hoped. She had prayed hard that he would call, stop by, anything.

"I know they couldn't find you. Was Seth upset about that?"

"I accidentally locked myself in the closet at church." She rolled her eyes at the absurdity of it now. "Thank God, Seth found me. I'm so grateful to him for that and so many things, but the reason he's upset is…"

Did she really want to rehash everything again? Right here in the hospital hall in front of strangers? Did Grant need to know this detail of her past? She continued with carefully chosen words. "Something bad happened years ago in college. I made a wrong choice and I don't think Seth will be able to forgive me."

They walked the rest of the way to the elevators in silence. Grant turned to her. "I don't know what you and Seth argued about, and I know it's none of my business, but I know Seth. He'll come around."

She shook her head. "Not this time."

Grant hugged her before getting on the elevator. "Let me know if you need anything. I mean it, Aimee. I consider you a friend, too." He smiled at her before pecking her cheek.

She trudged back to Luke's room and lowered to the couch. Was Grant right? Would Seth ever find forgiveness toward her actions?

It was a huge ordeal to overcome. She would remain tough and prepare for the worst, because Seth may never get over what she did. She couldn't blame him. Being honest from the beginning of any relationship was her new mantra. No way would she continue to make the same mistakes again.

~

September wrapped a heavy blanket of humidity over Point Peace that Seth was certain rivaled the heat of hell. He called practice early and drove to the cemetery. Sitting in front of Kevin's headstone didn't comfort him, but it never did. Sometimes if he had a question, he found the answer and came away with some semblance of solace. Tonight, the katydids sang so loud, it made him remember fishing with Luke. One of the last evenings he'd visited with Luke and Aimee, the child had quizzed him on every sound he heard and every bug he laid eyes on. Aimee told him later that was the child's way of keeping Seth there, of keeping Seth's mind off what time it was and if it was Luke's bedtime.

He swiped his face as he walked to his truck and took the road heading north, instead of south, toward home. The further he drove inland, the more he thought of the days when he and Kevin were just learning to drive and when they thought it was fun to speed through the narrow streets of Point Peace. It was a wonder they didn't get hurt back in those days, or hurt someone else. The sky blushed overhead, the soft orange light cast shadows over the Ridley's driveway which faced the four-way intersection of their subdivision. A yellowed SUV was parked in front of Charles's truck. Seth pulled to the curb and cut the engine as the Ridley's front door opened.

Aimee stepped onto their porch but turned her head back toward the living room. She raised her hand and waved as Charles walked outside behind her. The old man spoke as they trudged to her car and then he gave her a hug before he closed the driver door.

He sank down in his seat as she backed out and drove away. She hadn't see him, probably hadn't even glanced his way. Charles stood on the driveway until Aimee was out of sight. Seth knew the moment the man caught a glimpse of his truck.

Charles walked down his driveway, never taking his eyes off of Seth's 4x4. Once he reached his mailbox, Charles lifted his hand and waved.

Waving back, Seth shook his head. He couldn't sit here like an idiot, especially now that Kevin's dad had seen him. He cranked the truck and drove straight, making a slow turn until the passenger door was even with where Charles stood on the street.

"Nice night, Seth."

"Yes it is."

"Are you visiting someone?"

He had sat in this very spot night after night either dropping Kevin off after practice or waiting to pick Kevin up. He'd slept over at this house a handful of times over the years, but most of their gatherings were at Seth's parent's place. There was more entertainment at the Garrett's sprawling beach house. More toys than what the Ridley's modest salary could afford.

"I was coming to visit you and Mrs. Ridley."

"Jeff said you cut practice off early tonight. Is everything all right?"

Seth cut the engine and walked around to the passenger side. He leaned against the hood and peered up at Kevin's childhood home. "Nothing wrong with the team. It's just me. I can't concentrate these days."

With the newspaper and mail tucked under his arm, Charles sank his hands inside his trouser pockets. "I know what you mean." He thumbed toward the house. "You're welcome to come in. Clare would love to see you."

"Thanks, but it's late and I've lost track of time. I'll come by this weekend."

The two stood in silence another beat. Charles eyed him for a moment and then cleared his throat. "We just had an interesting visit from Aimee McClain. Says she knows you."

"Yes, I know her and Luke very well. The festival was in Luke's honor."

"Seems you all knew each other some time ago. She told me about the night of the accident, explained her part in it."

Air filled his lungs until he thought they might blow. He balled his fists at his sides and fought to steady the rapid beat of his heart. "Yeah, I just found out about her view of things." His words seemed nonchalant. "I don't know what to make of it."

"I remembered reading her name on the police report. It named Aimee Holmes as a witness. I didn't know she'd walked in front of your car." Charles wiped his nose with a handkerchief and stuffed it back into his pocket. "I remember you telling us someone had said they would help you, and you described a girl. I guess that was her."

"It's awful what she did."

"Yep. Sure is. I can't say I haven't thought about doing something similar after Kevin died. Hell, even before he died I thought about taking my life. Things get tough and I start thinking maybe the family would be better off without me. Seems I'd always end up talking to the preacher or your dad and I'd straighten myself back out."

Seth eyed Kevin's dad. "If I'm honest, I guess I'd have to admit to thinking along those lines after Kevin died." He shook his head. "I always ask God why. Why wasn't it me?"

"I didn't ever blame you, Seth. You know that, don't you?"

He swallowed hard but words wouldn't come.

Chapter Nineteen

Cards fanned in front of him, Josh sat at the end of Luke's bed. Despite his normally easy-going manner, Josh sent Aimee a tentative smile as he pulled a card from the deck. She and Luke had started a game of Uno when Josh arrived. She tried not to think about the fact the young pastor was also Seth's best friend. Curiosity as to whether Seth had asked Josh to visit had crossed her mind. Of course as a member of Hopewell Church's staff, visiting sick was probably part of his duties. Nevertheless, she was grateful for his presence.

In the days since she'd told Seth about her role in the accident, Luke had missed him, asked about him every day. Multiple times a day.

Seth's absence had nothing to do with blood counts, but the friendship Seth had developed with her son had a large impact on Luke's attitude. Luke had experienced a few low days during the last month, yet this rapid-fire decline scared her. Though his sitting position was slouched at best, today was the longest he had sat up in bed. Now, after only fifteen minutes, his eyelids were growing heavy. It took more effort for him to hold up his hand of cards. His energy waned. One card game and he was exhausted.

Telling Luke about the accident didn't seem important compared to keeping his spirits elevated. She'd prayed Seth would visit Luke anyway, despite her. This morning, when she knew he would be in class and unable to answer, she left him a message with Luke's current status and asked him to visit. Hours later, there was no response. Not even a text. Beyond the point of feeling sorry for herself and her son, Aimee was about to visit Seth herself and give him a piece of her mind.

Luke made his play. His card read: Draw Four Wild Card. "The color will be red."

Aimee scrunched her face in mock disgust as she drew four more cards from the stack. "Red? Why red?" Her hand consisted of blue, yellow, and green cards. Even the new ones she'd drawn didn't contain a single red.

Luke giggled as Josh drew from the deck. "Josh didn't have a red card either."

Two more turns and Luke won the game. As Aimee tallied the points, the nurse entered.

"Is it dinnertime?" Josh asked.

"I'm not hungry." Luke said.

Aimee cleared the cards away as the nurse checked his port and took his vital signs. Luke lay back against his pillow as the nurse left the room. "I'm sleepy."

"You don't want to play anymore?" Aimee

asked.

Luke turned toward the window.

Josh crossed the room to answer a knock. At the sound of familiar voices, Luke looked back at the door as the Garrett family entered. Bonnie led the way, followed by Cory, and then Tom waved as he strolled toward him.

"Where's the birthday boy?" Tom said.

"Right here," Luke raised his arm, with IV tubes hanging below his elbow.

Cory took a seat beside Luke and began asking Luke about his action figures sitting on his tray. Tom flanked the opposite side of Luke's bed and joined in the conversation Cory started about the toys. Bonnie smiled at Aimee. "How is everything today?"

Aimee laid her hand gently on Luke's head. "He's been tired today. This is the first time he's perked up."

Tom reached for something at his feet. "Let's get right to the presents, birthday boy. What'd say?"

Luke beamed at the bright green wrapped present Tom sat in his lap. He placed his hands on top and then raised his eyes to Tom and Bonnie. "Where's Seth?"

Tom stood and looked back at his wife. Aimee didn't miss the questioning exchange between Seth's parents.

Bonnie smiled down at Luke. "Seth couldn't come with us, hon, but he will come to see you." Then, she looked at Aimee and nodded politely.

Luke frowned and lowered his head. Aimee

closed her eyes for a moment, hating to see Luke wanting someone who may be out of his life for good.

She studied Seth's parents. Had he told Tom and Bonnie about her past, her mistakes?

Did they, like Seth, hate her now, too?

Bonnie smiled as she held out a birthday cake for Aimee and Luke to view. "I made this especially for you, young man."

Luke's grin spread from ear to ear. The first genuine smile in days. "Mom, it's got my number on it."

"Your baseball jersey number and that's how old you are today." It seemed like yesterday when she held her new baby the first time.

"Eight years old." Bonnie nodded. "You'll be eighteen before we know it."

Heat swelled inside her chest. She fought tears back as she moved to the end of the bed beside Bonnie. With shaking hands, she moved stacks magazines and books off the table. She helped hold the box down while Bonnie pulled out the cake.

"Maybe we can freeze the cake until Luke can eat it. They had to put his feeding tube in yesterday. It's been a busy weekend." Even her voice wobbled. She glanced back at the door, hoping Seth would walk through the door as if nothing was wrong. Where was he? What he was doing?

"I'm sorry, Aimee. I should have asked if you if bringing the cake would be okay."

"It's fine. What is a birthday party without cake? I appreciate it."

With the cake on the table, Luke pushed up to a straighter sitting position. "Mom, eat a big piece of cake for me." He looked around the room at Josh and Tom. "Everyone have cake. I don't mind."

The adults broke into laughter at Luke's enthusiasm. Bonnie patted her shoulders at first, then Aimee found herself wrapped in the older woman's arms. "Thank you," she whispered.

Bonnie's arms tightened around her. "You're welcome, dear." Bonnie pulled back and eyed her critically. "You're nothing but skin and bones."

"She hasn't eaten in days," Luke said.

"I have eaten," Aimee scoffed. "You happened to be asleep."

"Aimee, go get some dinner first, then you can have cake. We'll stay with Luke." As she talked, Bonnie pulled paper plates and forks from the paper bag Tom had sat on the vinyl couch.

Josh stepped forward. "Aimee, I'll walk with you to refill my coffee before I hit the road."

Once they were alone in the corridor, waiting for the elevators to arrive, she met Josh's eyes.

"Are you eating regularly?" he asked.

She shrugged. "I nibble." She couldn't remember the last day she'd eaten a full meal. Aimee's appetite had fled in the face of Luke's illness and Seth's absence. Normally, a homemade birthday cake would make her mouth water, but even that baked goodness couldn't stop her stomach from churning.

"I'm sure I don't need to remind you if you get sick, you'll be no use to Luke."

Nodding, Aimee stared at the elevator doors,

willing them to open. "I'm afraid..." Deliberately, she cut her words. She barely knew this man.

"You can talk to me."

The doors opened. "Hey Aimee," Grant stood at the threshold, smile wide. "I was coming to check on you and Luke."

Aimee brushed past a young couple with their toddler. Josh held his hand over the doors until the family boarded. Beside her, Josh shook his hand.

"Were you guys getting something to eat?" Grant asked. "I mean, I'm not interrupting anything, am I?"

Aimee stood between the men.

"Nah, I was going for coffee," Josh said. "Aimee was going to grab a bite to eat."

"Allow me," Grant led them toward the buffet line. Grant insisted on paying for Aimee's meal and Josh's coffee. He carried her tray to the table.

Once seated, she nibbled on her salad as Grant and Josh talked about the remarkable game Seth's high school baseball team had played against a rival school.

"Seth said he'd take the team to the State Championship, and he's doing what he set out to do," Grant said.

Josh nodded. "He's determined."

Beside her, Grant nudged her. "Seth organized the whole fair for you and Luke. I guess his mom helped some, but he is a project manager extraordinaire."

She swallowed hard, but a lump blocked her airway. She studied her mix of lettuce, carrots and cabbage, shifting the vegetables from one side of her plate to the other. "I-I really appreciate everything."

"Grant—" Josh started.

"I know you do, Aimee," Grant continued, "I want you to know we all care about you and your son. Everything is going to turn out for the best, I feel it."

Across the table, Josh smiled at her. "You've got a lot of people praying for Luke."

"I told you, Aimee. We're not just Seth's friends. We're your friends, too."

Her wary emotions bubbled under her fingers couldn't hold a fork. She placed it on the table and fisted her hands in her lap. "I can't eat any more."

Josh nodded and scooted his chair back from the table.

"You barely ate." Grant said. "Do you want something else?"

"No, thank you." Aimee slid the plate over. "It's hard to eat with so much on my mind."

"Did you and Seth work everything out?" Grant asked.

"Grant!" Josh scolded.

She chuckled. "It's okay, Josh. Grant actually stopped by after Seth and I had an argument and he was encouraging me." She gripped her hands in a lame effort to hold her composure. "Some things are unforgiveable."

Josh reached across the table. "It will work out, Aimee. I mean, I don't know the argument you and Seth had, but I know you mean a lot to him. Forgiveness is not impossible, but it can take time. Seth is not a person to hold hurt, or a grudge, for long."

"Thanks."

Grant put his arm around her shoulders and winked. "I upped the Annie with old Seth. I told him if he didn't make things right with you, then I was going to start dating you. If that doesn't light a fire under him, I don't know what will."

Josh leaned back in his seat and put his palm over his face. "Oh no, you didn't."

She shifted her confused gaze from one man to the other. "I'm not seeing the elephant in the room."

"It's okay. As long as I've known Grant, he has a knack of taking Seth's girlfriends."

Grant raised his hands in mock defense. "Aimee is different." He met her gaze. "I have too much respect for you to date you for impure reasons." He glanced back at Josh. "Besides, we already made a pact that we're friends." He then gave her a sly grin. "But if you have any single friends you'd like to introduce me to, I'd be completely amicable to meeting them."

Aimee was laughing now. It was so good to laugh. "You guys are the best. Thanks for lunch and making me forget my worries."

"We're taking this show on the road. The Josh and Grant comedy hour." Grant raised his hands as if he could see the words on a billboard in lights.

"I think I'd better keep my day job," Josh said.

At the main floor elevators, Grant hugged her. "I'm headed out." He pecked her cheek. "I have to get to the station early in the morning. I'll stop by and see you and Luke next weekend."

Aboard the elevator, Josh grinned when she met his gaze. As their conversation slid to Seth, Josh shrugged. "Seth has been dealt a tough hand of cards in life. He works hard for everything he has attained. Some may see it as him getting what he wants, but Seth puts in longer hours than anyone realizes. I think that's something you both have in common."

They walked in silence toward Luke's room. "What about forgiving? Does he forgive?"

Josh paused beside Luke's door. "I've known him almost my whole life and he gets angry, but he cares with all his heart. I think he's so busy blaming himself for past mistakes he doesn't realize he needs to let others know he forgives them."

~

Seth boarded the elevator with a handful of passengers. As the elevator ascended, his heart drummed. Part of him longed to see Aimee, despite everything. The other part of him wanted to stay far away from her. Luke was the most important person in their triangle. Going six days without visiting the boy had been too long and Seth couldn't help berate himself for his selfishness.

Staying away from Aimee had won over keeping in touch with Luke. He hadn't wanted to call the hospital room because he figured she would answer. Yet he could hear her voice every day. His thoughts were filled with her, even when he tried so hard to stay busy. Even though her decision twelve years earlier had altered his entire life, he couldn't put her, or the kid, out of his mind.

Familiar oncology nurses greeted him as he passed them in the hallway. After wiping his hands on his jeans, and inhaling deep, he knocked on the hospital room door.

Mom smiled. "Come on in. Luke wants everyone to have cake."

Amazing how his mother could act normal in this abnormal situation. She had that way about her, able to ease the tension no matter the occasion. She stepped back allowing him entry. His gaze touched on his sister and father who stood near Luke's bedside. The bathroom door was open but darkened inside.

Where was she? Something had to be wrong.

Dad grinned as Seth approached. A tool set containing wrenches and screwdrivers of various sizes lay open on Luke's right side, while a toy helicopter and a boat balanced across his lap.

A smile split Luke's pale face when he looked up. "You're here." Gray shadows hung under the child's eyes and his cheeks were gaunt and pale. His neck and shoulders slumped, as though he could barely hold up his own emaciated weight. Though the way Luke straightened at the sight of him couldn't be ignored.

Shutting his eyes to maintain control over the moisture filling his vision, he wrapped Luke in a bear hug. When they broke apart, Seth lowered to sit on Luke's bed

Face to face, Luke narrowed his eyes. "Where have you been?"

His tight smile barely formed. Had Aimee told Luke why he hadn't come around? "I've been getting the team ready for the State Championships."

Luke grinned. "Really? I bet they're excited. They're gonna win."

"I hope so."

His smile faded and a prominent frown took its place. "Mom thought you might not come back."

He shook his head. "I'm here, Luke. I'm not going anywhere."

"Home is here." Luke's mouth was firm.

He took the child's hand and squeezed. "I love you, Champ."

Luke's sad blue eyes sobered him.

"You'll be coming home soon," he hoped the reassurance in his voice would renew Luke's confidence.

The child seemed to age decades in the few moments that passed. "I doubt I'll ever bust out of this place."

"Sure you will. They won't put up with you forever," he joked and gave Luke a gentle fist bump.

Luke giggled, but a cough seized, sending his body into a jerking fit.

Bonnie rushed forward offering Luke water. Dad rubbed his narrow back while Seth held his breath, sitting there useless, helpless. When the hacking cough subsided, Luke lay back, his head falling back into an awkward position. Bonnie fussed with the pillows until he appeared more comfortable. Pushing the buttons on the bed, the hospital bed lurched down.

"We're good, Mom." Seth said it gently and

then focused on Luke. "I was joking, Luke."

He nodded. "I know. I'm glad you're here." Luke pushed the table holding his toys away and leaned back against his pillows.

"I'm sorry it has been so long since I visited."

Luke swallowed and closed his eyes a moment. "I need to ask you something."

Seth continued to hold Luke's hand, waiting. He closed his eyes as tears collected in the corner of his eyes.

He exchanged glances with his parents before fixing his attention back on his young friend. "What's on your mind, Champ?" He squeezed Luke's hand again.

"Mom's been crying a lot. And, I wanted to ask you if... if you'd take care of her for me."

Seth leaned closer while his mother turned away, toward the window. Beside her, his father shook his head. Oblivious to the others in the room, Luke went on. "I mean, take care of her if I don't get a donor."

"Luke, you are going to get a donor and the transplant is going to be a great success. Don't worry about things like this. Your mom is strong and she's going to be fine."

"She misses you, Seth. I don't want Mom to cry any more. Can you help her?"

"Anything you ask Champ, I'll do it." The click of the door handle drew Luke's attention.

Aimee stepped inside, faltering when she met Seth's gaze. Josh followed and raised his hand in greeting, then closed the door behind him. As Aimee seemed to thaw, she collected herself and turned to lay her purse on the couch.

"Did you have a good meal?" Mom asked.

"I had coffee," Josh replied. "Grant stopped by and Aimee had a salad."

Mom sent Aimee a look of mock warning. "Now, Aimee, I can tell by the look on Josh's face that you hardly ate. Now, you must eat before you can have cake."

Aimee avoided his gaze even while she moved closer to Luke's bed. Finally, she raised her eyes to his. "We appreciate you making it. What a nice surprise."

"I got your message." Their eyes held until Seth shifted his focus to Josh as his friend laid a supportive hand on Aimee's shoulder. He was glad Josh had visited Luke, and was helping Aimee, but his gut twisted into knots when the image of Josh and Aimee sharing a meal invaded his thoughts? Images of Grant and Aimee danced through his thoughts as he recalled his last conversation with his college friend.

"You two had dinner together?" He tried to sound lighthearted. "And Grant was there too?" Seth's neck heated as his frustrations rose.

Josh shook his head at him as if he were reading his thoughts. Jealous?

He avoided looking at Aimee, though it was hard to ignore her completely. Her hair was pulled into a messy ponytail. Her blue eyes were hidden behind a pair of black rimmed glasses Seth had never seen before. He didn't even know she needed glasses. Even beyond her lenses, he couldn't ignore the heavy bags under her eyes. She looked thinner.

Guilt punched him in the gut. He'd done this. His reaction to her honesty, combined with Luke's health decline, was taking its toll.

He wanted to leave but as she fussed with Luke's blanket, something kept him planted. He'd missed Luke. He'd missed Aimee. He couldn't deny she was as much a part of his heart, as her child.

Josh shuffled toward the foot of the bed with Cory standing beside him. "I'd better be going." He turned and shook Tom's hand, hugged Bonnie and Cory, then turned to Seth with an outstretched hand. "Good to see you, buddy." He raised his eyebrows when Seth hesitated before shaking hands. He smiled as he slapped his hand against his best friend's.

Tapping on the door silenced everyone. When Luke's doctor entered, Aimee moved forward. "I have an update." He glanced around the room and back to Aimee.

"Maybe we should step out," Dad said.

"No, please stay." Aimee held her palms out. "Luke and I consider you all family. We can talk while everyone is here, Dr. Hilton."

"We've found a match for Luke, a full match." The doctor's face brightened. "The donor has been through every single test and is a perfect match. The date has been set for the harvest."

As he announced the date, Aimee smiled down at Luke. "Ten days, buddy. We only have to wait ten more days." She kissed Luke's head.

"Seth—" Mom started.

Dad tugged Mom's hand and shook his head.

Meanwhile, Cory hugged Aimee, Josh and Mom sang praises as Seth met his father's gaze. Dad nodded to him and Seth tilted his head forward in return. Then he realized he still held onto Luke's hand.

"It's really going to happen, Seth." Luke squeezed his fingers.

Seth couldn't say anything at first. He wanted to tell Luke and Aimee his news, but this was Luke's moment. He'd tell them soon. Lowering to his knee, he kissed Luke's hand and splayed it against his tear strained cheek. "I told you that you'd be busting out of here soon. I never had any doubt."

His gaze collided with Aimee's. "Thank you," she said.

Everyone began to make excuses to leave shortly after the doctor left. Outside, the sun had completely set.

"Before we leave, let's pray." Josh gathered everyone in a circle around Luke.

Luke held his hand out to Seth. He looked to his left, "Mom?"

Within minutes they all joined hands around Luke's bed. Seth kept his eyes shut tight and concentrated on Josh's words, but he couldn't ignore the soft sounds of Aimee's breath rushing in and out.

He'd finally met a woman to spend the rest of his life with, only to discover she had been involved in the worst night of his life. Now, he was vested in her life, her son's life. He couldn't throw his feelings for her out like some greasy rag. It was time to seek a new peace. It was time to move forward and stop looking back.

Chapter Twenty

The next day, Seth returned to the hospital. Clutching a gift bag, he knocked on Luke's door.

Though he had full intent on the visit, he'd purposely failed to warn Aimee of his visit. Her eyes rounded when she opened the door, her surprise at his presence unmistakable. "Come in," she swung the door wide and stepped back.

He crossed the threshold. "Is it okay that I stopped by? I should have called."

"Seth!"

Aimee smiled at Luke's response. Seth stood beside her a moment longer, and finally leaned forward, wrapping her in a hug.

After a moment, her arms bundled around him. When they broke apart, he hustled toward the child's bedside. "Hey, Luke," he drew his small body close in a bear hug. Luke held on, as if holding onto Seth for dear life.

"Man, you're strong," he joked as Luke's grip finally loosened on his neck. "What's in those IVs? Superman juice?"

Luke giggled and glanced at his mom.

With hesitance, Aimee joined them at Luke's bedside. "Luke was just talking about you."

"You were?"

"Yeah. When I'm out of the hospital for good, I want you to help me with baseball. I want to be a pitcher just like you."

Seth looked down, pretending to itch his eyes. The moisture hit his fingers quicker than a broken pipe spewing water. "I'll be here, Champ."

"Promise?"

Lord, please let this transplant be a success. He smiled at the kid. "I promise."

"What's wrong?"

"Nothing. Allergies make my eyes water, that's all. I'm glad you want me to help you with baseball practice." Seth raised the supersize gift bag. "Here's your birthday present."

Luke's eyes popped and his smile gleamed as he gripped the box and yanked it from the confines of the slick, decorated bag. "Mom, look!" he held out the latest gaming system with both hands above his head. "And he bought me three games, too."

Aimee picked up the games from Luke's lap, "It's exactly what you were asking for Christmas. What do you say, Luke?"

"Thanks a bunch, Seth!" The boy leaned forward and threw his arms around his neck.

"You're welcome."

Luke settled back against his pillows and stared at the box.

"Do you want me to hook it to the hospital's television?"

"Yeah!"

Seth pulled the contents out of the box, and connected cables and wires to the television. Images on the screen danced with the introductory slides for the game Luke chose to play. He scooted over so Seth could sit on the bed beside him and they could dual electronic football.

Luke laughed. "Wow, you totally missed that pass. I thought you'd played before."

He scratched his beard. "I guess I'm out of practice. Want to go again?"

"Yup, if you don't mind getting beat again."

Across the room, Aimee chuckled. "Wow, Luke. Watch the attitude."

Her laugh warmed his heart. "He must be feeling better."

She smiled back at him as she wiped the countertop around the sink dry and repositioned a short stack of magazines. A new game ensued as she tidied the couch, folded a blanket and placed it on one end of the sofa. She glanced his way, only to quickly return her focus on the task at hand.

She went into the bathroom, closed the door. Water ran a few moments, then the door cracked open and she returned with a wet washcloth. Only then did she return to Luke's bedside and instructed him to wipe his hands so he wouldn't dirty the new game controller.

She looked away as soon as Seth's eyes locked with hers.

Luke yawned as Aimee wiped his face and neck.

"Time for a nap, Champ."

The child scooted over in the bed.

Seth leaned forward and kissed his brow. He scuffed his fingers playfully over Luke's head. "Listen, I've got to go out of town for a couple of days." He met Aimee's gaze and held it before returning his attention to Luke.

"Are you coming back?"

"Yes, I've been asked to speak at my old college."

"Will you be back for the transplant?"

The date had been set for the harvest, his part in the process. Seth was both ecstatic and scared. "If it's okay with your Mom, I'd love to be here."

Luke put both hands together in a prayerful plea. "Mom? Please?"

She smiled at her son, a sigh escaping her red bud lips before she raised her gaze to him. "It's fine, Seth."

Luke nodded, then cuddled under the blanket and closed his eyes.

"Guess I'd better go."

"Thank you." She shut Luke's door and followed Seth into the hallway.

Her eyes were the color of the sky on a sunny day, her lips were full and moist like the petals of rose bud. He moved a loose strand of her hair away from her shoulder before he could stop himself.

She took his hand, clasping her fingers tight around his. "Thank you for the game system, the games, and the time you spent with Luke this evening."

He looked at their joined hands. As if her touch created the central point of their electrical connection, the sensation hummed along his extremities, clearing a path down to his feet. It was time he started being honest, real, where she was concerned. Yes, he cared deeply for her. He just didn't know how to handle the feelings that remained, or the lack of trust that had infiltrated.

"I haven't done anything." The transplant could fail. No, he hadn't done anything yet. All he had to do was show up and go through a procedure. His stomach twisted into knots at the anticipation of the coming days, but nothing would keep him away.

Chapter Twenty-One

The next day, Seth took off running before dawn. His feet pounded sand until he reached the boardwalk, then hit the sidewalk that lead to the park. Cutting along the perimeter of the property, Seth attempted to avoid the throng of weekend tourists.

"Seth! Hey, Seth!"

Grant jogged alongside him, smile beaming.

"What's up?" He was winded, while Grant looked like he'd barely broken a sweat.

"This is a beautiful day, isn't it? Are you going to see Aimee and Luke today?"

"I'm leaving for Athens in a couple of hours. I saw them last night."

"I called her a few minutes ago. I'm going by this afternoon. They need all the support they can get."

Seth eyed Grant as they jogged through Point Peace Square, slowing their pace as they reached the shops and more tourists. They walked the rest of the way to the wharf where boats were docked.

A large sign for Martin Tours showed the location of Josh's family's business. Josh's cousin Levi was speaking to a group as a large fish hung beside him on display, the catch of the morning.

"You two aren't dating any more, are ya?"

He stopped and looked at his friend. "What's it to you?"

"Heard you two broke up," Grant bumped his arm with his fist. "If you two are just friends, then I want to take her to dinner. If you don't mind, of course."

He rubbed his neck. "I do mind, but I can't dictate who she dates." Seth paced ahead, then stopped short, fixing his stare on Grant. "By God, man you'd better not treat her like a piece of meat."

Grant narrowed his eyes. "What kind of person do you think I am?"

Shaking his head, he blew out a frustrated breath. "I'm sorry. I didn't mean to accuse you of treating her with anything other than respect—"

"That's not what I heard, old man."

Seth stiffened at the jab. Age bothered Seth, and Grant knew it. Aging meant getting weaker and he liked to be the top dog, the strong man, the confident one. Grant's comment, something he usually took with humor, hit him wrong today.

He'd been a coward when she trusted him with the truth. He accused her of lying when all she was doing was trying to protect him. Now, his best friend was stepping into the picture. He'd been so hard on her. He'd hurt her.

"You do still care about her." Grant crossed his arms.

Raking his hand through his hair, he looked across the crowd. "I'm in love with her, Grant, but I've screwed up. She was honest with me about something in our past and I pushed her away."

"I know. I happened to stop by and see Aimee after you two argued. She was really upset." The two ambled down the path toward the beach, stopping near the gate. Grant leaned against a post. "What exactly has you two so messed up? I thought you just met her in June."

Grabbing a piece of grass, he lifted his gaze to the boardwalk and eyed an older couple fishing off the pier. A strong Atlantic gust of wind blew their line as they cast out bait. The wind whipped around him, and sun's heat bore down as Seth squinted across the glistening waves.

"She was there. The night Kevin died." He crossed his arms. "I remember I had looked down at my phone. I only meant to look for a split second, but it was longer than that. Kevin yelled out and I looked up. Something was in the road and I swerved. I tried to correct the wheel but I panicked and ended up turning the wheel too far. The car went off the embankment and flipped, or so I was told. I don't remember. When it landed, it slammed against a tree on Kevin's side."

Seth swallowed. Talking about it twelve years later was still difficult. He shared Aimee's account of her events the same night. "She was trying to find help and she was upset over her father. Aimee said she was the person in the road. Apparently she had deliberately walked in front of my car because she wanted to end her life."

Grant trudged a few feet away, shaking his head.

"What's up? This is mine and Aimee's issues we're talking about."

"You blamed her?"

"At first, yes. She was there. I was there. We both did the wrong thing and Kevin paid the price."

"Obviously she wasn't in her right mind." Grant lowered to the grass and leaned his elbows on his knees.

Seth squatted beside him. "I agree."

"Because the Aimee we know and love would not hurt anyone or anything."

He rubbed his face. "You're right."

"It wasn't Aimee's fault, it was my fault." Grant rubbed his fist over his eyes and looked at Seth. "I helped you work on the Camaro, remember?"

"Yeah, we were replacing belts, checking the fluid levels. We checked the brakes."

"Seth, I didn't finish my part. I told you I was done with the brakes but I didn't finish checking all four. I checked two. A couple of my friends showed up and we started talking. They were going to get beers and I went with them. I told you guys I had to go study." He forked his fingers through his long hair. "When I heard about your accident, I knew what had happened. You trusted me to have fully checked everything. I didn't know you were taking the car out. I thought we'd have time the next morning to finish working on it."

Seth shook his head. The facts of that fateful night were a tumor, growing at a rapid pace. "God,

Grant."

"I know what I did, Seth. I've been trying to make it up to you and your family all these years. I couldn't believe Kev died and then you were in the hospital all those weeks. Your parents were freaked out and not sure you were going to make it. I should've said something. I've felt guilty all this time."

"Me, too."

"This is why you can't blame Aimee. I didn't know her side of the story until now, but she's still living in hell with Luke sick." Grant stood and faced Seth. "I'm sorry I let you down, but I won't allow you to continue to treat Aimee like this."

He glared at Grant.

"I care about her, too."

"Let me speak." Seth leveled his gaze with his younger friend who had become as close as Kevin and Josh were to him. "You didn't let me down. Kevin and I checked the car before we drove it. I know you didn't finish what you started. I knew you were a young punk who was thinking of yourself."

Grant's eyebrows narrowed. "A punk?"

Seth grabbed him with his left arm and pulled him in a headlock. "Yeah, punk." The two grappled until Seth's post-operative shoulder started hurting. "Ow, let go."

Grant straightened but punched his uninjured arm, hard.

"We checked each other, too. Nothing that happened that night was your fault."

His friend exhaled and relief washed over his

face. "Thanks. Now you need to go to Aimee and tell her the same thing."

"You're right. That night was as much my fault as it was hers. I should have been paying attention." Seth lowered his head to his hands. "I've been a complete jerk to her. She may not take me back."

"If she's not interested in you anymore, maybe she'll go out with me."

Seth shook his head.

They stood and started walking. Grant paused when they reached his Jeep. "Here's the deal. If you don't let her know how you feel, I am. I'm going to step into your territory and I'm going to take her out."

Seth glared back at him.

"Watch and see if I don't. None of us are perfect."

"I know." He lowered his gaze to the gravel below.

"Then tell her how you feel."

"All right." He pointed his finger at Grant's chest. "But you leave her alone, do you understand?"

Grant narrowed his eyes. "She's my friend, too."

"Friends only."

"We'll see how things go with you."

Seth shook his head as he walked away.

Chapter Twenty-Two

Seth exhaled as he opened the door to the sanctuary. He hadn't wanted to come this morning, but he knew he'd never hear the end of it if he didn't follow through on his mother's request. He just needed space, some direction after Aimee told him about her part in his past. Going to the scene of the accident had confirmed he didn't belong there. On the drive back, he fully intended to go home, but he detoured and ended up spending the night on Aimee's couch. What was worse, even after she'd filled in the missing pieces of his memory following the car accident, he'd stayed under her roof, wishing the distance from the living room to her bedroom would dissolve so that she could be in his arms.

Was he wrong to have these feelings for her? Her actions that night had led to Seth veering off the road. A move that took Kevin's life. How could he want to be with someone who had thought so little of herself that she would try to end her life? She hadn't cared how it would affect others.

Except he knew that wasn't true. She'd gone all of these years knowing the truth and trying to change. The giving and kind person he met months ago wasn't the same person who'd walked in front of his car twelve years earlier.

Yet, that same person, that college-aged Aimee, had not run from what she had done. She'd stayed by his side.

The donation day was only days away. In less than a week, he would undergo a procedure to withdraw his healthy bone marrow which would then be transported and donated to Luke. He wanted to tell Aimee and Luke about his part in the bone marrow donation. He'd become too invested in their lives to stand back anonymous.

What if the transplant didn't work?

No. He would not accept it. Failure was not an option.

As he pulled open the sanctuary door a packed house bowed their heads as Josh lead the congregation in prayer. Only a smattering of parishioners noticed Seth's entry and he nodded to a couple he recognized. Not wanting to distract anyone, he stood quietly and scanned the room. His parents usually sat on the right side of the large sanctuary, they weren't in their usual spot this morning.

His gaze swiveled to the center and he caught a glimpse of chestnut curls cascading over the back of the pew. His heart flipped like an Olympic diver inside his chest. Beside Aimee, his sister was seated to her left and then his mother on Cory's left.

"My good habits?" He mumbled, wondering if Aimee's presence was pure coincidence. He had a hunch his mother had dove head first into her treasure chest of meddling and pulled out a fast one. Nevertheless, Seth moved up the aisle as Josh ended prayer and called all children to go with their leaders to Children's church.

The children filed toward the stage and exited alongside their leaders. Seeing the kids stampede out brought sweet memories. How many times had he raced up this very aisle? With Kevin and Josh, the boys usually got reprimanded for shoving each other in church.

If Luke McClain had been there, he would have been first in line. Knowing Luke, he recognized the boy's determination. He was just like his mother in that sense. He deserved his second chance.

Seth was going to be a part of Luke's second chance.

As a woman got on stage to sing, Seth took the empty seat on the pew with his family and boldly glanced left.

Aimee tugged her bottom lip and lifted her gaze.

"Is it okay if I sit here?" Seth whispered.

She nodded and clutched her hands in her lap.

"I didn't know you were going to be here."

"Same here," she replied as her gaze lowered to his lips. "I'm sorry."

"Nah, it's fine. Surely we can share a row in God's house."

She faced the front.

As Josh took his place behind the podium, Seth

eyed Aimee again. His heart hammered until his lungs hurt. He grabbed the stubby pencil stuck near the hymnals, scribbled a note on the back of the bulletin, then passed the paper to her lap.

Aimee's eyes narrowed and she shifted her hips. Her purse, and his note, fell to the floor in a clatter that garnered attention of folks across the aisle. Beside Aimee, Cory cut her eyes at Seth. He grinned back as Aimee flipped her head back up, his note securely in her hand and her purse collected and quiet on the ground. And once more, she shifted her hips. If she was trying to scoot further away, the move had sorely backfired, only succeeded in moving her hip and thigh against his. As she read his note, her hand trembled.

Seth wanted to take her hands and kiss her fingertips. He wanted to tell her it would all be okay. That he cared deeply for her. Would she be able to forget how he treated her when she was honest with him? Would she ever feel comfortable being straightforward with him after he'd acted so childish?

She glanced his way, but this time he drew his eyes down to stare at his feet. Was it wrong to want to be with her? Was being with Aimee a betrayal to Kevin? He'd lived most of his adulthood blaming himself for Kevin's death. But the blame had not been his completely. The woman he had fallen in love with, who seemed to hold his future in her hands, who was everything he wanted, but she believed she was the one who had been the proximate cause of the accident.

Except that wasn't true. Fault for the accident

was still in Seth's hands. He'd been the driver. The one in control, the one who'd taken his eyes off the road too long. Seth shut his eyes.

Lord, please help me. Help Aimee and I get past that horrible night and our actions. I know you've forgiven us for our sins. Please help us forgive each other and ourselves.

He inhaled as a feeling came over him. He eyed Aimee's hands clasping the pencil and note he gave her. An urging appointed itself in his heart, in his mind. Should he?

He shook his head, willing the service to end so he could get away from her and from the painful feelings and memories. He balled his hand in a fist. That wasn't want he wanted. He didn't want to be away from her at all.

What if he told Aimee he was sorry? What if he said the words she needed to hear? What if they started over? They both had a broken past but weren't they both due a future that held a promise of happiness?

Pencil poised, she scribbled a note on the bulletin beside his message and passed it back to him.

He read the note, then met her gaze. She shrugged.

Grinning, he focused on Josh on stage, speaking of forgiveness. The heavy burden he'd been carrying all these years seemed to lighten. As the congregation stood and sang, Seth reached every note. He caught Aimee looking up at him, eyebrows raised with curiosity.

When the music subsided, Mom hustled to the

podium as if she were accepting an award. It was hard to feel sore about her meddling. She was such an expert at putting her nose where it didn't belong, he admired her skill. Because of her meddling, he was beside the most beautiful woman he knew, and he had made a decision where she was concerned.

Mom smiled and Seth knew she was looking at him.

"As most of you may already know, the Children's department is complete. Aimee McClain finished the beautiful murals adorning the walls downstairs, and I want to add, she completed them ahead of schedule. Aimee is with us today. Unfortunately, her son Luke, who I know you all have been praying for, is back in the hospital. However, Luke is only days away from a bone marrow transplant." Bonnie paused as the congregation applauded. "Before you leave today, we invite you to stop by and tour the children's department. Aimee will be downstairs, and I would love for you all to give her a Hopewell church welcome. Look for Seth, who is also with us today. Seth will be her escort. Thank you."

~

What was Bonnie Garrett thinking? Aimee's heart pounded as she gathered her bag and started toward the rear door of the church. "I'm going to the ladies room," she explained to Cory as she slid by her and exited on the side of the pew opposite of Seth.

Why in the world would Bonnie put her in close proximity to Seth after all the pain she had caused him? And Seth! He sat right next to her and wrote her a note in the middle of service. He wanted to speak with her after church. She couldn't take any more, she flung open the back door and hurried to the grassy quad between the sanctuary and the fellowship hall. She couldn't stand to see the disappointment in his eyes.

Sniffing, she swiped her eyes as she stepped into the sunshine, all sorts of curse words rolled through her brain. She glanced up at the blue skies. "I'm sorry to use foul language while in Your house, but You must understand how hard this is for me."

"Are you talking to yourself now?"

She whirled around and crashed into a wall of muscle. Her knees wobbled Jello-like, and she swayed. Reaching forward, there was nothing to hold on to except Seth.

His hands, oh those hands, grabbed her by the waist, steadying her. Once again, he caught her before she fell, always there. His eyes held humor and she couldn't help but focus on the gold flecks she adored. But he couldn't keep saving her, not when she'd cost him so much.

Steady now, she stepped away from his grasp, and headed toward the stairs, holding the railing for dear life.

"Are you alright?" He sounded concerned.

Liquid heat bubbled in her stomach, burning clear up to her chest. How was she going to handle being beside him this afternoon to meet the congregation for God's sake? She wanted him beside her but she didn't deserve him. And, she was angry that she was still drawn to him after all that was between them.

"I'm fine." The response was gruff and hateful. Yet it wasn't Seth she hated. It was herself, their situation, her actions of long ago she couldn't take back.

He came up beside her, keeping up with her quick pace.

"You don't have to go with me. Just because your mother orchestrated this whole mess does not mean we have to follow through." She hurried toward the parking lot. "I'm leaving."

"Wait, please."

She whirled around. Was that amusement in his eyes?

"Mom promised everyone you would be in the Children's Area. Can't you give her ten minutes?" His mouth formed a tight smile. "I'll be right beside you."

They crossed the parking lot to the rear of the fellowship building. He guided her onto the elevator. As soon as the doors closed, he pushed the ground floor button. Once the elevator began its decent, he pushed the emergency stop.

"What are you doing?"

"Why are you blaming Mom?"

She started forward, reaching around him to release the stop. He jumped in front of the stop button. She pierced him with one of her meanest looks. "Seth!"

"Tell me."

She tried to dart around him, but each time she went one way, he went the same way, blocking her ability to push the button to restart the elevator. They danced back and forth until Aimee blew out a frustrated breath.

She crossed her arms over her chest. Her skin tingled where he'd held her. "I told her everything yesterday and she still asked me to come. I had no idea you would be here."

"What do you mean you told her everything?"

Exhaling, she looked down at her pointy dress shoes. "Everything."

His hands clasped her arms below the shoulder. "Look at me, Aimee." When she refused, he loosened his hold. "I'm sorry."

She lifted her gaze.

"When you told me about the accident, I handled it really bad. I hurt you and I'm sorry. I never meant to hurt you."

"I never meant to hurt you."

He took her hand. "I'm going to forget. If it takes the rest of my life trying, I'm going to forget that day. I don't want to forget Kevin, but I want to forget the mistakes we made."

Closing her eyes, she inhaled.

With her hand clasped between his, he stepped closer. His face was so close to hers she could feel his breath. "Let's start over. Let's be friends." Her fists gripped his shirt. She didn't dare splay her fingers across his chest, didn't dare. He was so close, she was sure he was going to kiss her.

His movements stilled. "Do you want to be friends?"

"I need your friendship." She needed him.

He smiled. "Good. We're friends." He hugged

her, then took an admirable step away.

"Seth, I know the trust between us is gone, that you feel you can't trust me any longer because I wasn't honest with you. But the truth is I thought I was protecting you. I was wrong. As part of us trying to be friends, we have to work on getting past this."

He nodded. "I agree."

Hoarseness bubbled over her words as she fought to restrain her emotions. "Seth, I'm sorry Kevin died. I'm sorry you were injured. I'm sorry I ruined your career. If I could take it all back, I would—"

"Don't say another word." He stepped forward. "I forgive you." Searching her eyes, he took her hands and held them to his chest. "I forgive both of us. God has already forgiven us. If He has, then who am I to do anything apart from His will?"

She stared at him as she muttered, "Thank you." She'd had plenty of time to think about what she should've said to Seth. Although he said the words and she accepted, something had shifted. She had disappointed him. She could see it in his eyes. "Look, I don't want to argue anymore. It's painful being with you and pretending everything is alright when it's not. Luke is the only one that matters, and I'm to the point I don't care about your feelings or my own, but I do care about him. I won't tolerate anyone hurting him—"

Seth raised his hand. "I agree completely."

When she opened her mouth to speak, his fingers touched her lips.

"I don't want to be anywhere else, Aimee.

Wherever you and Luke are, it's where I want to be."

Her eyes burned with moisture. "But what about—"

"Can you forgive me for how I've acted in response to you these last few weeks?"

Words were difficult. "Of course, I forgive you."

He moved closer then and took her face in his hands. "Don't cry." He kissed each cheek then her temples, and brushed a light, friendly kiss on her lips. Then, he stepped back.

"Are you ready to face them?"

She touched her lips, nodding as they separated.

He released the elevator lever. The doors opened moments later at the children's department. Seth motioned for her to go first.

Aimee's pulse sped as she stepped into the fellowship hall, but it had nothing to do with the crowd of church members waiting.

"She did a wonderful job!" Someone said. And another person pointed at the ark and said, "Look at the detail."

The crowd's conversation created a cacophony filling her ears. Even though they were admiring her work, she wanted to run and hide. She wasn't accustomed to the praise and attention.

Bonnie stood near the exit. "What took you two so long? I was about to call the fire department about this elevator. I noticed it stopped. We'll have to have maintenance check that."

She corralled them through the sea of church

members. She planted them beside the mural of Jesus and the children. Seth had stolen a kiss from her in this very spot.

"Now, stand right here so everyone can meet you."

Aimee wouldn't have been surprised had Bonnie given them both a pat on the head. As it was, Seth's mother had already turned to a couple. "Joe and Susie, how are you?" Pleasantries exchanged, Bonnie went on. "This is Aimee, artist extraordinaire. And, you remember Seth?"

More people filed in, coming toward them like a herd of cattle, minus the mooing. Pressing closer to the wall, she couldn't help bump Seth's arm until he situated his hand around her waist. Escape was impossible.

"Just relax and go with it." His lowered voice hovered at her ear.

Aimee nodded at Seth's advice, inhaled and smiled at the next person approaching. Her smile remained as she greeted the next person and another, digging deep to bring the extroverted side of her to the forefront. She answered questions and made small talk. For a moment, she and Seth worked as a team. It felt good.

A middle-aged man stopped in front them. "Ms. McClain, I'm Ken Brown. I'm principal at Heinz County High School."

"Please, call me Aimee."

Seth introduced himself as he shook Mr. Brown's hand. "You're a little far from home. Glad you could join us for service today."

"It's good to meet you Seth. You're the reason

I'm here. I saw Aimee's murals on your social media pages." Ken shared he and Seth were members of the same online group.

"The Internet makes the world much smaller, doesn't it?"

Mr. Brown smiled. "It does. I reached out to Hopewell's staff and found out about this event, so my wife and I decided to make it a weekend trip." He handed Aimee a business card. "I am interested in hiring you to work at our school." He gave a brief explanation of the images they wanted. "The school has been there for decades. It definitely needs some updating."

"What is the size of the project area?"

Mr. Brown provided an approximate square footage of the gym and the cafeteria. "Are you available over Fall break? If not, Christmas break? Working during the two weeks the staff and students are out of school would be preferred. The high school is hosting a wrestling meet in January and I am hoping to have everything complete by then. I do realize you have a family of your own so if that time doesn't work, we could table it for spring."

By now, the crowd had waned until all that remained was Aimee beside Seth as the principal expanded on his thoughts for new murals at his school.

Sloan and Tiffany slid up beside her with Granny Lena and Aunts Tippy and Velma tagging along.

Granny piped in, "What were you saying? You want to hire Aimee up in Heinz County?"

"Why that's three hundred miles or so from here." Velma tapped her cane on the tile floor. "I used to date a boy from Heinz county," she added and nudged the principal's prim wife.

Aimee glanced over Ken's contact card in which he had attached an offer for the job. The amount represented a commission she had not expected. Commission on top of materials for the job was enough to help pay for other debts, beyond Luke's medical bills Seth had helped with, which she'd been chipping away one a crumb at a time. The money would help her give Luke some of the bigger presents he had been wishing for Christmas.

"Mr. Brown, I can't accept the job. I appreciate it, but a job this size would take me several weeks to complete. I can't leave my son alone for that length of time." She handed the paperwork out for Mr. Brown to take when Lena stepped closer.

"Just a minute. Let's think about this a moment."

"We can help you!" Tiffany exclaimed, elbowing Sloan in the process. "Why, Luke will be fine with us. You've already given all the medical releases you need."

"Tiffany and I know what Luke needs, we know his local doctors." Sloan reminded.

"Luke can keep me company during the day while the girls are at work," Granny Lena said.

"Mr. Brown," Aimee refocused on him. "My son is about to have a bone marrow transplant and there will be several weeks, possibly months, that we will be dependent on how his body responds to the transplant. I wouldn't want to commit to your school with things so uncertain for me at the moment."

She excused herself and stepped outside the perimeter of family. Lena kept close on her heels, spewing her words of disdain, "Aimee Louise, this is ridiculous. I saw that offer. Don't pass it up."

"Granny, I can't right now. Thank you for your concern."

"You need all of the help you can to redeem yourself after what you did all those years ago. I never would have imagined you would have done such a thing. Now the Miller name is smeared."

Aimee faced her small, delicate grandmother. "Don't you worry about the Miller name... no one outside of the Garrett and Ridley family knows my part in it. I assure you that you and Granddaddy won't be affected by my actions."

She turned toward the parking lot, but Granny's voice stopped her. "I don't understand why you didn't call me, tell me you were in pain. Lord knows, I understood. I still miss your mother. And even though your father drove me crazy with his irrational decisions, I loved him like a son. I love you."

She lowered her head and trudged toward her grandmother. "I love you, too. And I'll never make a mistake again of not leaning on my family. No matter how far away we are from each other."

Granny smiled and opened her arms. After they embraced, her grandmother wiped her eyes. "Now get. Luke's probably wondering where you are. I'll be by to see him this afternoon."

"He'd love it." Granny returned to the

fellowship hall and Aimee crossed the few yards to Tank.

"Wait up, please."

Seth jogged toward her.

"Where are you going?"

"Back to the hospital. We're being transported to Atlanta tomorrow." She rested her hand on Tank's hood.

"I'll come up there as soon as I can."

With a nod, she moved to the driver's door.

"Why did you decline Mr. Brown's offer?"

"For the reasons I told him. Why?

"I just hate to see you pass on an amazing offer like that. It could lead to more jobs."

She flung her purse across the front seat and turned to him. "It's okay. I can't concentrate on a project of that magnitude until Luke is in the clear."

"I understand." He glanced across the parking lot, as she slid behind the wheel. "Good luck at the game."

"What?"

"Your team?" She raised her eyebrows. "Going to the championship tomorrow, right?"

He chuckled. "Yep, that's tomorrow. I guess I've been preoccupied."

Their gazes held another moment. He seemed like he wanted to say more, but he just stood there, looking at her. She shoved her keys in the ignition. "I've got to go." She reached beside him to pull the door shut.

Seth blocked her. "Wait. I wrote you the note in church, but I never explained myself."

Eyeing his hand on the steering wheel now, her eyes widened. "Didn't we cover that in the elevator?"

He flashed a smile. "That wasn't it."

Shaking her head, she proceeded to turn the ignition. Tank roared to life. "I need to get to Luke and relieve your dad."

"Let me know what room number Luke is in once you two get settled."

"We'll be at CHOA. I'll let you know." Seth didn't budge. "Anything else?"

"Yep," he snaked an arm around her shoulders and the other around her waist within seconds. She had little time to think as she was pressed against the seat. He stopped, his face inches from hers.

"Seth, we're in the church parking lot. What will people think?"

"They'll say it's about time I came to my senses." His lips covered hers in one swift, yet soft, action. She cupped his face as he deepened the kiss, pressing her against the seat, as she wrapped her arms around his neck and brought him closer. He loosened his hold as his kisses grew shorter until he gradually pulled back.

Her eyes fluttered open to find him holding her at arm's length, waiting for her. "Something we discussed earlier is bugging me," he said, "about us being friends. I want you to have an abundance of friends in this world, but please don't let any other friend kiss you like this." He studied her before going on, "I don't want to control you or your decisions, but I do want to stake my claim right here and now. This is my declaration for our future.

And Aimee, I want it to be ours. Together."

Chapter Twenty-Three

The letter she wrote lay across his chest.

Seth tucked his arm behind his head and gazed over Aimee's penmanship. She had told her son's donor how thankful they were for him. She included a letter from Luke. Aimee had no idea Seth was her son's donor. And keeping the anonymity was challenging.

Seth couldn't deny the comfort he gained from her letter. It had arrived the day before, and he had read and re-read it last night. He hadn't been able to sleep. Going under anesthesia made him nervous. When he read Aimee's letter, he could hear her voice. He wanted to call her, but he wasn't ready to tell her about his part yet. Soon enough, they would know.

"Please," he said as volcanic emotion rose inside his chest, expanding until he thought he may burst into pieces. Leaning forward, he covered his face with his hands, suddenly without words.

What if it doesn't succeed? Complications could arise long after the transplant. Seth had read numerous accounts of successful transplants, except once the marrow reached the patient, the patient's cells didn't accept the foreign bodies.

Oh Lord, he wasn't ready to accept death as a final result. He couldn't bear it if the bone marrow transplant failed. Surely, God was behind the procedure's success.

He raised his head, wishing Aimee was with him. He looked over her letter, his fingers nimble as they unfolded the cream-colored paper and caressed the looped strokes of her handwriting, a unique mixture of print and cursive.

The door slid open. Seth folded the letter as Mom walked in, followed by Cory and Dad.

"They're on their way to take you to surgery." Mom kissed him on the forehead as if he were a child. "We're going to take your bag and will see you in the recovery room when you're through."

Mom inhaled as she held his hand against her stomach. "You'll be fine."

"Are you saying that for my sake or your own?"

She kissed his cheek as the nurses and anesthesiologist walked in the room.

"Mom," Seth handed her the folded letter. "Will you hold onto this?"

"Of course."

"It's from Aimee."

She looked at the folded paper and nodded in understanding.

Dad kissed his forehead. "Love you, son."

"Love you, too, Dad."

"Are you ready, handsome?" Gillian, a pretty

blonde nurse who had been with him since he arrived that morning, smiled warmly. Seth gave her a quick grin in return, then lowered his eyes to Aimee's letter his mother held. His heartbeat quickened. Despite everything, despite the accident, despite Aimee's hesitation in trusting him with the truth, Seth's heart had been made to love only one woman.

~

The next morning, pink shifted to blue across the Atlanta skyline, as Aimee sketched Luke's newest friend in the Zone, the Children's Hospital's play area. Little Kelly's blond pigtails were still long enough to fasten with bows.

"Throw the ball to me." Rosy cheeks against creamy porcelain skin reminded Aimee of a fragile doll. Except the kids that had to reside here for days and weeks at a time weren't fragile. They were tough. Fighters.

Luke laughed as the ball sailed across the room. His smile was hidden behind a mask that protected him and Kelly from any foreign germs which could create havoc in their already immune compromised bodies.

"They play so well together," Kelly's mom, Jennifer said. Talking to her had come easy for Aimee, especially since there were so many similarities with the illnesses their children fought.

"I'm glad they met. It sounds like they'll be confined to their rooms for a while."

"Yes, but I don't care. I'm so grateful each of them are blessed to have matching donors and they will be on their paths to healing."

Aimee nodded. Fortunately for Kelly, her bone marrow donor would be her older brother. And just like Luke, Kelly would receive the transfusion this weekend.

As Aimee and Jennifer talked, Aimee sketched. It felt good to be able to draw something, someone, who was here and in the present. Before she was honest with Seth, she could only sketch the meadow where Seth's car had run off the road. She drew many roads that went on and on without end. And later, when Tank broke down on the bridge, she drew and painted many bridges. Perhaps it was her subconscious trying to work through her path in life.

Sighing she lay down one pencil for a larger one. She had so much to be thankful. She had been honest with everyone in her life. There were no more secrets. Her past could rest where it belonged. She was free.

Her son had someone out there who was his match in every way that counted as far as bone marrow and chemistry was concerned. Aimee prayed she would be able to meet Luke's match someday, or maybe just get a letter from the man so they would know a little about him. Did he have a son of his own? What did he do for a living? Where was he from? She craved any detail to complete the picture of the man who was giving her son a second chance.

She eyed little Kelly, coloring in shorter strokes across the paper to finish the little girl's round face. Aimee drew longer lines to fill in her plump little arms and legs. She gave detail to Kelly's clothing;

lace along the hem of her dress and pink flowers around the collar. After a few moments, Aimee gently tore the page away from her pad and handed it to Jennifer.

The young mother's face brightened. "Thank you, Aimee," Jennifer hugged her. "This is the most beautiful portrait of Kelly."

Too soon, it was time for Kelly and Jennifer to leave. Aimee and Luke said their goodbyes and continued up the corridor. While Luke received the foreign marrow, and afterwards, he would be under more supervision and roaming the hospital halls would be off limits for a while.

They found the library, chose a couple of books, and Luke settled at a table. They read together for a few moments.

"I'm tired," Luke whined. When they reached his room, his face brightened. "Seth's game is on, Mom."

She pushed the volume up as her attention focused on the television. "They're announcing the teams."

The opposing high school was announced first. Though baseball season usually did not start until the first of the year, this had been a special tournament Seth had involved his school in during their off season. Each team had played various games and tournaments throughout the summer to reach this level in the championship. This was it. This was the World Series for the high school level of baseball.

Next, they announced Point Peace High. They announced Seth's name, but soon announced he wasn't able to be present. The commentators moved on to the assistant coaches who were present. Their pictures flashed on the screen.

"Seth's not there." Luke leaned back in his bed and frowned. "Where is he?"

"I don't know." He said he was going. Of course, he would be going.

A knock interrupted their confused silence. Aimee was half-way across the room when the door opened. Seth stood on the other side holding a dozen shiny balloons.

Luke scooted off the bed and hurried toward him. Seth stopped and let Luke run to him.

Luke raised his arms. "Pick me up."

"I can't, champ, but I missed you."

Luke wrapped his arms around Seth's waist. She saw perspiration beading across Seth's brow and his face was pale. He grimaced as Luke held on to his waist. "Wow, that's some strong grip you've got."

Aimee moved closer. Her heart beat so fast, she couldn't catch her breath. "I didn't know you were coming. The game is about to start." She gestured toward the television. "We were wondering where you were."

He forced a smile.

"Is something wrong?"

Seth shook his head, "No, no." He shoved his hands in his pants pockets. "I've got something I need to tell you and Luke. Some news. Good news."

"Better than what you told me day before yesterday?"

"Tons better."

Aimee smiled at him. "Have a seat."

She helped Luke settle on his bed, and then turned around to face Seth. He hung back. Normally, he helped Luke get into bed. Of course, he usually carried Luke like an airplane.

Hunched over, he trudged toward the bed. "What happened? Are you hurt?"

He shook his head.

"Sit down. You're pale." She took him by the elbow and guided him to the couch.

"Let me sit beside Luke."

Aimee held his arm as he slowly made his way to Luke's bed. "You're clammy and sweating. Dear God, Seth, do you have a fever? You're going to have to leave."

"Wait, Aim—" He caught her gaze in that instant. "I'm not sick. I just had surgery and I was supposed to stay in bed longer, but I told them I would rest over here."

"Surgery?" She took the balloons and set them in the corner of the room as Seth slowly pulled his shirt above the waistband. "I'll show you."

She looked at Luke and then stepped toward Seth. He untied his gray cloth pants and folded the elastic waist band so that the top of a bandage showed. The gauze was taped against his skin beside his hip. He showed Luke and Aimee the front and turned and showed them he had a bandage on his lower back.

"You see, for the procedure I had, they put me to sleep. They had to put a big needle into my pelvic bone in the front and back."

"What for, Seth?" Luke's eyes exuded concern.

"That's where they withdraw bone marrow." Seth took Luke's hand and he held his other hand out for her. But she couldn't move.

Could it be?

"Come here, I know it's a shock, but I need you." She trudged forward, not moving her eyes away from this amazing miracle.

He shifted his gaze to Luke. "From what I understand, the doctors are getting my marrow prepared so that they can bring it to you."

A tear fell from her eyes as she lowered to the edge of his bed.

"I'm getting yours?" Luke exclaimed. "Yippee!" He threw both hands in the air, his IV tubes slung here and there, "Yippee!" he yelled this time.

"Come here, you wild kid," Seth laughed as he hugged her son then he grabbed her hand, squeezing it. "I love you, son. I wanted to hang with you and your mom until your procedure is done. Maybe I can lie here on the couch tonight? Would that be okay?"

"You can sleep in my bed, Seth. You don't look like you feel so good." Luke patted Seth's shoulder.

"I'm going to be fine. I just had to get over here to you two. You and your mom are all I need."

Seth met her gaze. When he reached for her, she enclosed his shoulders with her embrace. Her hair shielded his face, surrounding him with her sweet scent.

Tears pooling in her eyes, she kissed him and

leaned back. "I'd hoped it would be you. I didn't think it could be possible."

He kissed her left hand and stroked her fingers. "Something's missing." Seth reached around Aimee for his jacket and pulled out a red bag. He presented the small box to her.

"I have a question I meant to ask you a while ago. You don't have to give me an answer today."

"My answer is yes, Seth. Yes."

"You haven't heard the question."

"But my heart already knows. And my answer is still yes."

Napping, Luke snuggled the teddy bear Seth bought him months before, as Dr. Hilton and his assistants marched into the hospital room carrying a syringe filled pure, golden stem cells.

Dr. Hilton began the injection, pushing the contents of the syringe into Luke's sleeping body. "What are you thinking about, Mom?" The doctor asked with a sweet smile.

Seth sat beside her and she looked at him, squeezed his hand and looked back at the syringe.

"It's the most beautiful thing I've ever seen." As the procedure unfolded, she thanked God for the doctors, their wisdom, and the nurses. "I'm so grateful for all of you." She turned to Seth. "Most of all, I'm thankful for who the cells came from."

He put his arm around her shoulders and hugged her. "I can't believe Luke's sleeping through this. He's missing the excitement."

The doctor chuckled. "The days ahead will be filled with plenty of excitement. I wish I could say it will be easy, but it will be trying on his little body. We have to make sure his cells don't try to destroy your healthy cells. Physically, Luke may be sick and in pain for a while. But we'll get through it. We'll be with you all every step of the way."

Seth held her hand as their gaze's locked. "And I'll be with you, and Luke, every step of the way. I promise."

Epilogue

One year later, Aimee rode in the back seat of Tank as the highway south of Savannah stretched open toward an orange and pink horizon.

"We're late," she sighed.

"We're almost there." Beside her, Luke stretched his neck and back to see around the seat to the road ahead. As Grandpa Paul turned off the main highway, Luke scooted to the right side of the back seat and rested his elbow on the open sill.

"Are you nervous?" She asked her nine-year-old son who had faced the challenges of bone marrow transplant with such bravery, and now, his health was almost one hundred percent restored.

"Nah, we practiced a lot." Luke gave her a long look, eyeing her from head to foot. "What about you? Scared?"

"Not scared. A little nervous." She smoothed the soft tulle of her skirt. "Do I look okay?"

"You look like a pink marshmallow."

Eyes widen, she tilted her head. "Is that a good thing?"

"Oh yeah, Mom. Pink marshmallows are cool."

"Well, you're a very handsome date."

His smile stretched from dimple to dimple.

Aimee cranked down her window and clung to the door. The warm ocean air floated inside the cab, blowing her hair off her shoulder. Following the bone marrow transplant, engraftment, and dealing with the fevers that affected Luke during the one hundred days post bone marrow transplant, she and Luke were finally taking a break. Absent were the bruises on his skin, replaced by a golden hue from his time outdoors. He possessed a nice tan from spending the summer enjoying football camp and baseball games. Luke still watched from the sidelines, but his time would come.

His white blond hair was grown out long, almost touching his shirt collar.

"Almost there, Sweetheart," Grandpa said from the driver's seat as he pulled off the highway and headed down the gravel drive. A few palm trees lined the property the closer they came to the beach. Grandpa pulled Tank to the edge of the yard and got out. He opened Luke's door letting Luke got out, then Aimee slid over. Grandpa smiled as she placed her hand in his and stepped out. She straightened her full, floor length skirt.

Dressed in matching satin dresses, Sloan and Whitney waited on her at the base of the steps. She only needed to step upon the bridge which led to the dock where her personal party awaited. To her right, Whitney hugged her then scooted behind her to straighten Aimee's train. On her left, Sloan handed her a bouquet of flowers. Grant and several groomsmen stood side by side dressed in matching suits.

"Come on, Mom. Seth's waiting."

Luke and Grandpa waited just a few steps away. Luke now held a pillow with two rings tied securely. Grandpa extended his elbow toward her. Garlands of tropical flowers wound in white tulle wrapped around the railing. Lanterns lined the path to the bridge and along the horizon, the sky deepened to fuchsia and lavender. Along the bay on either side of the bridge, boats holding acquaintances and family members watched from their railings, their moors tied off and anchored close to shore and swayed with the tilting waves. At the sight of Aimee, a harp began strumming a soft marching melody and Cory played a guitar near the altar.

Her cousins led the way, with Sloan as her matron of honor. As she neared the walkway, the dock, lit with more lanterns, came into view. The altar was decorated with white twinkling lights, white tulle wound with pink and white roses came into view. Only a small bridge was between Aimee and her future.

She stepped upon the dock and Seth moved toward her. Josh, their minister, waited on Seth's right and Tom, Seth's best man, was on his left. Luke took his place beside the man he called Dad now, who rubbed his shoulder with loving reassurance and whispered. "Good job, son."

Grandpa answered that he was giving her away and after he kissed Aimee's cheek, he placed her hand in Seth's palm. As the harp played the last cords, Seth grinned and whispered, "Glad you could make it."

With a flirtatious blink, she smirked. "Sorry I'm late."

"Yeah, I thought Tank broke down again, or you got locked in another closet. I was ready to organize a search party to come find you."

"Not necessary. You see, my luck has taken a turn. For the better."

"I'm the lucky one." They faced Josh, exchanged vows and rings, making promises of forever. "You may kiss the bride," Josh said.

Seth smiled as he cupped her face.

"Is this a dream?" she whispered as he lowered his face to hers.

"If it is, then I hope we never wake." Seth's expression was void of humor. His gray eyes were serious and loving and he was completely focused on her.

Aimee's smile could not be dissolved and she giggled.

Seth narrowed his eyes playfully. "Can I kiss you now, Mrs. Garrett?"

She wound her arms around his neck and pulled him closer. He had seen her at her best and her worst. He knew her darkest secrets, and she knew his. Together, they found forgiveness and love. As his lips reached hers, she sighed, "Now and forever, Mr. Garrett."

The End

ACFW Genesis Winner and multi-contest finalist, Christy has always enjoyed entertaining others. Christy wrote her first book, a mystery, while in seventh grade. Currently, Christy writes heartwarming southern romance, novels set in her home state of Georgia. Married to her high school sweetheart, Christy has a daughter, a son, four furbabies: Thomas: a nosey German Shepherd; Josie-Bobo: an adorable English Bulldog; and last but never least, Twitter and Ranger, two very loud Parakeets.

Connect with Christy online:

Facebook:https://www.facebook.com/authorchristylashea/

Instagram:https://www.instagram.com/christylashea/

Twitter:https://twitter.com/ChristyLaShea

Website:https://christylashea.com/

https://christylashea.blogspot.com/

Made in the USA
Coppell, TX
19 September 2021